The Right Wrong Man

Pamela S. Wight

Near.Perfect.Press
Tiburon, CA

This is a work of fiction. Names, characters, places, brands, media, and incidents are either the product of the author's imagination or used fictitiously.

Published by Near.Perfect.Press, Tiburon, California, 2013

Cover design by Suzanna Stinnett; photo by Shara G. Coletta.

ISBN: 978-0-9899324-0-0

Printed in the United States of America.

The Right Wrong Man/ Pamela S. Wight. -- 1st ed.

Dedication to GCC, always my right man.

"Love does not begin and end the way we seem to think it does. Love is a battle, love is a war; love is a growing up."

– James Baldwin

As Gregory and I raced our final mile, the sun rose, and I saw the shifting shadow.

"Huh," I said. Gregory ignored me, outpacing me by a stride and allowing sweat to drop into his hooded brown eyes.

I used to love running this last surge before my body stopped, heart pounding, blood coursing through my veins. I'd pretend I was flying, feet off the ground, hair swinging behind me, legs like a panther's. But with Gregory joining me on these early morning runs now, there was always this competition thing going. No conversation, no smiles and kisses before we warmed up and began a leisurely mile before the more steady second and third one. Just a serious, straight-ahead, running-is-my-life stride.

I saw it again – a shadowy shape moving to the left of us, behind the huge oak trees that led to my neighborhood. A creepy tingle slid up my spine, despite the mid-September warmth.

But Gregory was two strides ahead now, grunting and pulling with his taut, tanned legs. I ignored the shadow, and the fear, and pushed myself harder than usual. Two blocks, now one, and yes! I reached him as we both touched the banister of my front deck together. I smiled with delight; Gregory turned his back to me, bent down, hands on his knees, breathing in large thankful gulps.

"Tie, again!" I said. His shoulders bunched up, then straightened as he turned to me, blank face quickly changing to a satisfied one.

"Good going. Great run." He looked toward the east where the sun was unveiling a sky of pink and peach. "Hafta shower and get off to work." He leaned over, gave me a sweaty kiss, and then bounced up the stairs into the house.

"Sore loser," I muttered under my breath. And he didn't even lose, we both won, as far as I was concerned. But that was my Gregory, competitive, yet sweet and romantic. Well, I didn't know if I should actually call him "my" Gregory. He'd only moved in this weekend, and that was his idea, not mine.

I caught a shape on the periphery of my eye and swirled right. Nothing was there. But I knew I saw something. "Who is it?" I called out. Silence, except for the sound of cars passing down the street, the early commuters, and the birds singing as if it were spring and not September. Their last hurrah before fall really set in. I took one step up the wooden staircase of my old Victorian cast-off, and felt a hand grasp my shoulder. I would have screamed, but another hand was over my mouth.

CHAPTER TWO

"Sorry, Meredith. Sorry. I didn't want to scare you. It's me. I'm going to take my hand off your mouth now. But only if you promise you won't hit me."

I glared over the large male hand that covered my mouth and contemplated biting it. But sure enough, it was Parker, my ex-boyfriend, the one I hadn't seen nor heard from in over six months. Our last communication with each other hadn't been on the best of terms. I nodded my head gently, and he let go. But I still glared.

Parker put his hands out as if in supplication. "Dumb, I know, but I had to get your attention without

Mr. Fitness Fanatic seeing me. Who is that guy anyway?"

I continued to glare. I've been told, by Parker among others, that I have a good, strong, intense glare, the kind that could make a baby sob and a grown man get on his hands and knees and cry uncle.

"Okay, none of my business," Parker said. "I get it. Particularly at 6 in the morning when you haven't heard from me in so long. But that's your fault, of course."

I opened my mouth in disbelief. My fault? I wanted to turn away and leave, but we were standing in front of my house, and Parker happened to be blocking the staircase that led to the front door.

"What is it Parker? I need to get moving." I took one step and he stepped in closer to me.

"I'm starting this out all wrong, Meredith. Listen. I need to talk to you. Without the sunrise racer. Can I come in once he's gone? And, if so, could you make me some breakfast? The kind you used to make – eggs and bacon and black coffee that's too strong and the best in the world? Please?" He gave me his classic Parker look, with the wide-open expression of a sweet, innocent boy who believes every word he says, and who wants more than anything for his listener to go along with him.

"I don't think it's a great idea."

"Why not? Look, I'm kind of in a desperate situation. Aren't you the least bit curious to hear what I have to say? And didn't you miss me a little?" Parker's ocean blue eyes beseeched.

Yeah, I was curious. But I was also still scorched from the end of our relationship. But I didn't want him to know that.

"I'm out of bacon," I said.

"Eggs will be fine." Parker put on his serious expression. He didn't like to be serious; he liked to be cool and in control of his conversations. I guessed it went with his job. But now, his eyes clouded a bit, and his right-cheek dimple even flattened. "Merry, I haven't eaten a real meal in a day and a half. I don't want to be seen here, but I really need to talk to you. Please?"

I tried to stop it, but my heart tightened, as if the fairy godmother of love had swooped in and put her fist around the organ and squeezed it. Damn. "Okay. Gregory should be gone in," I looked at my watch, "twenty minutes. I'll go in now. Knock on the door in 25."

Parker touched my arm in thanks and then, as he so often did, he disappeared. He was in front of me one second, the next one, I couldn't see him anywhere. How did he do that?

But, more importantly, why was he doing that now?

CHAPTER THREE

I scraped the runny fried egg off the bottom of the frying pan, slid it onto a piece of burnt toast, threw the food onto a small plate, and deposited the entire foul-smelling affair in front of Parker.

"Just the way I like it," he said, ignoring my frown and sighs. Gregory had left ten minutes ago, and like magic, Parker had reappeared at my front door, charming his way in for some breakfast.

"Parker, it's 6:30 in the morning. Why are you here, and what's the 'desperate situation' you mentioned dramatically at the front door 30 minutes ago?"

Parker ate greedily, gulping down the hot coffee as he stuffed the obviously appreciated breakfast in his mouth. I noticed his hair was a little longer than usual, the brown ends curling at the nape of his neck. His color was good, though his blue eyes were bloodshot.

I stood, still dressed in my running shorts and tank top, although I had thrown on my old faded sweatshirt over that. My sweat had dried, and I needed a cool shower and a blow dry. My hair was pulled into a tight ponytail, leaving my face exposed and vulnerable. The last time I'd heard from Parker he was "doing a job" in Columbia. I remembered being relieved at the time that I no longer had to worry about him. He wasn't mine to worry about.

"Things have changed," Parker began. "I've changed. Well, I'm going to change, and I wondered, it's kind of complicated, but..."

I sat down next to Parker, my mouth open. "Okay," I finally said, "where's Parker and what have you done with him?" The man I knew never stuttered, never left an unfinished sentence, and never seemed anything less than self-assured.

He gave me a weak grin. "I've missed you, Duchess."

Not wanting to respond to his nickname for me, I turned my head and looked out the window. The Japanese maple Parker and I had planted a little over two years ago swayed gently with the breeze.

Parker stood up, his blue jeans looking as good on his 6'3" frame as I remembered. Somehow, pants always fit him in all the right places. Not too tight as if he was showing off, but tight enough to show he could show off if he wanted to. He placed his dirty dish in the sink and looked over at me as if seeing me for the first time.

"I've missed you more than you realize."

"That's for sure, since I sure haven't heard much from you," I said. Inside, my heart was thumping like a rabbit running from a coyote. Not wanting him to notice, I continued to speak to him nonchalantly. "What's really on your agenda Parker? Why did you show up here, unannounced, following me like some super shadow, asking for breakfast like it was the old days? What do you need? Just say it, and then you can go back to wherever it is you came from."

Feeling proud of myself, I leaned back in my chair. Yes! I truly was over him. I looked up at him with victory in my eyes and saw a gleam of something in his. Disbelief? Fear?

"I don't want to say goodbye like this," he said.

"We said goodbye quite a while ago Parker." I stood up. "I need to get ready for work. You know where the dishwasher is."

His laugh followed me up the stairs to my bedroom.

~~~~~~~~~~~~~~~~~~~~

I entered the steamy shower shaking with steamy emotions. After scrubbing myself clean of them, shampooing and conditioning my hair vigorously and wiping myself dry, I figured I was settled down. As I dried my hair I looked out the large bay window at the lavender-flowered hostas edging the lawn. We'd had it good for a while – Parker and I – but his work and long absences cut short any chance of a real romance. That's what I decided 12 months ago, and I was going to stick to my story.

The hair dryer made too much noise to hear Parker leave. To be safe, I turned it off for a few minutes, listening for telltale footsteps. Hearing none, I continued drying my hair. In my 30s, I was probably too old for thick wavy hair that hung to the middle of my back. When I complained about the time it took to dry it, Greg encouraged me to get a shorter cut. But I held back. I wouldn't have said that my hair was my best feature, but it was my sexiest. Parker used to love watching the different ways I fixed it, whether I made French braids or a tight bun in the back or just let it flow freely.

I tossed my head to get rid of those thoughts and pulled my hair into a tight ponytail, just to get it out of the way. I had a feeling this was going to be a tough day, and I didn't want to worry about my hair. After throwing on my favorite pair of black pants and lace blouse, and dressing it all up with my special string of pearls, I raced downstairs into the kitchen – a square room with old-fashioned white and black tiles and two tall windows, letting in lots of sunshine most of the day.

The dishes were clean and standing on the side of the sink. Parker didn't believe in dishwashers. I bought a nice new one when I purchased this old house a few years ago, and despite living with me for almost six months, Parker never used it. "Like to feel the soapy warm water on my hands," he'd say, "love actually feeling that grease come off with a little effort." I wasn't surprised. It fit his personality, wanting to get totally involved in a project, immersed in it, scrubbing clean what was wrong. Then I paused.

Parker mentioned he was in a "desperate situation." Was he unable to scrub something clean this time at work? I knew Parker well, or at least I thought I did. I'd never seen him cautious like he was this morning – unsure. What had changed? I stopped in the middle of the living room and stood still, realizing that I wanted more details. I cocked my head, listening, thinking that he had stuck around and was waiting for me to approach him again.

But he had disappeared. Out of sight. Not, unfortunately, out of mind.

CHAPTER FOUR

On my way back up the stairs to retrieve my purse, I stopped short. Something wasn't right. I looked around the entryway. Small table in place, front door closed tightly. But still. I walked through the room and glanced at the living room – all fine – and then again looked into the kitchen. Nothing out of place. But something was wrong.

I circled the tiny foyer once more, even looking up at the ceiling. Nothing. Then I concentrated on the three-corner oak table. It was just where it should be, but aha! My bone china figurine, "the Duchess" Parker used to call it, was out of place. I always kept it toward the front end of the table. It was a beautiful piece of curved delicacy, an English lady dressed in soft pink and blue, bowing as if ready to begin a ballroom dance. Parker brought it home to me as a gift after a business trip to England. More formal than I would expect from Parker, but he said her large white bosom, flowing out of her dress, reminded him of me. Thus, my nickname.

Now the figurine was facing the back of the table, her dainty face turned away. Why? Puzzled, I walked toward it, but I was afraid to pick it up. Had Gregory moved it? Was he angry with me? After all, he had just moved in, and I had practically pushed him out the door this morning. Gregory was probably my last best hope for a secure and loving relationship. I didn't want to blow it because of an unexpected visit from an ex-boyfriend.

Parker's sudden reappearance in my life was a mistake, of that I was sure. But I didn't like the way my heart drummed as soon as I saw him, like when listening to a great rock'n roll song. Wrong beat. I wanted to stay cool, calm, in control, not feel all these frustrating, uncalled for emotions just because this ex-boyfriend decided to "stop by."

The china lady hadn't moved an inch as I stood there contemplating her, not as if I expected her to. What was I afraid of? Well, I was afraid her change in position had something to do with Parker. Gregory wouldn't move her, because he wasn't spontaneous. If he had something to say to me, he'd say it. He wouldn't be obtuse. That was a Parker kind of thing.

I picked up the duchess. Time to stop this nonsense. I would just put her back where she belonged and get on with my life. But wait, what was this underneath her? A small scrap of paper was jammed through the little hole in the bottom, where it said "Royal Doulton Bone China." I pulled out the notepaper folded in quarters. I opened the first flap to discover blank paper, then opened it up all the way.

In big bold letters someone had written: "TRMFY." Whaaat? I threw the piece of paper down in frustration, but immediately bent down to pick it up again. This was one of Parker's little messages, no doubt. But what the hell was TRMFY? I knew he wanted me to wonder about it, ponder it, spend my day imagining what the letters meant. That made me madder. I looked at the black scrawl, and then I tore the piece of paper into dozens of tiny little pieces. Not once, I promised myself as I trotted back up the stairs, would I think about those letters.

Not once.

CHAPTER FIVE

Most days I took the T into the city, but today I decided to drive because I might need the car later on. Just a premonition, I supposed. My Mazda Miata jolted out of its tiny space on the street as if it had been left alone too long, and it raced over the bridge, just daring a cop to come along and stop us. I tapped my foot on the brake and slowed us both down. Too much gas swirling in Nelly's engine, too many thoughts carousing in my brain. Work, I knew, would help me focus. As an editor for a small medical publishing company, I could lose myself in the small, important details of publishing specialized textbooks.

Jill, my assistant, greeted me as I walked into my office. "Barbara Browning just called. From her yacht. Again. Wants to know when she gets to see the rest of the edited chapters."

"Hello to you, too. And how was your weekend? Mine was uneventful until early this morning, but never mind. Tell Barbara that if she hadn't written 100-page chapters, she'd have received the entire manuscript months ago."

Jill's eyes sparked interest. "Well, aren't you feisty. What did happen this morning?"

My assistant was too nosy for her own good. To her credit, she helped me stay organized and handled the authors I dealt with carefully and diplomatically. But, she was still young, just out of college, and constantly tried to butt into my personal affairs.

"None of your business, and yes, I'd love a cup of green tea. To answer your other question, I'm actually almost finished editing The Role of Occupational Therapy in the Public School Setting, and you can tell Barbara I'll send the chapters Fed Ex by the beginning of next week." I sat down behind my desk, hoping my assistant would get the message and leave.

"She expects you to hand deliver it."

"What?" I stood up again and frowned at Jill. "You didn't give her any ideas, did you?"

"Me?" the little innocent asked. "Of course not. She said how gorgeous it is in St. Thomas now. I may have mentioned you haven't been on a vacation in over a year. She indicated that she'd really like to go over the revised pages with you personally. Face-to-face. I told her you couldn't possibly leave town. She pointed out this is a large textbook contract, and that Mr. Flack had promised personal, intense editorial help, and that Mr. Flack had told her that's why he selected you to be in charge of the project." Jill stopped to take a breath.

I glared. "Terrific. Why would I want to go to the Caribbean in September? It's beautiful here. Gregory and I are planning to go to Mt. Washington for a little break in a couple of weeks. We'd like to visit New Hampshire before all the tourists in October."

Jill snorted. Most unladylike. "Gregory? Take a break? He's too interested in his work." Jill didn't like Gregory. I still didn't know the entire reason, but she thought he was too stodgy for me, and boring, including his career as an accountant. I didn't explain to her that, after Parker, that's just what I wanted. Boring.

"I'll have to think about it. This was not on my agenda. Now, can I have my cup of tea? With lemon?"

"Sure," Jill replied as she stepped backward out of the room. That always meant she had more to tell me. Terrific.

"Yes?"

"You also have three messages."

"It's only 9:15 on a Monday morning!" I sighed. "Okay, who are they?"

"Mr. Flack."

I groaned; she grinned.

Mr. Flack, CEO and publisher, liked me, for that I was grateful. But he heaped too many projects on me, explaining that the other senior editors couldn't handle them the way I could. But this was getting ridiculous. I had two nursing books, a neurology textbook, and Barbara Browning's, all with the same publishing date. Impossible.

"Maxwell Carter."

I groaned again. Another author. The neurotic neurologist who double checked every comma, and called to tell me about it daily.

"He wants to go over the diagrams for Chapter 3."

"And?" I asked.

"And some guy who wouldn't give me his name. He said you're supposed to meet him at 12:30 at Quincy Market, in front of some lamppost. You'd know which one he was talking about."

I groaned once more. That could only be Parker. I knew exactly which lamppost he meant.

Jill looked fascinated. "Who is it?"

"None of your business," I growled. "Now get me that tea!"

CHAPTER SIX

Twelve thirty-five and no sign of Parker. I was leaning against the lamppost, our lamppost, wondering why I was there. Parker was history. My history. When I had decided a little less than a year ago that Parker couldn't be in my future, he hadn't protested too much. True, I made the resolution when he was away, far away, in some jungle in South America. He'd been gone for three weeks, and the last time I'd heard from him, the phone connection had sounded like chimpanzees chewing on the wire. Between his, "I miss you," and, "I can't wait to get back home to you," I heard scratches as if bamboo shoots were climbing up the telephone pole, monkey screams, and a gunshot. He swore to me

that it was just a bad connection – not a lot of civiliza-
tion where he was hiding out right then – and that he
was safe and would be home soon.

But I couldn't take another sleepless night and
another day with my stomach twisted into pretzel
knots. He worked for the United States Drug Enforcement Agency, the D.E.A., and spent most of his time
out of the country in godforsaken lands where mur-
ders, kidnappings, and torture were routine occurrenc-
es.

Parker couldn't understand why his job bothered me. He expected me to let go, let him go, and
while he was gone, just go on with my life. When he
returned, whole, alive, we could continue to have a hell
of a good time together. And we did. Have a hell of a
good time. He was a fun-loving, thoughtful, caring,
gorgeous man, and I had found myself falling in love
with him. That was my problem.

Now, I heard the soft sigh of the lilting song,
and I backed away from the lamppost, looking for the
singer. "Singing in the rain, I'm singing in the rain..."
The goofy grin appeared, light-hearted and sweet, and
my heart leaped like a frog before I quickly knocked it
back into place with a swift intake of air. Parker circled
the lamppost, dancing like Gene Kelly and, for a second, he almost looked like him. Lean, lithe, light of
foot.

We had first met at this lamppost on a hot rainy August evening. I had left friends at Finegan's Bar near Quincy Market and was walking alone, umbrella closed up, allowing my face to feel the wet heat beat on my cheeks. I heard a chuckle and saw this handsome man leaning against a lamppost, watching me with an amused expression on his face. I was embarrassed and began to walk away, but he suddenly began to sing and swirl around the lamppost, "singing in the rain." Ever since, it's been "our" spot.

"Thanks for showing up, Duchess," he said, approaching as if he wanted to hug me, grin turning into a serious expression. I stepped back from the embrace and looked at the man. His eyes were tired and sad. I hadn't noticed the sadness earlier this morning. He looked unsure of himself, a rarity in this agent who thrived on aggressiveness and action.

I took my eyes off his, afraid of what else I'd find. "You're late, Agent Webb. And, after eating my food and cleaning my kitchen, you disappeared this morning." I didn't mention the Duchess and the slip of paper with the mysterious initials.

"I shouldn't have come in the first place," he responded. "I wasn't expecting that you'd have company."

I bristled. "I wasn't expecting an ex-boyfriend."

Parker's bright blue eyes flashed, and I knew he wanted to say more, but he bit it off and said instead, "Lunch? North End? Antonio's?"

"Not fair, you know I can't resist his pasta."

"Antonio's expecting us."

I moaned, and Parker shot me a satisfied grin. Antonio's used to be our favorite dining place – lunch or dinner – when Parker was in town. I loved his signature ravioli with pine nuts, spinach, and ricotta cheese. Parker claimed that the eggplant Parmesan was the best in the world. He should know, since he'd traveled to over 20 countries. "I haven't been back there since...."

"Yeah, well, Antonio always asks about you."

"I have an hour, Parker. Work is a mess and I'm way behind on deadlines."

"So what else is new?" He grinned. "Your ravioli is waiting for you. Come on, let's pick up speed."

The two of us walked quickly, companionably, down the streets toward the Italian section of Boston observing the sights and smells of a bustling metropolis. The weather was exquisite, as it can be in New England in September, and I allowed my mood to lighten. Damn it, it felt so good to be with him again. His stride was purposeful and strong, but he held my hand lightly and looked down at me frequently, as if to be sure I was really right beside him. Lightning pulses of chemistry shot between our fingers as I held on. I was confused. It felt so right, yet, what right did he have to be here, to be enticing me like this?

Almost a year ago when he returned from his trip, he found a note from me stating that I'd gone on vacation, that his clothes and suitcase and few household items were locked up in a storage facility, and that the relationship was over. He didn't fight for me. Instead, he just left me a letter, slipped underneath the door, which explained he was off again – Honduras this time – and that we could talk when he returned. He didn't call for two months. And when he did, I was too hurt even to try a civilized conversation. That had been the end of a beautiful but incomplete relationship. I mourned. I hurt. I dated a few guys, and eight months later ended up with quiet, secure, model-handsome Gregory, a perfect antidote for a female getting over her love for a traveling workaholic U.S. agent who thrived on danger.

Remembering this, I pulled my hand away from Parker and walked faster, leaving his side and looking around. A newsstand caught my eye and the blaring headline on the first page of The Boston Globe: "In Bogotá, US-Colombian raids net $35m in drug cash."

I stopped, dead in my tracts, and Parker walked right into my heels. "Ow!" I said. Parker didn't reply, but I saw his mouth set into a thin line as he read the headline too.

"Let's go. Antonio's, a glass of Chianti, and I tell you all," he said curtly. "Or at least all I can."

"No wine," I said back. "I'll never get a speck of work done this afternoon."

Parker just walked ahead, hand open waiting for mine. I ignored it and swore to myself that I'd hear his story, offer my sympathy for his dilemma, whatever that was, and be on my way to a safe, satisfying, secure life with my job, my house, and my new man, Gregory.

CHAPTER SEVEN

Settled comfortably on a corner of the north end of Boston, Antonio's overlooked the hordes of tourists and locals who patronized the Italian restaurants, cafes, bakeries, and churches interspersed throughout the district. I inhaled the sweet aroma of fresh pasta, enticing sauces, and cream-filled cannolis as we sat on wrought iron chairs at a table covered with a red-checkered tablecloth. Orange, red, and yellow zinnias decorated the center of the table, and a basket of fresh warm bread seduced me as I thought of the long line of people waiting to get a table.

"Helps to know the owner, capiche?" Parker whispered in his perfect Italian accent. He spoke five languages, fluently, but I was always forgetting which ones.

"This is a perfect setting," I agreed. Our usual table overlooked the street, tall windows opened wide to let in the early fall breeze. On other days, other times, it had been a romantic spot. But today, Parker had requested a more obscure table in the back corner, hidden from view by three tall, willowy ferns. As I munched on the soft, crusty bread, I felt bittersweet.

Purposely, I had forgotten how much I enjoyed being with Parker. His curled, pleased-with-himself grin, his crooked nose underneath beautiful expressive eyes that looked at me with an intensity that took my breath away. His well-proportioned body, with a strong stalk like a tree, arms and legs like sturdy branches, and a hard, flat stomach that was incredibly ticklish.

I shivered as I thought of our love making, and then I looked up to see a pair of gleaming blue eyes staring at my reflective face. "Penny for your thoughts?" he asked.

"No. That particular thought would require about a million pennies," I replied lightly, sipping my Pellegrino and willing myself to stop the memories. Despite our attraction to each other, the relationship hadn't worked. I needed someone I could call at 10 in the morning, if I wanted to, and see him in my mind's eye at a desk in a regular office building with a cup of steaming coffee and a stack of papers in front of him.

With Parker, I'd reach him only if his cell phone was working in the country he was visiting. And in my imagination, he was answering from a dingy bar or a drug kingpin's mansion where he was spying on the bad guys.

I shook my head as I sat there, erasing the good memories and making myself remember the bad. I looked up to see Parker staring at my neck.

"So, you still wear them?" He looked pleased.

My fingers moved to the pearls decorating my neck. Parker had given them to me on the first anniversary of our lamppost meeting.

"Yes," I replied.

"Good."

I shrugged my shoulders, trying to remove the memory of that day, when Parker had woken me up to a bedroom full of pink peony bouquets, and...

"You don't want the ravioli?" Parker asked.

"What? Oh." While I was in the middle of my reverie, the waiter had placed our food in front of us. "Smells delish." I tried a grin, but I knew it looked forced.

"Meredith, there's so much to explain, and I'm on borrowed time. Yours and mine."

"Well, some things never change," I interjected. "You were always running from one assignment to the other, from one crisis in Mexico to the next one in Guatemala." I placed a forkful of ravioli in my mouth and tried not to let him see that the sauce was burning my tongue. Damn.

Parker got that annoyed expression on his face, the one I hated. He had an agenda, and I had just interrupted it. Good. "Parker, you and I haven't spoken in six months. Having you pop in this morning was not a pleasant distraction. I have a life, you know. You left mine quite some time ago. Why this sudden interest in seeing me? And why couldn't you have just picked up the phone and said hello, or good-bye, or whatever it is you want to say?" I gulped down more sparkling water to douse the fire in my mouth and concentrated on my food. I really wanted to enjoy the pasta, but my stomach was twisting like a Slinky.

Parker stared back at me. "You, dear duchess, ended the relationship, not the other way around. I came home from Columbia and found that my life's possessions had been hauled out for storage, and that my girlfriend had flown the coop and hidden herself on some tropical island. Why didn't you call? Why didn't you wait until I got home, so we could talk it out?"

"Talk what out, Parker? You love your job; I hate your job. Your phone didn't work in the third world you were hiding in, or whatever it was you were doing, and the chance that you were going to come out of that one alive was iffy, at best. I figured I'd cut my losses before they – you – cut me. I just couldn't live your life."

"I didn't want you to live my life. I never wanted you to. I just asked you to be there when I returned, and then we'd continue where we'd left off." Parker's eggplant was untouched. He raised a finger and the waiter brought him a glass of Chianti, no other communication necessary between the two of them. I shook my head when the waiter looked at me questioningly.

"The last time I waited, Parker, you came home with a bandaged arm and a fever of 102."

"A flesh wound and small infection. No big deal. It healed in a week," he said, raising the wine glass to his lips.

"Bull shit," I said too loudly, my arm swinging up and accidentally hitting his glass, causing a drop of wine to spill on his shirt. Several heads turned toward us as I leaned toward Parker and whispered, "How was I to know how you'd come back the next time? In a body cast? A casket? Sorry Parker. No can do. You're a great guy. We had some good times, but my life is better now. Much better." I stuffed another forkful of ravioli in my mouth and chewed enthusiastically.

"I don't believe it. I've missed you every day since you threw me out. And there's no way you're satisfied with that, that, what's his name? Jeffrey guy."

Parker wiped at the wine stain distractedly, smearing it further.

"Gregory," I said, teeth clenched.

"Whatever. Boooring."

"How would you know? You saw him for maybe two seconds."

"Long enough." Parker sat back in his chair, sipping his wine and looking at me intently. "Listen, I don't want to argue. What we need is some time by ourselves. Some time alone. I'm changing my profession. No more drug chasing. No more traveling to places unknown. I'm changing ... a lot. And I'd like you to be part of the change."

I sat up straight, ravioli forgotten, lines of people forgotten, even burnt tongue out of my mind. "You're quitting? The D.E.A.? Can you do that?"

"I have to. We made a great catch in my last assignment, the one I was working on, actually, when I was with you. It took almost two years, but we got some of the bad guys, along with a spectacular stash of drugs and money. An almost successful operation. Except for one thing. We didn't get the main target, just his operatives. And my cover has been blown, so I have to disappear, change, make a new life. Or I'll have no life."

CHAPTER EIGHT

My appetite disappeared. The amazing man in front of me just told me he had to disappear. Did that mean he needed the witness protection program through the feds? My favorite ravioli looked mushy in its light red sauce, and a glass of wine seemed much more tempting. I looked up to find the waiter, just as Parker's cell phone rang. I asked for the Chianti as Parker looked at me apologetically, getting up to leave the table while he answered the call. The wine was delivered before Parker returned. I sipped half the glass before realizing that Parker wasn't coming back.

Damn the man. It was happening again. This was exactly the reason I was finished with Parker

Webb. Finished. How many other times had we made plans – the visit to my mom in New York City, the long weekend to Savannah to see my college friend - and we had to cancel, suddenly, because of Parker's job? A phone call, an urgent e-mail, a mysterious stranger at the front door, and he was out of there with a kiss, an apology, and a promise to "make it up to me" when he returned.

I sat dejectedly, watching the people walk by Antonio's. They seemed happy, these families and couples and friends, walking the streets of Boston with only the worry of where to eat on their minds. I, on the other hand, had a brain crammed full with questions and concerns. Why did he leave me like that, without even a goodbye or "I'm sorry"? Did he have to run? To hide?

This was why I liked Gregory so much. He would never leave me sitting alone at a romantic restaurant. He would have planned the entire outing so that he'd have plenty of time to devote to me. No lunchtime rendezvous. He rarely even ate lunch during the work week. But he'd have a 6:30 p.m. reservation for us, probably at the best restaurant near Symphony Hall. In fact, he'd probably also have tickets for a performance of the Boston Pops. We'd have a leisurely, quiet dinner, hold hands during the performance. No hurried assignations that would separate us for days.

Maybe Gregory wasn't as passionate as Parker, but he was always there for me.

Not surprisingly, Parker had, again, disappeared, but not before hitting me with the invisible bomb of his "desperate situation." Now I had to wonder if I would ever see him again, and if I even wanted to.

Unfortunately, I knew the answer to that question. Yes. Yes, yes, yes, I wanted to see him again. Not just to hear all of his story, but to smell his after-shave, to see him smile at me as if I was the only one in his world at that particular moment, to feel his arms around me one more time.

And mostly, as much as I hated to admit it to myself, just the chance that maybe, we could make love one more time. God, that sounded so cold. So male. I couldn't live with him, but the sex was enough to make me just want to get him into bed, at least one more time.

Making love with Parker had been different in ways I never could have imagined, as if what I knew about love and sex and passion were drawn in black and white in my memory, but suddenly when I was with Parker, it was all in living color. That sounded a bit naïve, considering I began seeing Parker when I was 30, a mature woman in every sense of the word. I had dated. I had had sex. I had even considered marriage one or two times.

But no man had ever done for me what Parker did.

From the beginning, the excitement was there, palatable, electrifying, from the moment we linked eyes at that lamppost. Before we ever physically touched, we felt each other, deep deep down in some visceral way that neither of us could explain. Within two weeks of meeting, we'd made love, but it hadn't seemed too soon. I felt as if we'd been undressing each other, feeling each other out literally as well as figuratively, since that first rainy night.

The sex was, well, how could I explain it without sounding trite or bombastic? It felt like I'd been standing on a cliff overlooking a waterfall all my life, wanting to be part of the waterfall, to feel that deep, fast penetrating water cascade over me, but I'd always been too afraid. Until Parker. When he made love to me, I jumped. The waterfall was more powerful, more pounding, more explosive than I had even imagined, standing on that cliff looking down.

I looked down now and realized I was holding an almost empty glass of wine, and that I was sitting alone at a table meant for two. My head began to throb. Damn. I was prone to migraines, but usually only when I got extremely stressed. I guessed meeting up with an old boyfriend who drove me crazy was stress enough. I quickly searched through my large purse and breathed a sigh of relief. My bottle of pills sat at the bottom like a whale resting at the bottom of the sea. If I took one of these tablets in time, the migraine could be reduced to an annoying headache.

The waiter sensed my discomfort and sidled up to my table. "Another glass of wine? Is your ravioli alright?"

"No more wine. A glass of water, please. And I have a favor to ask. Do you have a copy of The Boston Globe? I just need to see the front page." I looked at the older man imploringly, and he smiled at me as only Italian men can smile.

"Uno momento."

In two seconds he was back with water and the newspaper. "Grazie," I said as I swallowed a pill and then focused on the article I was looking for.

Bogotá - Authorities discovered $35 million yesterday in two upscale apartments – possibly one of the largest seizures ever of drug money – as part of a joint US-Columbian operation.

One man was arrested during the morning raids. In Washington, US Customs spokesman Floyd Denton identified the man as Felix Chativa Carrasquillo, and said he owned the apartments. He was arrested on a provisional warrant issued by the US Custom Service and the Drug Enforcement Administration, Denton said.

I remembered Floyd Denton. I met him when Parker took me to some Washington shindig during the holidays. He was a small, nerdy sort of man, with shifty eyes that never stopped roving. Parker said he was meticulous in his work, and although no one liked him, he was respected for his ability to open diplomatic channels between the U.S. and other countries. I read on:

Chativa was a major target of Operation Journey. I took a deep breath. Every time Parker left for a business trip when we were together, he mentioned that he was going on a 'journey.' I thought the use of the word odd then, but never questioned him. The investigation involved 12 nations and resulted in the seizure of about 25 tons of cocaine and methamphetamine and the arrests of 73 people around the world.

I put the paper down and drank the last of my water. Good God, this had been a huge operation, and all I had done was bellyache about the amount of time Parker was gone. Twelve countries! Twenty-five tons of drugs! Parker must have been thrilled when it all came down. But something went terribly wrong. Some of their information must have been faulty, because the big guy didn't get caught, and now Parker had to disappear.

I read the rest of the article, which of course didn't mention those details. Instead, it explained how the drug money was packed in bundles of $100,000 each, and that Luis Gilbert, commander of the Colombian national police, said it could be the biggest-ever haul of drug money in the world. At the Bogotá news conference, the US Ambassador and Gilbert congratulated each other on the operation, in which the D.E.A., the FBI, and Columbian police participated.

No mention of Parker's role, of course, or of the man who didn't get caught. I wondered who he was and what he planned to do to an undercover agent who tried to disappear when his cover had been pulled off.

I stood up, still unsure about what to do. The waiter approached me again, this time I assumed with the bill.

"Non, madam. It's already been taken care of," he explained with a charming grin. "Come back again, soon, though, with your boyfriend, no?"

No, I replied silently. I will not come back again with Parker. I probably will never see him again.

CHAPTER NINE

Back at work, I asked Jill if I had any messages.

"None from any unnamed man," she said with a grin. I ignored the remark and tilted my head for more. "One from Mr. Flack and one from your friend Shannon, reminding you about your dinner engagement tonight," Jill responded, sulking. She was waiting for me to explain about my lamppost rendezvous, but I didn't take the bait. She could sulk all afternoon, as far as I was concerned.

"Tell Mr. Flack I'll be up in 10 minutes," I ordered as I walked into my office and closed the door. Thank God, a reminder call from Shannon, my steady and sane friend. Boy, I needed to see a friend now. I called her back and left her a message that we were still on for the dinner we'd planned several weeks ago, and that I'd meet her at the Mexican restaurant in Harvard Square at 7:30. Then I called Gregory and left him a message (according to his secretary he was 'unavailable while with a client') and told him about my plans for dinner but hoped he'd still be awake when I got home. Gregory was an early to bed/early to rise kind of man, so the chances that he'd still be up when I got home were small. Maybe just as well.

Fortunately, the thrumming in my head had disappeared. I popped in a peppermint to clear my breath, brushed my hair into a neat chignon at the back of my neck, and braced myself for the meeting with my boss. If he called me twice, that meant he wanted something from me. Just what I didn't need.

Arthur Flack's office was in the upstairs' loft, all by itself. It was a huge room with high windows that overlooked the Public Gardens on one side, and Beacon Hill on the other. His tall, lanky frame was bent over a manuscript as I walked in. Without looking up, he re-marked, "Fine job on the Taterson galleys, Meredith. You worked miracles on that mess."

"Thanks," I replied. He didn't often dish out praise. Unlike many publishers, this man was a hands-on manager, and he oversaw every book that went through the system. Although he didn't have any medi-cal experience himself, he used the talents of his half a dozen board members, all with medical or therapy degrees. He expected, demanded, perfection from each book we published, and he damn near got it each time. I supposed that's why I liked working for him.

He stood up and looked at me. Six feet seven in his stocking feet, with white gray hair and light green eyes that never left a person's face. He intimidated many. I was intrigued. I knew that if I matched him, stare for stare, we'd always work well together, and the last three years hadn't proven me wrong.

"Now, about the real reason you're here," he said with a small smile.

"I'm just waiting for the other shoe to drop," I smiled back. Even though he could be cranky at times, he was a charming man, and he was trying to charm me right now. Uh oh, I thought.

"Barbara Browning has requested a one-on-one meeting with you regarding her book." I opened my mouth to protest, but he disregarded me and continued. "You're on the second set of galleys, so it's pretty clean. She's always been the kind of author that we need to treat tenderly, but as you well know, she's worth it."

I nodded. I did receive a generous bonus last year after we finished her first tome on occupational therapy. Practicing OTs, as well as nursing and OT schools, lapped it up hungrily. The last well-written,

definitive book on occupational therapy for children
had been published over 20 years ago, and it was out-
dated and boring. Barbara had a fresh writing style,
even though she was a pain in the neck.

"I take it that meeting her won't happen here in
Boston?" I asked, already knowing the answer.

"She wants you to go to her yacht, docked at St.
Thomas." He took one look at my face and frowned.
"You know, Meredith, most editors would jump at the
chance to go on a junket like this. All expenses paid. To
St. Thomas! You look like I've just asked you to visit
the basement and read the last five years' worth of
medical textbooks to see how many times the word 'hyperventilate' was used."

I winced. "It's not exactly good timing, Mr.
Flack. You've got me assigned to the book on nursing
care for the breast cancer patient, and the treatise on
male nursing, as well as ...."

"I've assigned the male nurse book to Jeff while
you're away, and Margery can handle the breast cancer
book permanently."

I tried to hide my disappointment. The cancer
book was fascinating. Plus, Jeff would edit the male
nursing book all wrong, and I'd have to spend double
the time correcting his blunders.   "And the neurology textbook?" I asked.

"That can wait. You're only going for four days,
Meredith. So, how soon can you leave?" He looked back

at his work, spectacles halfway down his nose, already dismissing me.

If I had to leave now, Gregory would be disappointed. After all, he had just moved in. And what about Parker? If I left now, I might never see him again. Of course, that might not be a bad thing, but I really needed some time to sort out my thoughts.

"Give me another day," I responded. "I'll leave on Wednesday."

Mr. Flack just grunted, and I walked out the door, anxious to meet Shannon and gripe while sipping a margarita or two.

CHAPTER TEN

I hugged the steering wheel of my convertible lovingly as I crossed over the Charles River toward Cambridge. The idea of hordes of commuters elbowing me for room in the subway, staring at me as I stared out into space pretending I was alone, didn't appeal today. It felt good to be enclosed in something familiar. But it took me 20 minutes to find a parking space blocks away from Harvard Square, so I was late by the time I walked into the packed crowd waiting in line at the restaurant. Knowing Shannon would be early, I pushed my way toward the tall pine reception desk and described my friend.

"She must be here," I insisted. "Tallish, red head, probably wearing an incredible bright peach or pink scarf around her shoulders ..."

"Oh. Sure. Next to the window." The young hostess gave me a once-over as I walked toward the back of the restaurant. I'm sure I didn't look like I belonged with the woman waving a long arm in my direction. Shannon was a buyer for a small boutique clothing store and carried herself and her clothes well. Despite her womanly frame, curly out-of-control red hair, and 5 foot 6 inch height, she appeared as sophisticated as a runway model. Compared to Shannon, I looked nondescript in my black pants and cotton top. I shrugged my shoulders as I reached my friend. Her heart was as large as her fashion sense, and I blessed her silently for being there, as always.

We pecked each other's cheek and smiled as I sat down with a large sigh and a quick glance for a waiter. "I don't know how you got us the best table in the restaurant, but thank you, and now I need a drink," I began.

Shannon's jade eyes twinkled as she removed her scarf, showing off a brilliant green silk blouse, and she huddled closer to me at the table. "And I know why, my secretive friend."

"What? Why?" I asked.

"Don't act so innocent with me, Meredith Powers. Don't forget, I've been in your life for many years, and I know all your secrets." Shannon was five years older than I. When I was in high school she was my best friend's older sister, but I never really knew her. After my freshman year at college, I ran into Shannon when I applied for a summer job at Nordstrom's, where she worked at the time, and a new friendship began.

"I don't know what secrets you're talking about," I began, but by the look in Shannon's face, I shut up. Just then, the waiter stopped by. "Perfect timing," I said lightly. "Margarita on the rocks, please, with salt."

"Would you like to order?" the tall, skinny young man asked, looking harried as he opened up his pad.

"Haven't had time to check out the menu." I hated it when a waiter tried to hurry you along. "We'll have our drinks, and then order, please. Shannon?" She still had half a glass of wine left and shook her head, impatiently tapping her shoes on the floor until he left.

"Now, are you going to tell me what's going on? Or should I call Gregory on this little ole cell phone and tell him that the fun is finally back in my friend Meredith's life?"

I frowned. Shannon didn't like Gregory any more than Jill did. Actually, I couldn't think of any of my friends who liked Gregory, but that was because they'd all been insane about Parker. He charmed them all, but so what? They didn't know anything about his real profession; we told them he worked for the U.S. Census Bureau and that's why he traveled frequently.

"How do you know about Parker?" I whispered. I don't know why I was afraid to talk about it. No one could hear us in this loud restaurant. But I whispered nonetheless, and stopped as soon as the waiter brought my drink.

"I saw him. This afternoon," she answered.

I sat up straight and took a large gulp of margarita, salt stuck on my upper lip. "You did what? When? Where?"

Shannon looked shocked. "You mean you don't know he's in town? That isn't your secret?"

"No, no. I mean yes, I did know, but I can't believe you just saw him."

"He was right here, in Harvard Square, bold and beautiful as ever." Shannon's eyes gleamed. She had been infatuated with Parker and, when we were dating, thought I was the luckiest woman alive. He was uncomfortable with her obvious admiration, but the two of them overcame this by developing a wisecrack friendship full of jokes and sarcastic comments. She must have been thrilled to see him. "It was the greatest coincidence. I had walked into Telford's, you know the cigar shop on Mass Ave? I was buying dad his favorite tobacco for his birthday next week. God, that's stuff is expensive. Do you know how much ....?"

I leaned over and touched her arm. "Forget the tobacco. What was Parker doing there?" I asked, dying to know what he was up to. I couldn't believe that he walked out on me at lunch, yet was able to stroll through Harvard Square. We used to go to Telford's together. Parker loved to take his time and select a really good cigar for an occasional smoke. It was a man thing, I guessed at the time. He never smoked it in front of me.

"I don't know. He never saw me. He seemed to be having an altercation with the owner, which surprised me, because Parker gets along with everyone. And then he raced out of the shop before I could let him know I was there." Shannon drank her wine thoughtfully, then looked at me as I took a gulp of my drink. "In fact, now that I think about it, Parker didn't seem himself at all. He looked agitated. His hair was uncombed. His shirt had a stain on it..."

"That was the Chianti."

"What?" Shannon was nonplussed.

"We had lunch today, well, part of lunch, and I spilled some wine on his shirt."

"Girl, you have a lot of talking to do. You haven't heard from that man in six months, and suddenly you're having lunch together, and he's looking weird. What in the name of love is going on?"

CHAPTER ELEVEN

Thankfully, the waiter returned to our table. Shannon ordered the fajitas, and as she pondered whether to have the chicken or steak, I thought of how little I could tell her. None of my friends knew Parker worked for the D.E.A., and I certainly couldn't reveal this secret now. On the other hand, I really needed to talk to someone. The waiter cleared his throat, and I realized he was waiting for me. I ordered the vegetable enchilada and asked for iced water and another margarita.

The crowd was getting boisterous, and I wished we had selected a quieter restaurant. Shannon stared at me expectantly.

"I truly don't know where Parker is right now," I answered. "He asked to see me, we met for lunch, but halfway through the meal he disappeared. Just made me glad I wasn't seeing him anymore." I took a large gulp of water as soon as the waiter set it down in front of me, and finished with, "that's the end of the story. So, now it's your turn. What's going on with you?"

"Ha ha, good try," Shannon responded. "I'm not going to let you off that easily. Don't worry, I'll get you to tell me more about Parker before the evening is through." She shifted her eyes over the tables full of 20 somethings, interspersed lightly with those in their 30s or 40s. "You know what? This place is getting too young for me. Never thought I'd say that. I'm 37 years old and feeling my age tonight."

I looked at Shannon's face as she took a small sip from her wine glass. Fine lines were etched around her eyes, but I thought they made her look even more attractive.

"What's the matter?" I asked.

Shannon looked at me rather wistfully, then responded, "I'm 37 and, finally, I met a guy who excites me. Someone I actually want to spend more than a day with." I opened my mouth and she shushed me with the palm of her hand. "I know, I've met some nice men, but none of them has held my interest for long. Except this one." She shook her head. "But there's a problem, so it probably won't work."

"What? What's the problem?"

Shannon just shook her head. "No. Can't talk to you about it. Not now, anyway. But we can talk about you right now. You had a magnificent specimen." She smiled at her words, but continued. "A man who is funny, smart, easy on the eye, and thought you were the best butter to spread on his bread. And yet, you let him go." She shook her head as if a teacher to a recalcitrant 5-year-old student.

"Butter?" I said, trying to lighten up the conversation. "I'm butter?" Again, I was placed in an untenable situation. Shannon didn't know about Parker's job, about my fears for him, about how little I really knew about him and what he did. She thought I wouldn't see him anymore just because he traveled too much. So instead, I just said, "Shannon, all is not as it seems. As you very well know is true in life. Besides, in my book, exciting isn't all it's cracked up to be. Constancy, reliability, subtlety, these things are fabulous attributes in a male specimen."

The waiter, thumping a hot steaming plate of enchilada in front of me, eyed me as if I were a man-eating plant. I looked up at him just in time to see him roll his eyes. Waiters hear all the best parts of strange conversations, I'm sure.

"Salsa on the side?" I asked, "and maybe some sour cream?"

"I'm sure you don't want the hot salsa," the sour-faced man said, then he quickly rushed away. Shannon smirked.

"So, now you're talking about Gregory," she noted as a plate of sizzling steak strips were placed in front of her by another server, a young woman. Shannon leaned toward the waitress. "Tell me hon, which would you want to date - cute, sexy and hot, or cute, boring and steady?"

The waitress looked at Shannon with a grin and answered, "sexy and hot eventually cools down. I'd go for the sure thing." I thanked her silently and began to attack my enchilada. Shannon took one bite of her fajita, sighed contentedly, then went back to the bone she was chewing on with me.

"So really, what's going on?" She smiled as I looked up with exasperation, nibbling on a zucchini slice smothered in cheese.

"Don't even try that on me. You're giving me a hard time about my love life, and giving me nothing in return. What gives with the guy who has 'problems'? Who is he? I didn't know that you've started to date a new man."

Shannon's eyes lit up like a bonfire on a cold night, but at the same time, her lips, usually in a wide smile, pressed together. "Don't want to talk about it. I do want to talk about you."

"Well, first of all, have you noticed that man sitting four tables away? He hasn't stopped staring at you for the past 20 minutes," I said, diverting her beautifully. Shannon blushed. Nothing like a blushing red head. "Ah ha. You have noticed."

"Not my type," she responded dismissively. "Worn gray trousers, decades-old blazer that was only cool in the '90s, uneven haircut and shifty eyes. Not interested."

I laughed. Not only had she noticed, she'd cut him down to size in one fragmented sentence. I had to agree with her assessment.

"Come on Merry, forget the unattractive Casanova and talk to me. Tell me your deepest dark secret," Shannon persisted.

I swallowed some of the surprisingly good shredded lettuce sprinkled with mild salsa. Then I felt a rush of adrenaline as I opened my mouth to talk about fears I'd kept quiet even to myself. "I never told this to anyone, but I wonder if I'm even capable of loving someone."

Shannon looked at me intently, smart enough to show no expression in her eyes. She just nodded her head to me in encouragement to go on. I took a sip of my second margarita, no rocks left, just a slimy green concoction.

"I mean, you tease me about my boyfriends and always having a man in my life. But think about it. In high school and the first two years of college, I didn't go out at all. Then I went crazy and dated guys for, what, maybe three weeks, one month tops. But then I couldn't stand any of them. There was one flaw or another – too loud, too short, too aggressive, too dumb. Remember?"

"But Merry, that's what dating's all about," Shannon protested, pushing her wine aside and leaning toward me. The crowd at the restaurant had gotten even noisier as the sun fell quietly into its resting place. I peered out the window; Harvard Square had become a dark place with bright lights advertising its treats: bookstores, clothing stores, bars, theaters. The center seemed different once the natural light disappeared, more magical and less frantic. I returned my gaze to my friend, who hadn't moved her eyes from mine.

"Let me get this out," I implored. "Just consider yourself my therapist for the night." Shannon leaned back and sighed, her dark red hair falling away from her face, showing gray circles underneath her eyes that I'd never noticed. "What I'm talking about is not exploring my options by dating different men. I'm talking about an inability to love, to actually give myself to someone, flaws and all. I know that no one is perfect. God knows I'm not. But I can't allow myself to get close enough to someone to love their imperfections, as well as the fascinating parts of their personality."

"Like Parker?" Shannon asked. I glared at her. She was getting into this therapist role a little easier than I wanted. I took a sip of the too sweet drink and reached for another bite of my enchilada. Time to change the subject. But I couldn't help the self-pity I felt for myself at that point. "You know what? I'm odd. That's all there is to it. I'm odd."

Shannon looked at me with amusement written all over her face. "Of course you're odd. I'm odd. We're all odd. That's what makes us even."

CHAPTER TWELVE

Shannon wanted to escort me to my car, but I insisted on walking her to the T stop at the center of Harvard Square, using our passes to continue through the turnstile. Our shoes tapped as we stepped down the concrete stairs into the cavernous tunnel to wait for her train. As I hugged her goodbye, thanking her for the dinner, and even more, the conversation, she plunged her hand into her huge pocketbook as if scrounging around for some errant piece of paper. Victory in her eyes, she brought her hand out, fingers clasped tightly around an object.

"I didn't know whether I should give this to you," she began, looking at the tracks as the noise of an oncoming train grew louder. "But here, this is what Parker and the guy behind the counter were arguing about." She opened her fingers and showed me a long, chubby cigar lying flat in her palm.

"That's weird," I began. The train rolled to a stop and Shannon walked toward it.

"I know, that's why I filched it while the guy wasn't looking," she nearly shouted, turning her head away from me to get on the car. "Parker wanted the cigar, the man refused to give it to him. When Parker left, the man put it on the counter to answer the phone, and, as they say, the rest is history."

"Shannon!" I screeched, more in shock than to make sure she heard me. She'd jumped onto the car and was waiting for the door to close. I couldn't believe she'd just picked the cigar up, hidden it in her purse, and left the shop, waiting until now to tell me about it. But this was just like Shannon. Always looking for drama, even if there wasn't any. Wouldn't she be surprised if she knew how weird Parker's stop at the cigar shop truly was, considering his sudden departure from lunch today? Shannon probably just figured she was giving me some excuse to see Parker.

"Good luck!" she yelled, but I could only see her mouth move as the train rolled away. Then I saw her expression change when she looked past me, so I twirled my head around and saw the retreating form of the man who had stared at Shannon when we were in the restaurant. Had he followed us to the station? I shook my head no. Everyone used this station. It was a coincidence. He probably missed the train – just as well for Shannon – and was waiting for the next one.

I put the strange cigar in the zippered pocket of my purse, walked back up the stairs to the fresh early September air, and started down the street toward my car, trying to remember where I'd parked it. As I walked, I mused about the stolen object now in my possession. What should I do with it?

The evening was pleasant, and when I finally escaped the busier section of the square and entered the quieter streets with ivy-covered houses and low-lit windows, I could see the sky sparkling with a million stars. I grew wistful, thinking about how I used to spend time years ago watching the sky and naming the constellations.

I heard a tree branch crack and startled back into awareness of my surroundings. A lone women ambling through a dark, quiet neighborhood, I needed to walk smartly, not like some bubble-headed princess.

Another crack of a tree branch, crunch of some leaves, but no one in sight. Normally, that wouldn't have scared me, but the back of my neck grew goose bumps the size of acorns, and I knew that my instincts were telling me I'd better watch out.

However, I refused to be intimidated. I walked decisively, angry that my heart was beating louder than a jackhammer. Purposefully, I stopped, just to calm myself. And then I heard a sound, a sound like a husky breath that was nearby, but hidden. I started to trot down the street toward my car. It was still half a block away. Damn. Why did I decide to play the brave female part and leave the T station alone? Shannon and I could have walked here, then I would have driven her back to the T. What a fool. A sharp breeze blew the tree branches around as if they were helpless marionettes, and I shivered uncontrollably.

Then I heard the footsteps. Heavy footsteps, running toward me. I broke into a run, finally seeing my car ten yards away. What should I do? The person was gaining ground. He'd probably get to me before I reached the car, or right when I got there. Wasn't that worse? What if the man got my keys, knocked me down, and stuffed me into the trunk of the car?

I ran faster, my shoes cutting into my heels and my toes squished tightly with each pounding step. Two cars away I swerved and ran toward a house with its lights still on, preparing to scream for help like an injured animal. I opened my mouth and moved my vocal cords, but not a sound escaped, not even a whimper. Nothing. I tried again, pushing my tongue against the back of my throat. Scream, damn it, scream. But the night was silent except for the moaning trees and the incessant footsteps, sounding closer every second.

I reached the stoop of the well-lit house and tripped on the first step. My knee crashed onto the cement, and I felt blood leak through my pants. Then strong arms lifted me up as if I were a rag doll and dragged me away from the house, away from the lights, away from the fantasy of shouting like a strong, independent, free woman.

I hadn't realized how firmly I was clutching my purse, its long strap twirled up and over my left arm, until the man, covered in some kind of grotesque woolen mask that just showed dark eyes, tried to pull it away.

"Give it up," he snarled.

I was having difficulty being a strong woman, maybe, but I was not a fool. I looked at him coolly and said, "Let go of me, and I'll give it to you." He loosened his grip and upon doing so, some of my strength and resolve returned. I let off a scream of magnificent proportion until he smacked his hand over my mouth.

Then I bit him.

"Bitch!" he shouted, still pulling at the purse and trying to press me against him, all at the same time. At this point I would have gladly given the handbag to him, but the strap was wound around my arm, and he wouldn't give me room to move. Instead, he rammed his hand into the bag, muttering unintelligibly until the outside light of the house came on, shocking both of us.

The door began to open, and, feeling safer, I pulled my purse back into my stomach and screamed. The masked man stepped on my foot, either in haste to escape or in anger at me; either way, it hurt like hell. A tired-looking, middle-aged man peered out his screened door, shouting, "What's going on there?"

"Call the police!" I yelled. But as soon as the homeowner had appeared, my assailant's grip had loosened. By the end of my proclamation, he was gone.

Nothing of the encounter was left except a red mark on my mouth from my attacker's grip, and a bloodstain on the knee of my pants.

CHAPTER THIRTEEN

The next 30 minutes were a blur. The lights blazed while the sirens screeched into the quiet neighborhood like unwanted guests. I answered questions for what seemed hours, but was surprised that when I was finally escorted to my car, it was only 10:30. The police had combed the area, turning up not one clue. They told me they'd contact me with more questions and any new information the next morning. I nodded numbly and drove home.

At first expecting an empty, unlit house, I crept toward my street, less than a mile from Harvard Square. While dealing with my fear, confusion and rage, I had forgotten that Gregory lived with me now.

Kind of. It had only been two days since he moved in with one suitcase, a couple of suits, a grill (he preferred his charcoal over my gas), and his running clothes. We weren't really ready to cohabit, and I think we both knew it. This was Gregory's idea of a preliminary "let's see what it's like if I'm around most of the time" kind of casual move.

But now, I was extraordinarily relieved to see a welcome yellow glow greet me as I found a parking spot near my house. The curtains were closed, and I was sure I'd opened them before I left in the morning. I turned the lock to the front door and immediately heard soft classical music emanating from the living room. Without thinking, I knocked my shoes off, one by one, and padded exhaustedly toward the sound. The last thing I expected was a relaxed looking boyfriend garbed in his striped seersucker bathrobe, knotted tightly at the waist, with a glass of port in one hand and a look of hot naked love in his doe-brown eyes.

"I thought you'd be home earlier than this," Gregory said as he handed me the small-stemmed glass and led me to the comfortable armchair in the corner of the room. "You look exhausted. Is everything alright?"

"Gregory!" I answered, not knowing what else to say. My hand trembled slightly as I took a sip of the thick golden liquid, feeling it sting sweetly as I swallowed.

"What's the matter? Everything isn't alright!" he exclaimed, now kneeling next to me. He took the glass from me and gulped a mouthful, as if needing some sustenance himself.

"I was mugged, or at least I think someone was trying to mug me. On my way back from Shannon's. Well, not Shannon's apartment. We ate dinner at Harvard Square. I walked back to my car." My voice quivered and I stopped and took a deep breath. "I was scared," was all I could end with.

Gregory looked nonplussed. "This just happened? You were just mugged? God, look at you, you're bleeding." He had just noticed the dried blood on my pant leg. My eyes were smudged from wiping tears away as I had driven home. "Are you alright? Why didn't you call me? Where are the police?"

Why didn't I call him? That was strange. I hadn't even thought of calling him. I figured he'd be in bed anyway; he was always asleep by 9:30 during the week, up by 5 a.m. I thought of calling Shannon, but she would have just arrived home, and I didn't want to worry her; there wasn't a thing she could have done for me at almost 11 p.m. My parents would be useless: my mom hysterical, my dad ready to hop in his car and drive the seven hours up to Cambridge from New Jersey. No, thank you.

I asked Gregory to sit down and told him about walking from the T, hearing the sounds, feeling the man reach me and try to grab my purse. I didn't tell him about the cigar. I didn't tell him what I was slowly beginning to suspect - that the attacker wasn't looking for money, but for a specific object. I just told him how scared I'd been, and that I wanted to sink into bed with the covers up to my nose.

Gregory couldn't have been more understanding or caring. He washed off my knee with warm water and then gently rubbed ointment on the large brush-burn and covered it with a Band-Aid. He left me alone as I changed to a long t-shirt in the bathroom, and when I came out, the bed was turned down, the lights dimmed.

"Are you feeling better? Do you have a headache? Should you take a pill?" Gregory had seen me suffer a couple of migraines over the past few months.

"No, surprisingly no headache. But I took a pill earlier today. Maybe that helped." Gregory looked at me questioningly, but I didn't explain.

"Okay, good. Everything's locked up. Your alarm is turned off. You're not going to work tomorrow," he said, voice firm. "You don't have to worry about anything. Sleep tight."

"But...." I began. I knew I should talk to Gregory about Parker; I needed to be honest with him.

I obviously had ambivalent feelings about an old boyfriend. I obviously wasn't sure I was ready to have a live-in boyfriend. But as Gregory slid into bed beside me, he put his finger near my lips, shushing me, and brought his lips to mine lightly yet seductively. It was a tender kiss, asking for nothing in return, yet letting me know how much he cared. He ended it with a light peck on my cheek and turned off the light. I didn't argue. I sank down in the comfortable bed, pulled the flannel sheets up to my chin, and turned my back against his.

As I listened to his breathing quickly change to the slow, deep sigh of sleep, I thought of his kiss. Sweet. Caring. Loyal. And, dare I say it, loving? Yes, I believed that Gregory loved me, and I didn't know what to do about it. Two men in my life, two men inextricably connected to me, two more than I ever thought I could handle, or need.

I closed my eyes, attackers forgotten, cigars forgotten, even the question of Parker's whereabouts forgotten for the minute. Instead, I explored my lips with my tongue, a smile on my face. Gregory was a good kisser. He loved me. Parker was an incredible lover. He wanted me. And who, I wondered, who was I in this mix of male madness?

CHAPTER FOURTEEN

The dream hit me like an arrow hits the center of a bull's eye. I rose in my bed as if sleepwalking, eyes open, mouth forming an O. But I was wide awake. The dream began to dissolve, mist floating from a cold river, evaporating into thin air. No! I had to hold onto it. The answers were there in every tiny detail.

I sat up straighter, my thin t-shirt pulling against my breasts, gathering in a bunch at the top of my hips. I remembered the voice – Gregory's voice – telling me to stop. To leave. To go away. Why would he say that? And then Parker's deep, loving tone, imploring me to "Smoke it. Smoke it."

I shook my head back and forth. Damn. The dream had made sense when I was in the thick of it. It had enveloped me like a fog surrounding a tree, sucking up all the moisture. I knew that my subconscious was trying to tell me something. But what?

I collapsed back down on the pillow. What had I read before about dreams and how to remember them? Ah, yes. I curled up into the fetus position, right ear snuggled against the soft pillow, and closed my eyes. If I positioned myself the way I had been sleeping, the dream would return. That's what the book said anyway.

I felt myself relax. My body grew heavy. I allowed my muscles to let go and my breathing to slow down. There was Parker, with smoke curling out of his mouth. What was he saying? I sank further into the pillow, and the dream. He raised his hand to his mouth and pulled out – a cigar? He puffed on it and looked directly at me, eyes pleading, speaking to me, but all that came out of his mouth was smoke.

I sat up straight in my bed again, wide awake.

The cigar! That's the bull's eye! I tore my t-shirt off and pulled on my blue jeans, only to look at the clock. 3:12 a.m. In disgust, I removed my jeans, put my t-shirt on again and threw myself back into bed, seeing the dream dissolve into a wisp of gray vapor. Gregory tossed in his sleep, then half awoke, asking, "You okay?"

"I'm fine," I replied as I squeezed my eyes shut. "Just fine."

When I awoke again, it was 7:40 a.m. Gregory was gone. He must have changed in the guest room. He left me a note, telling me to relax and take the day off and call him in the office. I curled the note up in my hand and pressed it close to my heart.

I thought of the way my heart beat last night when that man grabbed me and my stomach had kicked back like a horse against a barn door. I picked up the phone to call Gregory, but I dialed my mother's number instead.

"Mom." My voice was shaking, and I knew that she was immediately aware that something was wrong.

"Meredith? Sweetie? Everything okay?" But she didn't wait for an answer. "I'm so glad you phoned. We haven't talked in over a week. But you know, I just haven't been around. Donald had some time off and he took me to the most glorious new restaurant off Park and Fourth in the city. Chez Piazza. Have you heard of it?"

I didn't say anything, stunned at her insensitivity, but not surprised. What had I expected? It had always been about Mom, never about me, or even Dad.

"Well, it doesn't matter," she continued. "The next time you come visit me in New York, I'll take you there." She paused for a breath, and I waited to see if she would pull the conversation back to me. Ever since she'd begun dating Donald, she had a girlish lilt to her voice, and when we did talk, she went on and on about the places he took her. Donald was only one in a long line of suitors – Mom and Dad had been divorced for over fifteen years - so I was used to hearing about all the men in her life.

"Merry? You're awfully quiet. What have you been up to?"

"Just the usual," I fibbed, "until yesterday. But then I had a scare, Mom." My voice broke and I pushed my fingertips into the soft spot of my palm. I would not break down while talking to her.

"What? What's the matter?" She sounded genuinely concerned.

"Well, I went out to a restaurant in Cambridge with Shannon, you remember her, and on my way back to the car...."

"Meredith, I've told you over and over again not to go out at night by yourself. You act as if you're a man. Men can get away with it, but you're an attractive young woman. It's not safe. For a woman with a Master's degree you can act pretty stupid. Now, what happened?"

I gritted my teeth and stood up. This had to be short and simple. I should never have called her. What was I thinking? I wanted some motherly concern, a mom-hug over the phone, but instead I was getting the third degree.

"Mom, I'll remind you that I am a grownup. A 32-year-old woman who owns her own home and has a successful job. If I want to meet a friend for dinner, I'll meet a friend for dinner at 8 p.m., or 1 a.m."

My mother sighed long and audibly at the end of my statement. "Okay, dear. Fine. Then what lovely experience did you have after your dinner with a friend, at night, alone on your way to your car, as an intelligent 32-year-old woman?"

"Forget it, Mom."

"Meredith, don't do this to me. I want to know what happened. Now."

We were 300 miles away, but I could still feel the force of her personality pushing, demanding, reducing me to a skinny little girl who was always diminished by the thundering disposition of her mother. I sucked in a deep breath, stood tall and straight, and said in a strong voice, "As I left the restaurant some guy tried to take my pocketbook. I struggled with him, but he got scared off and ..."

"Did he get your wallet, Meredith? If so, you have to call all the credit card companies. I've always wondered why you have so many cards. Remember last year I suggested you cut some of them up? Now you know why. Watch out, or that thief will charge up hundreds of dollars and the credit card companies will hold you responsible."

I felt sick to my stomach. I needed to get off the phone. "No! He didn't get my purse or anything in it," I yelled. Why couldn't she just act concerned and get it over with?

Silence on the other end. "Well, are you alright? I'm coming up there. That's a horrific experience honey. I'm so sorry. I don't like you living in that town, which is really a city. It used to be a small neighborhood, I realize that, but look what it's become. You can't even go out for dinner without getting robbed and raped and ..."

"Mom, I'm okay. I just wanted to talk to you. I'm really okay. Relax."

"Well, what did you do when you got home? I hate the idea of you in an empty house as it is, but after that..."

"Gregory was here."

"Thank God." Mom loved Greg. She couldn't stand Parker, not that she ever saw much of him. Thought he was too cocky and too flighty for me. Not my kind, she used to say. Gregory, I guess, fit her bill for the right kind of man for me: steady, solid, good job, good looks. I couldn't argue with her. "What does he think about all this? Does he want you to move in with him? You know, that's not a bad idea..."

"Oh, there's the doorbell," I lied. No way I was going to tell her that Gregory had tentatively moved in. Nor that Parker had shown up and wanted to be back in my life. Well, that would be a lie anyway. Parker had revealed himself for a minute. He was out of my life, permanently. "Better see who it is. Talk to you later, Mom!"

"Oh." She sounded disappointed. "We never have long conversations anymore, Meredith. Think about coming for a visit, okay? Or I could come out there. Let me check my calendar."

"Right. Gotta go, Mom. Love ya." I hung up, felt my stomach unclench, and then heard the doorbell ring.

CHAPTER FIFTEEN

I laughed. I told my mom I had to hang up because the doorbell was ringing, and conveniently enough, it really did. I checked my watch as I walked toward the front door. 8:10. I should have been halfway to work by now, and I hadn't even called the office. Perhaps I should take Gregory's advice. But I couldn't afford to take a day off – too much to do. On the other hand, I was still shaky from the incident last night. The thought of driving into the city, or taking the subway, and trying to concentrate on Browning's treatise daunted me. Would I get anything accomplished, besides staring out the window, wondering if the thug would have hurt me if I hadn't been rescued by that sleepy man in the neighborhood?

I shivered as I opened the door to, well, to nothing. Nobody was there. I stepped out and looked both ways up and down the tree-lined street. No cars. No neighbors taking their dogs out for a walk, no mail carriers, no UPS truck. Nothing. Shrugging, noticing for the first time that it was an absolutely perfect day, 70 degrees, blue skies with puffy white clouds and a soft gentle breeze, I turned to go inside. I stopped when I noticed something fluttering by the Rose of Sharon bush, still bursting with amethyst flowers. Its pointy yellow stems directed me toward a folded piece of white paper in its midst. I opened it up to read the scrawled black writing: "Great Meadow. 9 a.m. TRMFY."

Parker. It had to be Parker. When we were together, we used to love going to Concord to run the paths of the meadow, a little known bird sanctuary and wildlife preserve. But why did he sign it TRMFY? What did that mean? But I promised myself I wouldn't think about it. Why didn't he just call me like a normal person and ask me to go to Great Meadow? And how did he know I was home? Questions raced in my head like speeding cars around a racetrack.

I locked the door after me, bolted it, and raced upstairs. I had 40 minutes to change, get in Nelly, and drive to Concord. I could do it. The question was, should I? As I pulled out a pair of running shorts from my dresser drawer, the phone rang. Damn.

"Hello?" I answered, out of breath.

"I hope I didn't wake you. I just wanted to make sure you're feeling better. Did you sleep okay? How's your knee?" Gregory sounded so concerned; I felt a twinge of guilt. I had barely thought of him since I woke up.

"Much better," I said quickly. "Thanks again for being there last night Gregory. You were really wonderful." I sat on the bed while I talked to him, realizing I was right. It had been wonderful, having Greg there. I felt secure. I was able to get a good night's sleep, despite the nightmare, because he was in the house, protecting me. I never felt as if I needed protecting, and generally I would growl at the thought; but last night, I felt vulnerable and needy and afraid. And Gregory was there, as always. So what the heck was I doing, running off to see an ex-boyfriend who was never around when I needed him?

"I'm glad I was there too. But I wonder if I moved in too soon. You didn't seem, well, ready somehow. All weekend, I got the sense..." he paused, sounding unsure of himself. "You know, we need to talk. The last thing I want to do is rush you, Meredith." The last thing I wanted to do was answer Gregory's questions. "Of course we can talk." I said. "Maybe we should go out tonight for dinner. You know, just relax and spend some time together."

"It's a date," he said. "So will you stay home today, rest up?"

"Yes, I'm going to take your advice. I'll call you later today. Is that alright?"

I heard Gregory smile over the phone. He had the nicest smile; it lit up his face and made him look relaxed, without a care in the world. "Sure. Take it easy. If you want, I'll make us dinner tonight. We don't need to go out."

I hesitated. "Let's wait and see, okay? And thanks, Gregory, thanks for everything."

I hung up slowly, looked at myself in the mirror, wide eyes, long hair loose and unbrushed. Then I pulled on my shorts and searched for my favorite sports bra.

CHAPTER SIXTEEN

Top down, sun shining, wind blowing in my face, I drove as if I didn't have a care in the world. My heart raced happily while simultaneously I felt guilty. Was it right to be in such high spirits? I didn't want to hurt anyone, or disappoint.

Speaking of which, I used my cell phone to call my dad at his office.

"Your mother just called and I've been trying to reach you at home," he responded before the end of the first ring.

"Well, hello to you too," I said, laughing. He loved his caller ID at work. He refused to have it at home, basically because he hated to talk on the phone, and once home, he didn't have to. If I wanted to reach him there, I called twice, hung up, and he called me back. One of his many quirks. His quirks were Mom's excuse to leave him when I was in high school. I found them endearing, but then again, I wasn't married to him.

"Sorry, Dad. I didn't want to worry you. I know you're busy with a big project."

There was an angry pause, then he said, "Merry, you are my biggest project, and you have been for 32 years." I smiled. I loved my dad. He reminded me of the absent-minded professor: glasses always falling down his nose, crumbled shirts and a pen behind his ear. He never remembered when my friends called me when I lived at home, and he often forgot to eat. He had a Ph.D. in pharmacology and spent days locked up in a lab. He still lived in the same house in the same small New Jersey town where I grew up.

"Dad, it was scary, but I'm absolutely fine. In fact, I took the day off and I'm driving with the top down toward Concord's Great Meadow. I remember how much you loved walking among the marshes."

"Gosh, we haven't done that in a while, have we?" I knew I could calm him down. Just change the subject a little, cute little trick my mom taught me. "Meredith, um, I've been thinking of coming up to Boston for a visit. A couple of things I need to, well I want to, talk to you about. But now I think I'll do it sooner rather than later. How about this weekend?"

Now this was concerning. My father rarely traveled. He hated planes, trains and automobiles. He preferred to walk, and many times that's how he figured out problems. Some weekends he'd walk 15 miles before realizing he'd better turn around and walk home. "Dad, what's wrong?"

He laughed. Dad rarely laughed; he usually was thinking too much. "Dad?" Now I was really getting worried.

"Nothing is wrong. Actually, I've met someone. Well, kind of met someone. I've known her for a while, but lately it's become more than, let's say more than an acquaintance."

I sat in my car, thankfully in the slow lane by now, breezing down Route 2 and thinking, 'the world is coming to an end....or at least to a weird tilt that will change the axis of the planet.' As far as I knew, my father hadn't dated since Mom left him. "That's wonderful Dad! I can't wait to meet her."

Dad cleared his throat, three times, and then said, "I just want to see you myself, first. Talk to you, you know?"

No, I didn't know. "Dad, I'm going to be away this weekend. I have to fly to St. Thomas and meet an author."

"St. Thomas?" As far as he was concerned, if I flew to Washington, D.C. it was to the ends of the earth. "Why St. Thomas?"

"The author is married to a retired banker, who bought a yacht, his life-long dream. They sail around the Caribbean, anchoring in St. Thomas. She hopes it's just a phase and they can return to their home in Maryland soon."

"Huh." Dad wasn't known for his conversation. "Meredith, isn't this a bit soon, after being mugged? Shouldn't you just stay home for a while? Your mother sounded quite concerned."

I felt the breeze in my hair and nodded at the 30-something man who ogled me in his large pickup truck. "Dad, I'm fine. Mom just exaggerates things, you know that." I could imagine Dad nodding his head in agreement. "Look, I'm almost at the Meadow. I'll call you in a few days, when I'm in St. Thomas. Maybe you can tell me more about this woman you're seeing."

"Maybe." He didn't sound so sure. I wondered what was wrong. All the people in my life were having love problems. Shannon with a man who had a 'problem.' Dad with a woman he wanted to talk to me about before I could meet her. Me with the disappearing ex-boyfriend and a new guy who had moved in, sort of. Mom was the only one who seemed happy with her love life.

We hung up, and I fast-dialed the office to talk to Jill.

"Hey boss, how are you feeling?" she responded when she heard my voice. I guessed she figured I was sick, since I wasn't at my desk at my accustomed hour of 8:30 a.m.

"I'm sorry I didn't call earlier, Jill. I had an incident last night, and ..."

"Oh, we know all about it. Gregory called us first thing this morning. He really sounded worried about you, Meredith. Poor guy. And poor you. Are you alright? Mr. Flack said you should take a couple of days off. Let Barbara Browning wait on her own high horse, he said, and that's a direct quote."

"Greg called?"

"Yeah. Told us all about the mugging, and how shaken up you were, and how he hoped you'd sleep in all day. You are in bed, aren't you Meredith? Or at least lounging on your sofa, reading a good book and eating bon bons?"

I was just about to hit my horn at some stupid 16-year-old hot dog who had cut me off the fast lane on Route 2. Instead, I gingerly placed my left hand on my lap while my right hand steered. The phone headset gave me two hands for safe maneuvering, but I was only able to give the driver a dirty look.

"Sort of," I said. "Listen, it wasn't that bad. The mugger didn't even get my purse. I'll be in tomorrow. Tell Mr. Flack I'll change my flight. I'll leave on Thursday."

"Okay, I'll do that for you, but are you sure? Gregory said..."

"Yes, positive," I said, cutting her off and turning off the phone. 'Gregory this' and 'Gregory that.' Since when did he take charge of my life? I felt my hackles raise and wondered why. Wasn't that one of his appealing qualities? He took care of me, as far as I would allow, and was always around. My security blanket, so to speak, but much more charming than a blanket or a stuffed animal. I shrugged and took the exit for Concord. The trees became taller and lusher. Hanging baskets decorated the front porches with colorful red geraniums and purple asters. Pink begonias and impatiens dotted the plush green lawns amidst mulched gardens. Even the sky looked bluer here. I turned onto Bedford Road and looked for the small, discreet sign for Great Meadow. Few people knew about this gem of a nature preserve, and I was looking forward to seeing it again. I hadn't been back since Parker and I split.

I counted only two other cars in the small lot adjacent to the Great Meadow, but neither of them was likely to be Parker's mode of transportation. Was he here? I stretched beside my car and looked around, but only saw a birder walking with his cumbersome equipment toward the path where the marsh lay. Tall cattails swayed in the breeze as red-winged black birds called to one another.

I stretched a few more minutes, then got impatient. Was this another aborted effort? Lunch, and now a clandestine run in which Parker never shows? I sighed with disappointment and began to jog on my own. My leg muscles were tight, but it felt good to loosen them in the late September warmth. My hair bounced behind me in a ponytail, and I breathed in the fresh air with relief. Maybe this was the way it should be. Forget about Parker. Forget about lost love and ugly chubby cigars. Just be happy with what I had now, a good job, a trip to the Caribbean, and a caring boyfriend.

A shadow lunged toward me from the river trees, and I jumped like the frog I'd just passed three strides ago. A noise escaped from my throat, part scream and part greeting.

Of course, it was Parker.

CHAPTER SEVENTEEN

With a cocky grin and a lift of his eyebrow, Parker raced ahead. "Not quite in shape, huh?" he called as he passed me.

"You're late," I responded. I kept my pace even, and he slowed down a little so we could talk.

"Wanted to make sure I wasn't being followed." This is how we used to talk when we ran together. Quick bursts of meaningful words. Short and honest. Maybe that's why I loved running with him when we were together. No bantering then, or skipping around our feelings or worries. It all came out on a hard six-mile run.

"By whom?" I asked.

"The bad guys," he dared to reply, staring straight ahead.

"Give me a break."

Parker broke his stride and almost stopped, so I slowed down to a jog and returned his stare. "I don't want to say too much. Some men are trying to hunt me down. I know too much."

"What are you going to do?" I picked up the pace again. I didn't want long sentences or explanations. I just wanted the truth.

"I have to figure out some stuff first. Then I'm entering the witness protection program."

I stopped so fast Parker was four strides ahead of me before he realized it. He turned and walked back to me, giving me time to hide my shock. "That stinks." I resumed running, slowly, because my heart was racing as if we were running three times faster. The witness protection program? I'd never see him again.

"Yeah, I'd like to avoid it, but it's not looking good." Parker stopped talking as we ran past a couple walking slowly on the path. They held hands and looked content. I pushed down a sudden pinch of jealousy, then looked at my ex-boyfriend.

"What do you want, Parker?"

"Doesn't matter what I want at this point." He turned his head at the noise to our right. A large goose had honked her disapproval at us as she moved with her mate and half a dozen goslings, in circles, on the marsh.

We both looked ahead of us again. No other interlopers, human ones anyway. That was the beauty of not working on a weekday. Everyone except that couple was at work. I wondered what their story was. I wondered why I cared.

"I'm going to have to go away for a while."

"The protection program, right now?" My face was flushed, my knees ached a bit. The sun felt good; the conversation hurt.

"No, not yet. I need to... Never mind. I'm sorry, Merry. Maybe I shouldn't have tried to see you first."

"Maybe not." I was angry. What was I supposed to do? What was I supposed to feel? We continued in silence, and then looped around the marsh and returned to the spot where the couple had been, but they were gone. Sweating and breathing hard, I slowed down at the place we'd last seen them. What was it about them that piqued my interest?

Their serenity, I realized. I wanted to be part of a couple that meshed together, relaxed, happy, able to just hold hands and walk quietly. I stopped my run so suddenly I felt lightheaded. Parker jogged slowly ahead of me, looking back quizzically. That was it! I wanted an easy, smooth relationship, one where I was sure about who I wanted to be with for the rest of my life. Sure of me, then, too, and what I wanted and needed. Look at me, I thought. I was running with an ex-boyfriend who didn't even know who he was, or who he could be, anymore.

I walked as I thought, looking out at the marsh covered with tall brown and green reeds, cat's tails, and grasses. The path was deserted, which I appreciated, and the silence was soothing. But a sudden swoosh like the sound of a hundred taffeta dresses moving in synchronization startled me. I jumped away from the marsh, and out of the corner of my eye I saw Parker turn quickly to reach my side.

Out of the reeds and low-lying water, hundreds of hidden ducks swirled up, into the air. I gasped, mouth open, head turned upward. The sound moved me as if I'd just listened to an organ recital at a large cathedral, and I felt connected to the land, the sky, and to myself. Perhaps a message was there, somewhere between the contented couple and the ducks. I just had to learn how to read it.

Parker stood in front of me, his eyes following the ducks' flight in the sky. "Spectacular," he said, but now he was looking at me.

"I need to go, Parker."

He smiled, the kind of smile he used when he was hurt. God, I hated it when he did that. He was such a macho man, yet he looked just like a little boy now.

"Let's cool down at the diner. Finish the conversation over a latte."

I nodded. What the hell. The diner was a little hole in the wall in West Concord. We'd never run into anyone we knew.

"Meet you there," he said quickly, and then, what else? He disappeared in a flash of blue shorts and muscled legs.

~~~~~~~~~~~~~~~~~~

Fifteen minutes later I was at the Red Dog Diner, which overlooked a creek and actually did include a red dog. Rover, an Irish setter mix, sat at the door and greeted all the customers. A waitress had once told Parker and me that Rover was the great-grandson of the original red dog, which had given us an idea of how long this place had been in existence. The owner/manager/cook gave me a nod to seat myself at one of the well-used leather booths, and I sat facing the door, looking out the window at the small stream of water that raced over large rocks.

"Breakfast, or just an iced tea?" How did he do that? Appear as if out of thin air. Parker's ability to seem weightless and invisible always amazed me. Today, I noticed, I was also annoyed. Why couldn't he be a regular guy like Gregory? But I knew the answer even before I considered the question. Because he was Parker, born to a successful father who traveled

extensively as an engineer for Boeing, taking his wife
and son with him to Australia, Germany, and Spain.
And those were the long, two-year stints; the family
also had smaller stretches of time in Russia and China,
not to mention Texas and California. Parker was
different from me in every way: home schooled versus
the same school system my whole life; the son of
sophisticated parents who married well, as opposed to
the daughter of a mismatched, unhappy couple; an only
child as opposed to being a younger sibling. He loved to
travel; I sank all my extra money in a small cottage. He
snowboarded; I skied.

"You're off somewhere, again," Parker said,
interrupting my thoughts. He wiped his hand through
his hair, messing it up even further, and looked over at
the plump, blonde-haired waitress who appeared at the
side of our booth as swiftly and effortlessly as a spy.
Maybe she was. Maybe she worked for Parker. Maybe I
was becoming neurotic.

"She'll have an ice tea and one of your iced
scones. I'll take a low-fat latte, heavy on the whipped
cream." I rolled my eyes. Parker and his whipped
cream. No self-respecting man used whipped cream on
his hot drinks. Gregory drank coffee, no sugar, no milk.
Like a real man. I coughed into my hand. Now I was
thinking stereotypically, as well as neurotically.

"So, what were you thinking about? Didn't look
like work. In fact, it looked like you were pondering the

meaning of the universe," he continued as the waitress brought our drinks miraculously fast.

"Nothing so expansive," I responded. "A little closer to home. Where is your home, Parker? I mean, in between all the trips."

His smile vanished from his face, a very fatigued face, I noticed. He looked down into his whipped cream as if reading his fortune, or his future, and when he looked up, I wanted to jump across the table and console him. Instead, I sat still as a stone as he said, "Let's just say that at this point in time, I don't have a home. And that is just one of the many things I miss about.... About you."

"My home?"

"The way you made me feel at home. When I was with you, I felt like I could settle down. Have a real life."

"Whatever that is," I said.

"Exactly," he agreed, then he took a sip and looked out the window at the swirling water around the rocks below. "And that is one of the things we should have talked about when we were together. I realize that now. I was afraid to wreck it. To wreck what we had by talking about anything too seriously."

"Well, you couldn't talk to me about your job. And your job is the reason I left you. So, we're back to square one." I squeezed some lemon into my tea and took a bite of the orange iced scone. So forbidden. So delicious. I looked down at my stomach. I had just run five miles. I could allow myself this one temptation.

"No, everything's squared now: the danger, the reason I worked for the D.E.A., even the reason I'm leaving them." The waitress walked over. Why couldn't she just leave us alone?

"Anything else, hon?" she asked Parker, ignoring me entirely.

"Not right now," he responded, not really seeing her, his eyes glazed. "Merry, we need to talk. But now's not the occasion. I'm going away for a while. Hopefully when I come back, you'll still have some time for me."

I looked down at my scone, suddenly not appealing. What? Parker wanted me to wait for him? Again? No thanks.

I stood up. "Fun run. Good luck. I'm sorry, Parker. We've already been through this, and I can't do it anymore." I walked out of the diner, not looking behind me, hoping he didn't follow. But he did. I felt him touch my arm lightly as I pulled open the car door. His touch reminded me of the possibilities of love. We'd had it once before. Or almost had. Perhaps if I could have learned to enjoy what was, instead of fearing what might become - but I don't operate that way.

With large steady hands encircling my waist, Parker pulled me close, making me feel feminine and sexy. His touch brought me back to our time together two years ago. He had always appreciated my body and the warmth we created together. We did create a lot of heat, those days, not just in bed, but in the way we looked at each other across the table at Antonio's, or when we raced each other along the Charles River, and in our laugher as we threw snowballs in the middle of January. I was never cold that winter. Not when Parker was home. I think Parker knew, back then, that what we had was special, not something to be thrown away. But I couldn't enjoy the times we were together when I so resented all the times he was far away. But hadn't that been part of the appeal? The danger, the distance, then the passion when we were reunited.

His arm now cradled me in his embrace, and I looked at Parker's long brown eyelashes as they closed and hid the fire in his eyes. The fire that I knew was burning for me. But what about Gregory?

"I loved you Parker. I know I did. But not anymore. I need to let you go. I hope you get the 'bad guys,' as you put it."

"Give me a break, Meredith. Listen to you."

Anger welled up in me as foamy and high as Parker's whipped cream had been. "By the way," I tried to begin nonchalantly. "Talking about bad guys. How come you were at the cigar shop in Cambridge? And why the interest in a particular kind of cigar?" Parker's arms released me and he stepped back, either in surprise or irritation. "And how come some goon tried to mug me for that cigar? Huh?"

Parker's face turned as gray as the rocks in the creek. He held me again, this time tightly on my arms. "What the hell are you talking about Meredith? Someone mugged you? And how do you know about the cigar shop?"

I pulled away from him and jumped into my car, wishing I had put the top up. "It's a long story. Needless to say, the mugging scared me silly. But not to worry. Gregory helped me out." I was being mean. I knew that. But I needed to get away from this guy. "Bye, Parker." I locked the car door. I could see by the look in Parker's eyes that he wanted to hop in the car and try to make me talk. But I was tired of talking. I honked the horn and waved as I pressed my foot on the pedal. For days ever after, I wondered how I could have been so nasty.

And if everything might have turned out differently if I hadn't been.

CHAPTER EIGHTEEN

As soon as I opened the front door I sighed loudly and kicked off my shoes. This was my ritual – no matter what, when I arrived home from work, or a run, or an evening out, I kicked off my shoes. That's why I never bothered to keep my shoes in a closet upstairs. Instead, I created a shoe shelf in the hallway closet by the front door that contained my sneakers, boots, high heels, low heels, and everything in between. But for now, I just kept my shoes where they fell. I knew that I wouldn't pick them up and put them away until later in the evening. Somehow, it felt better that way, as if all was right in my world if my shoes were allowed to land haphazardly and stay in that position for hours.

It drove me crazy the times that Gregory immediately picked my shoes up and put them away. He thought he was doing me a favor and never understood why it irritated me. I didn't try to explain it to him; I wasn't sure how to explain my shoe flinging needs anyway. I thought that maybe the kicking of the shoes was metaphorical – kicking away the day, in a sense. No matter how productive the day had been, or how difficult or long or taxing, it was always so damn wonderful to be back home, in my space, where I didn't have deadlines or grumpy bosses or nosy secretaries or arrogant authors to contend with.

I looked around me and groaned. What a lousy way to end a lovely run. Parker. I had been perfectly content before he decided to show up again. Now my head was a tangle of confused messages and feelings. I needed to erase him. And no better place to do that than here, at home, alone.

I always loved being back in the home that I created, with the soft pastel oriental rug underfoot, the lacy white curtains hiding the rest of the world but allowing a soft light to glow from the windows, the funky kitchen where I could sit and sip on a glass of water with a twist of lemon and contemplate what was really going on in my head. Like the freedom of my shoeless feet, the silence that surrounded me - except the slight bubbling of gas that escaped from my Pellegrino - the ability to be by myself and totally enjoy the company. As I sipped on my sparkling water, I started to erase. I envisioned a chalkboard, the old-fashioned kind we used to have as kids. I closed my eyes and imagined myself holding a soft gray eraser. Swipe. There goes Parker's head. Swipe. Swipe. There goes his body.

"Meredith! There you are!"

I jumped out of my seat as if struck by a sudden jolt of electricity. Gregory stood in front of me, pleased with his surprise appearance. I just wondered how to get rid of him and get back to my erasing. Then I wondered if he'd already returned my shoes to the hall closet. And finally, I realized he might be the eraser I really needed.

"Gregory! When did you get here? How can you be here? It's," I checked my watch, "11:15 a.m. You should be in the office!" I was more shocked than surprised. Gregory never left his office during the day. He rarely even took a 30-minute lunch break. He told me once that he loved crunching numbers to create a budget or plan a project, like an author loves words to create a book.

"I came to check on you," he said simply. He stood in the kitchen in his gray, pinstriped suit, yellow tie, and crisp white shirt like a schoolboy out of class. "I tried to call you here, but you didn't answer. I tried your cell phone too."

"Whoops. Sorry. I left it in the glove box of the car. Silly, huh?"

"Where were you? You're supposed to be resting, taking it easy." Gregory looked at me, taking in my running attire. "Well, I guess that's one way to settle down."

I relaxed. He did understand. He was a runner himself. It would make sense to him that I'd want to get out on a day like today and stretch my muscles. "Exactly," I replied.

"Where'd you go?"

I hesitated for a second. But why lie about it? "Great Meadow."

A shadow crossed his face. Just for a brief second. Then he recovered quickly. "Perfect. You and I have never run there. We should. I'm jealous you got to spend the morning there all by yourself. I should have taken the day off, but my boss would have killed me. Three projects, three deadlines."

"That's fine. I think I needed the time to myself anyway," I lied.

"Maybe we could go this weekend." Greg sidled up to me, stale sweat and all. He took my face in his hands and brought his up close. "I was worried about you." He looked good. Real good. His sandy-blond hair, just a tad long for an accountant, brushed the top of his collar as he bent down to kiss me. He smelled like fresh ink and zesty soap. He brushed my lips with his and smiled. "Too bad I need to get back to the office."

"Yeah," I murmured. "Too bad." Gregory was rarely spontaneous in the bedroom, or out. In fact, Gregory practically had to mark it on the calendar to find time to make love: date, time, a.m. or p.m. He was extraordinarily affectionate and thoughtful, but he admitted to feeling uncomfortable 'doing it' without being married. He laughed at himself, blamed his strict fundamentalist up-bringing, but couldn't seem to kick the habit. I think that's why he asked to move in with me – see if that would help.

"Gregory," I interrupted, sliding out from his embrace and sitting back down on the chair. "I haven't had chance to tell you about work plans that have come up. Forgot to mention it to you with the mugging and all."

Greg sat down at the kitchen table too, long legs sliding underneath the plaid tablecloth. I could tell he was tense. Damn.

"I have to go to St. Thomas for a few days. Second draft of the O.T. book I've been working on." Gregory became so still I wondered if he was okay. His brown eyes flickered – he was looking off at something. I turned around to see if he could see someone through the window behind me. But no one was there. "St.

Thomas?" he finally asked. "Where that author's husband owns the boat?"

"The yacht, yes."

"When do you leave?" Now Gregory's eyes were focused. On me. Intently.

"Thursday morning."

He barely nodded his head and stood up. "Are you mad?" I asked. "I'm sorry. I couldn't get out of it. I know you just moved in, and now I have to be gone, probably until Monday or so." I was confused. Was he mad or just hurt?

Gregory beamed a large smile my way. "Hey, relax. Not at all. It's work. I understand. Too bad I can't go with you, but between my deadlines and yours, it's not in the cards. Speaking of which, I won't be home until late tonight. If you're okay, that is." His face relaxed once more into the smooth, sweet accountant I knew, and he rubbed his hands on my upper arms.

"I'm fine. Call me and let me know when you're getting home." I raised my head and let him kiss me. A warm, happy kiss. Parker was erased away.

Until, that is, I took my shower and padded over to my dresser, towel draped Grecian style over my still-wet body as I poked in my underwear drawer. Where was my favorite bra? I was sure I had washed it two days ago and put it in here.

Then I felt it. The cigar that Shannon had given me the night before. The cigar that had caused me a cut knee and the fright of my life. The cigar that made Parker's face turn ashen when I mentioned it to him. When I had returned home last night, Gregory soothing me and helping me in bed, I had quickly hidden the cigar in that drawer – my regular depository for things private. Isn't that where all women hid love letters, found money, and sentimental objects? The cigar wasn't sentimental in my case, but it was a puzzle. And I had never found a puzzle I didn't want to solve.

After a quick blow dry to my hair, a fast smear of make-up, and a 10-minute drive, I parked the car on Massachusetts Avenue, one block from the center of Harvard Square. Walking swiftly in my comfortable sandals, blessing the gods of September that I still could wear summer shoes, I took a deep breath of air before opening the door and entering Telford's Pipe and Cigar shop. It didn't help. The smell of heavy, musky cigar pervaded every corner of the darkly paneled room. Two men talked quietly in one corner of the shop. One of them, gray-haired and weathered, looked intently at the other, younger man who slowly sniffed a long, brown stogie. The entire scene looked illicit to me.

I shrugged and walked toward the owner, Mr. Telford, a tall, virile-looking, gray- haired, 60-year-old who used to wink at me when I visited this store with

Parker in the past. Now, he just looked past me and out the store's front window. I smiled hesitantly, but his vacant look made me wonder if I had suddenly become invisible.

"Mr. Telford," I began.

"Yes?" He cocked one dark bushy eyebrow. He looked at me quickly, then looked away. He pulled his brown wool sweater closely around him, as if a cool breeze had just chilled him. The room temperature must have been 80 degrees. It was always warm in that store. Parker had once explained to me about the sensitivity of cigars and the necessity for just the right temperature and humidity, but I had tuned him out. Men who treated their cigars like cherished objects were infantile, in my mind.

"Mr. Telford," I repeated. "I'm Meredith Powers."

He raised his eyes to my hair, then lowered them slowly down the rest of my body. I suddenly felt exposed and frightened. "Yes?" he said coldly.

"Well, don't you remember me?" I asked, finally showing my exasperation. "I've visited your store before with Parker."

He gave me a look of total incomprehension.

"Parker Webb."

"Yes?" the obtuse man said, again.

For the first time in my life, I wanted to suck on a cigar so I could exhale the air right into the bastard's face. "Mr. Telford." I took a wider stance and raised my voice a notch. "Parker visited you yesterday. Around 1. He came to buy one of your 'finds,' as you call them, or to bring you one."

"Really?"

"Yes, really. Do you remember?"

A chime announced the opening of the door, and a dark, good-looking man with a thick black mustache, dressed in jeans and a navy blazer, walked in casually. Too casually, I noticed right away. He looked directly at Telford, and the warning shot from his brown eyes was as loud as a cannon. Telford cleared his throat and declared, "Sorry, I can't help you, Miss ...."

"Powers," I replied icily. He didn't remember me? But then again, he had hundreds of customers. Maybe Shannon had been wrong. Maybe she misread everything she thought she'd seen. Was I embarrassing myself?

I took out the chubby cigar, which I'd been hiding in my shorts pocket. By now it was soggy from my sweaty palm, which had been holding on to it like it was a lifeline. As I raised it up to his face, Telford took a step back and looked swiftly up at the new customer. The stranger strode up and plucked the odd-looking cigar from my hand.

"Most unusual," he murmured. He focused his gaze on Telford. "Bob, you never told me you sold these in your store!" He put his arm around the older man's shoulder and moved away from me.

"Wait a minute!" I shouted. The younger man turned expectantly toward me. Telford still faced the other direction. "I was in the middle of a conversation with Mr. Telford. I'm not finished. And I'd like my cigar back!" I could feel my blush turn from rose to crimson.

"Cigar? What cigar?" the man asked arrogantly. He turned his back on me and walked Telford to his back office, and closed the door.

I heard the loud click of a lock.

CHAPTER NINETEEN

On my way home from the pipe shop, I had an uncomfortable sense of dread. Well, why shouldn't I? The atmosphere in that once cozy and welcoming shop was downright spooky. I knew Bob Telford remembered me, yet he had acted like I was a stranger.

And what was up with that bizarre man? Creepy guy, in a dark, mysterious, sexy kind of way. If he hadn't acted so cold and nasty to me, I would have liked to use some of my girlish charm to find out what the heck they were hiding in there. But charm was the last thing of value I'd find in Telford's. Instead, there was a palpable sense of fear, as well as some unexplainable urgency.

I had tried to get more information. I knocked on the locked door and was completely ignored. The other salesman in the store looked like he was ready to shove me out. A customer who walked in as I was banging on the back door treated me as if I'd just escaped from prison and was looking for a hostage. I think I was mostly frustrated with myself. Not only had I acquired no answers, I had lost the one object in my possession that so many wanted. No, I hadn't lost it; it was taken from me, and very rudely.

I drove too fast down Massachusetts Avenue toward my own neighborhood, anxious to get behind locked doors. Gregory wouldn't be home until late, he'd said. Just as well. I wanted some privacy right now. I walked in the front door and immediately locked it behind me, then turned on all the lights of every single room. Childish behavior, perhaps, but it made me feel safer.

I changed into my black leggings and large soft gray sweatshirt and padded down to the kitchen, wearing my comfortable thick socks. Just as I opened the refrigerator door to take out a soft drink, I heard a bang at the front of the house – outside. I walked quickly toward the living room when a tumultuous crash tore through the front window. I screamed – dumb reaction but unavoidable. My heard pounded as if I was running a 10 K race, and my feet stuck hard to the wooden floor. I didn't know whether to race toward the broken glass or to the phone in the kitchen and dial 911. My pride, and curiosity, won as I walked swiftly to the front room.

The bay window wasn't totally smashed, as the sound would have suggested, but there was a huge round hole in it and splintered lines running like a web from the hole outward on the rest of the large window. I gasped as I looked down at the culprit. A baseball-sized glass paperweight was still rolling on the Oriental rug; in fact, it stopped as I stared at it in horror. Was it the same one I had noticed sitting on top of a stack of paper napkins at the table where Parker and I sat earlier today? Inside the heavy round globe floated the letters 'Red Dog Diner.'

Now, what was it doing here, smashing my window?

~~~~~~~~~~~~~~~~~~~~~

I called the police, knowing it was a useless endeavor. Two police officers, a 50-something-year-old man with a beer belly and a 20-something-year-old woman who never said a word but nodded her head at everything her cohort said, looked around the house, shook their heads in dismay, and left within 15 minutes of arriving. I called the handyman I've used in the past; he would come the next day to take measurements and order a replacement. In the meantime, I had a smashed window and no security system. I raced to the hardware store, still open, thank God, and bought sheets of heavy plastic and some tape the young clerk suggested. Thirteen minutes later my window was covered, though I doubted it would keep out a raccoon, much less a thief. Well, I wasn't going to worry about it. Gregory would be home by late dinner anyway.

The rest of the night was a blur. I tried to call Shannon, but just ended up leaving a message. I washed two loads of laundry and filed my nails. I began watching a DVD out of my collection – Pride and Prejudice - after Gregory called and said to eat without him, and fell asleep three quarters into the movie.

But at midnight, I heard a noise and jumped off the sofa, where I'd fallen asleep. I checked the living room and the smashed window, but realized thunder had wakened me. After drinking a small glass of milk, I laid down in bed and tried to sleep. For what seemed like hours.

I squeezed my eyes shut and gave myself a lecture, which went something like this: "shut up, shut up, shut up, shut up." But the mantra didn't work. My brain continued to race as fast as a cat chasing a ball of string. What an apt metaphor for my string of random, mostly useless thoughts. They were unraveling now at a most inappropriate time – 2:23 a.m.

How could Elizabeth not know, right away, that Mr. Darcy was superior in so many ways to Wickham? Was she really only interested in looks? Or was her pride that great that she couldn't see how similar Darcy was to her? Why are some women only attracted to good-looking men? But some men may seem good looking, when in reality, they're something else.

I was not going to get to sleep this way! I went back to my 'shut up' mantra, but on the third 'shut up!', my thoughts took over again.

Now Parker is not model handsome, but good looking in an athletic hunky way. God, he and I were so god damn good together for a while. Shut up Meredith. Think of Gregory. Gregory, now he's handsome any way you look at it. Huh. Hadn't thought of that before. He's so good looking it's almost scary. But what's there to be scared of? He's sweet, quiet, thoughtful, just the kind of boyfriend most women would die for.

I jumped out of bed. Shut Up! Walking aimlessly around the bedroom, I spanned the room, realizing that Gregory was invisible in this room. He'd left nothing – not a pair of pants, or shoes, or even socks. I walked into the guest room and opened the closet door. Yes, there were two suits hanging neatly in between my dresses, and one pair of shoes. I opened the dresser drawer in the corner. One pair of brown socks, some underwear, and a well-worn sweatshirt. He had moved in, but barely.

After walking thoughtfully back to my bed, I slowly rolled down onto the mattress, planted my head firmly on the soft pillow that smelled faintly of lavender, and closed my eyes.

Sleep refused to come.

3:16. At this rate, I wouldn't be able to edit anything at all tomorrow, much less catch up on all the extra work that must have stacked up after missing a day. Have to sleep. Sleep Sleep Sleep. 99 98 97 96 95

Oh shit. Warm milk. That's what I needed. I should get out of this bed and fix myself a cup of warm cocoa. But would that help? I'd just wake up an hour later to pee. Plus, chocolate is a stimulant. Well, maybe just half a cup. But did I really want to get up? Oh no. 3:42. Shut up. Shut up. Shut up.

CHAPTER TWENTY

"Where were you last night?" I had waited four and a half miles to ask the question. I didn't want to sound like a nagging girlfriend, yet I thought Gregory should have volunteered the information by now. He had appeared at 6:15 in the morning, knowing I'd be stretching outside on the deck for my run. He came prepared, wearing black running shorts and a long-sleeved fitted shirt that nicely showed off the results of his three times a week weightlifting. In fact, he looked so good that I bit my tongue and didn't ask the question right away.

He had called around 8 last night, sounding hassled and telling me not to wait for him for dinner.

"But hey, maybe I can make it for dessert," he'd added. "And, well, you know, then some more dessert after." Gregory had a hard time talking about sex. It had taken him ten dates before he kissed me. Five more before he tried to reach third base. Some would call him old-fashioned. Shannon just called him strange.

But he never showed up anyway, probably one of the reasons for my sleepless night.

We took off down the relatively quiet streets of north Cambridge just as the rosy apricot sun was making its appearance. We didn't say much, getting into stride and matching breath for breath. I told him about the broken window (amazingly, he hadn't noticed it) and he blew out a disgusted breath regarding the lack of police response. I let him go in front of me when we had to run single file. His tall lean frame sat on two well-muscled, blond-haired legs. Not a bad sight to start my day. But now, 40 minutes later as we approached my home, I finally asked him.

"Where were you last night?"

Gregory's open face closed for a split second, so fast I wondered if it was my imagination. Then it opened up again, he smiled apologetically, and answered. "I ended up working until 11:30. Third quarter reports. I didn't call because I knew you'd be in bed by then. I just went to my apartment."

"Oh," I said, surprised. I thought he had moved in with me, officially, but maybe it was better that he could stay at his apartment sometimes too. "When does your lease run out?"

"A month and a half," he replied.

I swallowed that with a large gulp of water from the Evian bottle he handed me, and that's when I saw Parker, standing against the front door, cocky grin on his face, sharp blue eyes targeted straight for Gregory.

Gregory stopped short, as if he'd just run into an invisible wall. He watched Parker walk down the deck stairs toward us, his arms open wide as if to hug me.

"Meredith! Meredith Powers. I thought this was the house," Parker said in a maddeningly false cheerful voice. "How the heck are you? It's been quite a while." He squeezed me hard, as if I were a sponge, and then turned to Greg.

"Meredith? What's going on?" Gregory walked slowly toward me and Parker, his sweaty blonde hair tousled like a child's.

"Oh. Gregory, meet Parker." I looked up at my ex quickly. "He was once my friend, I mean, he was my friend, and now he's, I mean, he's still a friend, an old friend. Parker, this is Gregory." I could have killed Parker. What was he doing here? Again?

Parker lifted an eyebrow higher than any eyebrow should possibly be able to go. "And Gregory is?"

Greg looked at me, dark brown eyes lit with a huge question mark of his own.

"You know what? I'm late. Gregory and I just had a long run. I need to shower. Parker, nice to see you, but next time call me – at a reasonable hour, and we'll catch up. Greg, I know you have an early start today too." I stood there, waiting for Gregory to follow me up the stairs. Instead he planted his feet on the concrete sidewalk and stared at Parker as if seeing a long lost brother who he'd never liked in the first place. "Gregory?" I repeated.

"In a minute, Meredith." Gregory looked at me with a slow sweet smile. "Why don't you take your shower first. I'll be right up."

Not bloody likely. I moved myself between the two men, but faced Parker. "Was there a reason you were looking for me?" I asked bluntly.

Parker didn't miss a step. "Actually, I've been out of town for a while, and soon I need to leave for another extended trip, so I thought I'd look up some friends I haven't seen in a while."

"Well, I imagine that's just about all your friends, isn't it?"

Parker just smiled in return. "Yours was my first stop, and I would have kept on going when I realized no one was at home; however, I noticed that you're missing a window."

Oh. Parker noticed my plastic sheeting. Of course he had. "Just some adolescent punk," I explained. I hadn't told Gregory about the paperweight. Couldn't tell Parker now. It's not like it was a secret, but I knew instinctively that it was not something to share with either of these men.

"Oh good." Parker stood up straight from leaning on the banister. "So the police caught the little weasel."

"No," I replied slowly. "I didn't say that. The police didn't seem at all concerned about a little vandalism on this street, unfortunately. Now, Gregory and I really must get ready for work. Thanks for dropping by. Give me a call before you leave for your next trip." I turned my body around quickly, allowing my long ponytail to swish like a frisky colt. What the hell was going on? I sighed audibly, avoided looking at either Parker or Gregory, and ran up the stairs into the house.

As I dried myself after my shower and patted on some baby powder, I heard Gregory knock on the door.

"Almost ready!" I called out lightly. I pulled on my bathrobe and opened the bathroom door. Gregory stood there with his arms across his chest.

"That was strange," he began.

I nodded my head in agreement.

"You've never mentioned this Parker guy, but when you and I first met, you told me you were recovering from a bad relationship. Was he the one?" I could hear the timidity in Gregory's voice. He didn't really want to know the answer. My heart beat a little faster for him. I was being unfair to him, and all he'd done was be a thoughtful, sweet boyfriend to me. I thought of my conversation with Shannon two nights ago. Was I doing it again? Pushing away a wonderful man because of my own problems?

"Yes," I answered.

"He wasn't like I imagined him. I thought he'd be this big tough guy, good-looking in a young Mel Gibson kind of way, you know?" Greg laughed. "But he didn't look so tough to me. He looked pretty worn out. Do you think he'll bother you again?"

I didn't know what to say. Yes, he'll bother me again. He'll bother me for the rest of my life, if I don't get him out of my system.

"No, I don't think so Gregory. I'm sorry I never told you much about him. I just didn't want anything to do with him. Um, could we talk about this later?" (or maybe not at all, I thought to myself). "I don't want to be late for work, after missing yesterday. I have a lot to do before my trip."

Gregory looked thoughtful. "Sure. Sure, I know what you mean. Go ahead and get ready for work. I'll take my shower. If you leave before I get out, let's just connect by phone. See what our plans are for tonight."

"Okay!" I was relieved. He didn't seem anxious to ask any questions. Good. The less questions, the better. Besides, Parker was erased, I reminded myself. Gone!

~~~~~~~~~~~~~~~~~~~~~~~

Of course that was anything but the truth. I put the top down, drove one block into my commute, and stopped at an intersection. Mr. Parker Webb jumped into the passenger seat as if he were a modern-day cowboy jumping onto someone's modern-day horse.

I swallowed a scream. "Parker!" I shouted. "What are you doing?" Stupid question. He was harassing me, that's what he was doing. The real question was, what was I going to do about it?

"Just keep driving," Parker said out of the side of his mouth, looking out the window and avoiding my glare. "This was the only way I could get your attention."

"I thought I made it clear I didn't want your attention," I shot back. I looked at him, and then looked down where he was looking. My lap. There was a lot to look at. I chose my short red plaid skirt today, topped with a crisp white blouse, and black leather flats. The outfit made me feel feminine and bossy, all at the same time. I wanted to look feminine for Gregory; I needed to be bossy at work. I had to get a lot done. However, I had forgotten how much the skirt rose up when I sat down.

"Stop looking," I warned. Parker's head shot back up and his mouth lost its silly grin. "Now, what do you want?"

"Don't go back to Telford's," he demanded. "Lock your doors at night. Don't drive this car to work, take the T." He paused two seconds, then added, "And get that stupid window fixed."

"Anything else?" I asked sarcastically.

"Don't trust Gregory." He folded his arms across his chest, still looking ahead.

"Good God. Parker. I thought you had to leave." I turned my blinker on and took a sharp right onto Longfellow Bridge. It didn't have to be that sharp, but it felt good.

"You won't hear from me again for a while. I can't phone you. Just be careful, that's all I'm asking. Don't turn here." My left hand blinker was blinking.

"This is the way I get to work," I protested.

"Go straight."

For the heck of it, I listened to him. We drove in silence for two blocks.

"Turn right on Center Street here, stop at the curb."

I did as he directed. He didn't hop out of the car this time, but chose the civilized route – he opened the door. "Meredith, please. Just look out for yourself." He leaned over and planted a warm loving kiss on my lips. "Be careful."

And then he was gone.

CHAPTER TWENTY-ONE

The morning was uneventful at work, and for that I was eternally grateful. I just wanted life to get back to normal, whatever that was. A nice quiet relationship with Gregory, a happy working environment with a cheerful secretary, a....

"Meredith, do you really expect me to type up this entire review by noon?" Jill asked in a plaintive whine. "Did you forget?"

Oh, I had forgotten. A week ago Jill had asked for a half day today; she and a friend had snagged Red Sox tickets. The Sox were playoff hopefuls again.

"I really need Jeff to get my review on the Mateson book by 3 so he can ask any questions before I leave work tonight. I'm on a plane, remember tomorrow morning."

"I'll have it on his desk by 10 tomorrow," Jill promised. "He can call you on your cell if he has any problems." I just nodded my head. The kid deserved her Red Sox time. "I have to leave in about an hour and a half," she added.

"Okay," I agreed, looking down at my desk, which was hidden from view because of the stack of papers strewn from one end to the other. "Don't send me any calls, take messages. And I don't want any visitors either – particularly from proofing!" I grimaced and Jill smiled.

"Not even that guy downstairs, the one who has a crush on you?"

"Jill." My bossy attire was not working. She loved to tease me about any man she thought had an interest in me. Any man but Gregory.

"Okay, okay, I'm leaving." But I noticed the smirk on her face. My attention was quickly diverted, though, to a poorly written page. I crossed out the redundancies and put in commas where they belonged. Sounds quieted, the room brightened, and my concentration thickened as I did the job I was sitting there to do.

An hour later, my muscles stiffening, I realized I needed a yoga break, something I required at least twice during my regular editing day. I stood in the puddle of sunshine on my office floor, breathed in, breathed out, and stretched. I was beginning to feel in control again. I was beginning to feel calm. Less stressed.

Until I heard Jill shout out, "I don't think that's a real good idea," and then my office door swung open.

"Baby, how are you?"

"Mom?" I uncurled from my yoga position on the floor, oddly enough, the child's pose, and slowly stood up. What was she doing here?

"I know you told me you were okay, but when Donald heard about your mugging, he insisted that we drive up and check you out ourselves." At that, a large bulky form slunk in from the outer vestibule. Donald. He looked at me noncommittally. Donald didn't know me, and I figured Donald didn't give a damn about how I felt after the mugging, so something was up.

I walked up to Mom and gave her a quick hug. I didn't know what to do with Donald, so I pulled my arm out in front of me, Donald took my hand, and we shook. The day was getting more and more surreal, and it was only noon.

"Mom, the mugging was nothing. I'm fine. I was just shaken up for a couple of hours, but I'm fine. And you know I'm getting ready for a business trip."

Mom looked at my yoga mat lying next to my desk, and then looked back up to me. "Busy at work,

huh?" she asked, scanning me up and down. I didn't
know if she approved of what she saw, or disapproved.
"I suppose yoga is a great de-stressor, but don't tell me
that mugging didn't freak you out. I know when my
baby girl is frightened."

Oh no, she hadn't called me her 'baby girl' since
the day she told me she was getting married to Larry,
the boyfriend before Donald. What horrible news was
she going to tell me this time?

"Mom?"

"Oh, okay, I see you're doing fine. And I don't
want to get in the way of your trip. Donald and I have
been dying to see the exhibit at Boston's Museum of
Fine Arts for weeks now, and this seemed like a good
opportunity to do that – to find out what's really going
on in your life and to see the show." She put her finger
to her mouth and paused. "However, we were hoping to
take you and Gregory out for dinner while we're here.
Donald's been dying to get to know you. What do you
say?"

I rolled my eyes, and then quickly turned
around hoping my mother didn't see. Gregory and I
needed to be together tonight. Alone. I needed to
straighten some things out with him. Alone. The last
thing I needed was my mother interfering.

"You know mom, I'm not sure what Gregory
has planned for tonight," I lied.

"Oh, it's like that!" she chortled. She dug her elbow into Donald's well-hidden ribs and said, "They want to be alonnnnnnne, tonight."

I looked at my mother as if I was looking into the deepest, darkest mystery of human kind. How could we have possibly come from the same DNA, the same gene pool? It seemed implausible to me, nearly impossible. I thought back to the time when I was a pre-teen and convinced that my parents had adopted me. Now, at 32, I had those thoughts all over again.

"Welllllllll?" she wheedled, cuddling up to me like a cat with a well-trained owner. "How could you ignore the obvious, Meredith? Gregory is gorgeous, he's smart, he's got a good, steady job, and he loves you. Your other boyfriends..." (and here, I knew she meant Parker) "...were less stable, less reliable."

Mom put her hands out in front of her and used them like a scale, balancing them up and down. Gregory, I assumed, was on the right, since that hand was lowered almost to her knees, and Parker was on the left. "Piece of cake!" She smiled at me, light blue eyes sparkling, but not as much as the diamonds on both of her ring fingers. Donald was a prominent New Jersey banker; in Mom's estimation, he did her proud.

She frowned at me when I didn't respond. Gregory could put rings on my fingers, but unlike my mother, I wasn't into glitz or, what's it called, bling. On the other hand, Gregory was as steady as the desk we were standing by. I knocked on the wood twice and said, "You're right, Mom."

"Call me Glory," she whispered. "Remember? Once you turned 25, no more Ma or Mom or Mother. We're equals now. Just call me Glory, like the rest of my friends."

I nodded my head, even though I knew I would never consider my mother a close friend.

"So what about it?" she continued. "Let Donald and me take you two lovebirds for dinner. We insist. We're staying in the city. The Four Seasons. We made reservations near there, some place the concierge recommended."

I nodded my head again. "Let me call Gregory. I'm sure he'll be pleased." And he would. Gregory thought my mom was great – fun and glamorous and beautiful. He didn't understand my problem with her and decided it was just a mother/daughter thing. He was probably right.

~~~~~~~~~~~~~~~~~~~~~~~

Gregory and I decided to meet at the bar forty-five minutes before Mom and Donald arrived. "I'd love to see them, but we also need a little time to ourselves," Gregory had responded on the phone when I'd told him about my mom's proposition. Now we sat next to each other at the trendy bar. As I sipped on my glass of wine and examined Gregory's face, so handsome in a preppy kind of way – short blonde hair, expressive brown eyes, newly shaved face with fair skin and ruddy cheeks – I felt myself relax for the first time in days. Whatever had I been thinking, meeting Parker for lunch, answering his mysterious and convoluted messages, and a day later, following him to Concord on a wild goose chase? Or should I say wild duck chase? Parker had always been unpredictable, but I had forgotten how unsettling it was.

"Try the bread sticks," Gregory said. "They've got thyme or chive, or something like that, in them,"

Dutifully, I took a bite. "Rosemary," I said.

"Who?" he asked, seriously.

I laughed. That was the problem with dating an accountant. So literal. And not a great amount of humor, but so what? Gregory was the most compassionate man I knew.

"What?" he asked. He placed his arm on the back of my stool; I loved the look of his starched white shirt. His tie was still tight around his neck, his jacket neatly folded on the chair next to us.

"I don't know, I'm just happy to be with you," I replied. He smiled and leaned back a little, and I realized that he'd been a little uptight. "Greg, I'm sorry about the last few days. You know, with the scare in

Cambridge and then Parker and stuff. I just want to go back to the way we were before all this happened." I moved my hand from my lap and placed it over his, resting on the bar. The bartender approached, but I shook my head no, and he left. We looked into each other's eyes like we were in love, and for a second, I felt a sense of contentment.

Then, breaking the spell, I heard my mother's voice and within seconds, she and Donald found us. They were early.

"Ah, we thought we'd get a great table before you two got here. Come on – it's a perfect setting." We followed the two of them, my mom in a sexy black pants outfit and Donald in a dark business suit. They had selected an out-of-the-way round table in the corner, covered with a stiff linen tablecloth and beautiful silver candlestick in the center. Mom's face looked youthful and serene as Donald helped her to her seat, and I wondered if she'd had another face lift.

"Gregory, you look even more handsome than I remember," Mom said without even blinking an eye. "It's been months. What's new? Meredith doesn't tell us much. I think she's been trying to keep you all to herself, but it's time we got to know you a little better." She settled back comfortably in her seat, looking smug. I knew she was just trying to be a mom, trying to wriggle her way into my life, but I resented it.

On the other hand, I was leaning forward, anxious to hear what Gregory had to say. After all, what did I really know about him? Gregory rarely talked about himself; when I asked him about his past, he mumbled something about preferring to live in the present. I knew he had graduated from Princeton with a degree in economics and international relations. I knew he received an advanced degree from Harvard and worked at State Street Bank as an 'accountant,' but I'd never been to his office.

Gregory shrugged, looking uncomfortable. A waitress handed us our menus, and he looked at his as if the answers to a riddle were listed inside.

"I know what!" Mom said suddenly. "Let's play ten questions."

Gregory looked at her warily. "About the menu?"

"No, no" she said quickly, a little frustrated. "About each other. This will be fun. A good way to break the ice."

Gregory's expression closed like a front door on a windy day.

"Glory, most people don't like games like that," I said.

"Like what?" she asked, mystified.

"Well, like charades or What's Your Line, or Ten Questions." My voice had raised with my annoyance level.

"You know what? I could use a glass of wine," Donald interrupted. "Come on, let's order a bottle. Gregory, do you prefer white or red? There's your first question."

"White," Gregory said.

"Perfect. There's one question down. Chardonnay or sauvignon blanc?"

Mom threw her menu down. "That's cheating. I'm serious. I'd like us all to get to know each other better."

Gregory motioned for the waitress to come over and pointed to a line on the wine list. She nodded and left. Then he looked at Mom and said clearly, "I already know everything I need to know about Meredith. She's beautiful. She's smart. She's funny, and she likes me. What else is there to know?" He got out of his seat and moved over to my side of the table, bending oh so slightly and kissing me lightly on the mouth. I felt a delicious tingle from the tips of my toes to the top of my head, and I shuddered. I looked up and saw the blissful smile on my mom's mouth, and heard her voice inside my head, Honey, if it ain't broke, don't fix it. I returned the kiss, blushed, and looked back at the menu.

That's when I saw it. The initials. TRMFY. Right under the listing for the entrees, between the roast wild duck with orange gravy and the ginger-marinated flank steak. I made a little gasp and knew my face had just changed from rose to gray.

CHAPTER TWENTY-TWO

"What?" Gregory asked.

"Oh nothing, nothing," I lied. Again. I seemed to be making a practice of lying to Gregory. Why did I lie? Why not just come right out and say, "Oh, look at this crazy word written on the menu. TRMFY. I wonder what that means?" Talk about ten questions, I could have asked everyone at the table to make a guess. Then maybe I could figure out what Parker was up to.

Better yet, I could just tell Gregory the truth, something like, "I made a crazy trip out to Concord yesterday because I thought Parker might need me, but don't worry, he didn't, and you, you are the only love of my life." But I didn't say it because it wasn't true. There it was. In black and white and sorry all over. Why couldn't I be sure that Gregory was the love of my life? It would make everything so much easier.

Instead, I said, "Excuse me. I need to go to the rest room." Gregory stood up half way as I left the table. I tottered in the sexy black heels that I hated, looking right and left like I was a chicken who'd just lost an egg. Where the hell was Parker? He had to be around. And what did TRMFY stand for? I rushed into the ladies' room, sure I'd find him sitting on the counter with a sly little grin on his face.

My heart even did a couple of flip flops as I raced toward the marble sinks. But no Parker. Fool that I was, I opened each stall, making sure no one was hiding there, waiting to surprise me. But again, no Parker. How did he do that? And how did he know which menu I was going to read?

I took a quick look at myself in the mirror, noting the bright startled blue eyes, the flush to my cheeks, the slight look of panic in my expression, and I took a deep breath and walked purposely back to our table. After I sat down, I surprised Mom by reaching over and grabbing her menu. No initials between the duck and the steak. I handed the menu back to her, ignoring her questioning look, then picked up my purse and put it back down again.

Oblivious to everything, Donald released a loud sigh, saying, "Tough to make a choice, but I'm going to order the duck."

Mom looked up at him as if she was going to respond, but instead her eyes gazed beyond him to the bar and widened in recognition. "Merry, isn't that, you know, your friend?"

My heart tumbled into my stomach. Shit. She just saw Parker? I turned my head to where she was looking, but didn't see him. "What friend?" I asked, trying hard to sound nonchalant.

"You know, the one you met when you worked at Nordstrom's. Shelley? Shelby?"

"Shannon?" I looked again to where Mom's eyes were focused, and sure enough, there was a red head and a gorgeous green silk scarf thrown around laughing shoulders. "Shannon!" I said again, loudly.

Shannon glanced over to where we were sitting, and a look of shock, and then distress, covered her face like a black veil. I stood up to walk over to her, but she had turned her body again and walked away, quickly. Who was she with?

"Gregory," I burst out, "something's not right."

"What? They have vegetarian on the menu, back page," he said distractedly.

"No, I mean...." What did I mean? I turned to Mom and Donald, who were both looking at me, waiting. "I'm sorry, I'm not very good company. I'm stressed. I have an early flight tomorrow. I haven't packed."

Mom looked back toward the bar. "That's so strange," she said, ignoring my words. "I swore I saw your friend with..." She looked over at me as if asking me a question, but not opening her mouth. "So, was that Shannon?"

"I think so," I answered. "But she was leaving. I'm not sure she saw me."

"Ah ha." Mom responded.

"Ah ha?" I waited for more comments.

"Ah ha, that's all." Mom's gaze grew thoughtful, very unusual for her. "So why are you so stressed?"

"Remember I told you I was leaving tomorrow to visit an author? I always get anxious before traveling, you know that."

"That's your father's fault," she said. Then she shut her mouth. For the rest of the night the meal was subdued. Gregory seemed preoccupied. Mom was definitely thinking about something, but she wasn't sharing what it was. Donald focused on his duck. I couldn't wait to get home and cover my face under the bed sheets.

~~~~~~~~~~~~~~~~~~~~~~~~

Gregory and I had our own cars, since we met at the restaurant straight from work. I arrived home first, finding a parking space only half a block away. Miraculous. It was a windy and starless night, and I clasped my arms around myself as I got out of the car and walked toward the house. Even though it was only mid-September, the air suddenly felt like late fall. The tree branches swayed dramatically, as if trying to warn me of some danger ahead. The sound of the still-green leaves dancing against each other in the black ink background of 10 p.m. chilled me beyond the 55-degree temperature. I had left my sweater in the office, and my cold hands did little to warm the goose-pricked skin on my arms.

I stopped in front of the door and couldn't move a muscle. Funny, what fear does to the body. Instead of giving extra oomph to flee, it paralyses into inaction. I had heard a noise, almost indistinguishable with the sighing trees and the frantic chirping of the late summer crickets, but a noise none-the-less. A noise that was more human than insect or wind, the sound of a snapping twig and an intake of air.

Finally I gained enough spirit to swirl to the left side of the house, where the sound originated. In a split second, I saw a flash of something. Was it a face? A light colored jacket? Then I wondered why I was being so stupid, standing here alone at night. Didn't that mugging two days before teach me anything?

Then again, maybe it was just my imagination. I fumbled for the keys in my purse and opened the door more quickly than I'd ever done before. As the latch clicked open, I exhaled loudly and slammed the door behind me. Damn Parker for getting me so spooked, and damn me for giving him my attention. This could not go on. I would not think of Parker any more. He was out of sight. He had to be out of mind.

As I packed my carry-on suitcase, folding underwear and shorts as carefully as my two sundresses, I heard the key scrape the lock of the front door. Gregory was finally home. The door opened with a bang and a muttered curse. He must have tripped over my shoes. Again. Whoops.

I continued to pack, adding suntan lotion, hair blower, make-up, and a nightie. As an afterthought I added my pearls, suitable for all occasions. Then I heard a glass break, a louder mutter and "damn, people who don't put things away where they're supposed to..." Unusual for a man who normally was so unruffled.

"Gregory? Everything alright?"

His steps sounded heavy on the carpeted stairs, but his face brightened when he saw me standing in the bedroom, a pair of flats in one hand and a toothbrush in the other.

"God, you're nice to come home to," he said immediately. Then he grimaced, "even though you don't know how to clean up after yourself."

"I'm sorry, it's just that..."

He waved my explanation away. "Hey, it's your place. I'm just tired. Your mom got quiet tonight, didn't she?" He began to unbutton his shirt, not waiting for my reply when he added, "it's just been a bear of a day. How 'bout I open a bottle of wine and we just relax for a little while. What do you say?" When he stopped talking, he looked at the open suitcase on the couch and then at me. "Oh shit. Oh yeah, you're leaving tomorrow."

"Just a short trip."

"Suntan lotion? Bathing suit?" he smiled, but the smile wasn't in his voice.

"Well, I'm going to the Caribbean. We're working on her yacht at St. Thomas harbor."

Gregory wagged his head in disapproval, and turned to leave the room.

"Wait. It's just for a few days. Not even a week."

"We just moved in together, Meredith. And now you're leaving."

I didn't know how to answer that.

Gregory looked at the bed, then looked back at me, an idea forming in his head. "Maybe I should go with you. Take a quick break from work. God knows I need to get away from there."

"No!" I said too emphatically.

He looked at me quizzically. " 'No' because you don't want me there, or 'no' because...?"

He was giving me an out. Thank God. "Greg, it's going to be all business. Barbara is needy; she's going to want my full attention. I'll be editing with her all day, probably into the evening too. I'm staying at some cheesy hotel right at the harbor. It just won't be fun for you. For us. Let's go away on our own schedule, not because of work."

Looking satisfied, Gregory shook his head in agreement and left, mumbling something about not being able to leave work right now anyway. He looked so distressed; I put down my shoes and followed him downstairs to the living room, where he had turned on the T.V.

"Hey," I said, pulling him back toward me. "I'm really sorry. I don't want to go." And that was the truth. I really didn't want to go. He made me feel good. Wanted. Gregory pulled me into his arms, his shirt still on but unbuttoned.

"Remember when we first met?" he said, lips warm and sweet against my ear.

I nodded my head and smiled. "I still don't know what you were doing out there at 6:15 in the morning. You obviously weren't awake," I said, with a fond pat on his butt.

Gregory and I met on the bike path somewhere between Lexington and Arlington. Once Parker and I were no longer together, I had begun to run more frequently. I lost weight. My sexual appetite decreased, and at first I thought that was all about giving up Parker. You know, give up chocolate for Lent, lose seven pounds. In this case, give up a lover who adored you, lose the hips, and go down a bra size.

The more I ran, the more I had to run. By 6:00 every morning I watched the sun rise as I pounded the pavement, just a few other diehard runners out there with me. We never acknowledged each other, just looked straight ahead, lungs filled, then emptied, then filled with rejuvenating dawn air, focused on just one thing. The running. I reached the stage of euphoria by mile five and used that emotion to get through the rest of the day.

"Hey, I didn't mean to trip you then," Gregory said, interrupting my thoughts.

"Well, I still have the scar on my knee to prove it," I laughed, pulling up my pants leg. "Oh no, it's gone now, because of the brush burn I just got."

Gregory pulled me into him, tighter. "Just be careful out there, okay?"

"Out where?"

"You know. There. At St. Thomas. Just be careful."

"Of course I will," I replied, touched by his concern. When he had tripped me on that run, he stopped my rather destructive obsession. I got healthy again. Clear-headed. I lifted my lips up to his and gave him a long luscious kiss. "I'm so glad you're with me, Gregory," I whispered. Then we walked back upstairs together.

CHAPTER TWENTY-THREE

I didn't like to travel. It was not just because I was a homebody, needing to sit on my own comfy couch in front of the fireplace, eat in my kitchen, or sleep in my own bed. I did love my house and the way I'd accessorized it to fit me, but it was not what I missed most when traveling.

I missed my work, and the daily routine of fixing myself a lemony scented cup of tea in my travel mug, roaring out of the neighborhood at 7:40 a.m. in my convertible, arriving with a grin to a chorus of hellos from the proofers and editors and Jill and even Arthur Flack. I enjoyed settling down in front of my computer, an author's manuscript in front of me, facing the daunting challenge to change a poorly written piece of medical jargon into a seamless piece of useful medical literature. A sense of satisfaction arrived every day when, at 1 or 1:30, Jill knocked lightly at my door and announced, "You really should take a break, you know." I was always amazed to learn that I'd been cutting and slashing and red marking for five hours straight.

This job gave me a purpose, a direct line from home to work, back to home and a run, some dinner, and maybe a 60-minute read or an hour T.V. show before dropping off to a good night's sleep. My life felt complete, organized, safe and secure. Parker, of course, used to laugh at my love of the regular and the routine. His job brought him the opposite satisfactions. That difference should have forewarned me about our problems before the relationship got as complicated as it had.

And now. Now Parker had disappeared after reappearing and leaving me cryptic messages; Gregory wanted to move our relationship up a notch; and my publisher was pushing me to leave it all and pamper a spoiled author. My easiest response would have been to refuse and stay in the safety of my Boston brick office building, inside my little white box of a room, happily editing out clichés and misspellings and run-on sentences. But instead, I packed up my nine-year-old Samsonite - never felt a need to replace it since I never

intended to go far – for a four-hour flight to Miami,
then a quicker flight on a smaller plane to St. Thomas,
so I could handhold a skittish, demanding author on
her rolling, sophisticated yacht. Blah. But I respected
Arthur, and I loved my job, so here I was.

I sat in my first class seat, compliments of
Arthur, contemplating the upcoming flight. I sighed
the sigh of the damned and tried to close my eyes as the
flight attendants prepared for departure, but the noise
and jostling of coach passengers still getting settled
made it impossible to rest. My eyes wandered to a seat
two rows ahead of me. A man had just stretched his
arms in front of him, and the way he turned made my
heart twist.

It was the shape of his head.

The shape of his head reminded me of Parker,
and I suddenly missed him so badly I ached from my
toes to my scalp. I tried to close my mind from the
memories, but the effort was useless. I remembered
how I used to give Parker head rubs; he craved them
and begged me for them more than a back or neck rub.
I'd move my fingers delicately, at first, through his
thick brown hair, feeling him shiver with delight, then
put more pressure on my fingertips as I massaged his
scalp. He had a funny little bump on the top of his head
to the right, and it was sensitive to the touch. An old

wound, he would only say. I kissed it at the end after every rubdown.

I missed that shape of the back of Parker's head. I missed the look on Parker's face as he turned and moved in to kiss me. I missed....oh damn. This was ridiculous. I closed my eyes so I couldn't see the man's head in front of me, then I squirmed in the leather seat and exhaled louder than the plane's engines. I was here, not happily, but at least I had some room and space.

Now, if only I had both seats to myself. I looked around me; first class was only half full, while I knew that the seats in the back were loaded. I checked my watch. Five minutes to take off. I crossed my right index finger over the middle one. Please please please please. No seatmate. I didn't mean to be grouchy or unfriendly, but I had too much to think about, worry about, without some nosy, talkative stranger bothering me.

Two minutes left. The flight attendant was handing us our menu. Good sign. The engines seemed to be revving. Even better sign. I closed my eyes in relief and therefore jumped six feet when a loud, husky female voice said, "Sorry deary, I guess I need to climb over you."

Shit. Double shit. I opened my eyes and smiled half-heartedly. "Oh, I'm sorry." I hugged my legs together and slanted them to the right, so the hefty woman could move past me to the window seat. I didn't like the window seat. I needed the aisle, where I could feel some sense of freedom if I wanted to escape for the bathroom or the emergency exit.

My only view now, I noted as the stranger sat down heavily, was of a large 60ish woman with short graying hair, hideous plaid green shorts and a tent-like maroon blouse. Silver earrings in the shape of sharks dangled from her large ears. Her face was opened up like a map: cheerful and full of directions. Oh no, I muttered to myself. A busybody. I could see it on her face; I could smell it somehow. The woman opened a container from her tote bag and the aroma of freshly baked chocolate chip cookies drifted across our two seats.

"Never know what they'll offer for dessert," she said with an apologetic smile. "Want one for the ride up?"

I shook my head no in thanks and looked out the window on the other side of the plane. For the ride up? Jiminy.

I closed my eyes in self-defense until I felt eyes staring at my flattened hair, and sure enough, when I turned toward the stranger, she was looking at me quizzically, as if trying to recall something. I moved my tongue around my teeth, a useless but hopeful teeth-tongue brushing, and looked around for the flight attendant. A bloody Mary sounded awfully good just about now.

"Let me guess," the woman said as if we'd been in a dazzling conversation for the past half hour. "You're not from Boston, you're going home to Florida. Not Miami. No no no no. You live in, what, Boca Raton? Key Biscayne?" She looked at me so happily that I almost wanted to lie and tell her she was right. But I wasn't feeling nice. Plus, I never lied. Or at least not unless there was a really good reason to.

"I live in Boston. Just flying to Florida for business." That wasn't really a lie. I was flying to Florida, then had to make a connection to St. Thomas, but she didn't have to know everything. Besides, I had a feeling that the more I told her, the more she'd try to wiggle into a long drawn-out conversation. In preparation for that, I pulled out a thick paperback and placed it on my lap.

"Well, you look too relaxed and pretty to be from Boston," she informed me, ignoring the book. I wondered what the hell that meant. I guessed she didn't like Boston. I looked at her, one eyebrow cocked up just a fraction, and that was all I had to do. "Nice place and all, don't get me wrong, but everyone in Boston is so busy and harried and stressed," she continued. "Not like us Floridians. Now we know how to live. Take it day by day. Listen to the ocean. The waves tell you what to do. Life is meant to be enjoyed, slowly, in and out, gently."

Oh God. I nodded as if in agreement, didn't permit my mouth to open, and grabbed my book just as the attendant finally responded to my little red light. "Tomato juice, please, with a twist of lime." I knew if I started drinking something stronger, with this seatmate, I'd never stop.

"Oh, that sounds delicious," Mrs. Busybody said to the attendant. "I'll have one of those too." She paused in time to stare at me carefully, as if memorizing my face. "No pleasure on your business trip?"

I put the book down slowly. "I'm pretty busy right now with work, so I doubt that I'll have time to take a day or two off," I answered nonchalantly. The less I told her, the better, I decided. She just stared at me, as if waiting for more. "I keep telling myself that life will slow down," I babbled. "I know I need to make a few changes soon, slow down and, as you say, smell the ocean." I laughed at my own twist of words. Fortunately, she laughed too.

"You know young lady, there's an expression you should keep in mind when you think about that change. It goes something like, what is it now?" The woman tapped her long fire-engine red fingernails on her forehead, as if the knocking would release the information from her brain. I just looked at her, practically holding my breath, wondering if she would remember what she wanted to say, and if so, that would satisfy her for a while and she'd leave me alone.

"Ah yes! I remember." She cleared her throat. She was once a smoker, I surmised, but was no more. 'Life is change. Growth is optional. Choose wisely.'

I stared back at her, mouth open. For some reason, her words were surrounded by bells, charming little bells that tinkled with prophetic urgency. Life is change? Growth is optional? Choose wisely? Choose what? About whether to grow or not, and is that really a choice? But in my agitated state of mind, my choosing seemed more personal. Parker or Gregory? Exciting or dull? A safe life or a fun one? In that one instant I hated that woman. Hated her for making me think about choices and men and the life that was spread out in front of me like some enigmatic, roiling ocean. I picked up my book, nodded my head slightly, and began to read.

She poked her finger on my shoulder. "As a matter of fact, choice is what life is all about, don't you think? The choices of what we do, where we go, can make or break us."

"Sure," I said. Then I went back to my book.

"Which means, we should always be careful of what we do, and where we go."

This was getting ridiculous. I looked at the woman, a line etched between my eyebrows, and said, "I suppose so. But for now, I'd like to forget heavy conversation and just relax with my book."

My friendly neighbor finally seemed to get the message. She looked out the window as if pondering her own choices, and surprisingly, I fell asleep for the rest of the flight. I woke as the plane landed; she was the first to gather her tote and jump out of her seat.

"I need to quickly claim my baggage, since my husband is waiting for me in his car," she explained as she waved goodbye. I watched her rush off, wondering if the Miami bag handlers were really that much faster than those at Logan.

I searched for a restroom as I strode through the Miami airport looking for my next flight's gate. But I paused as I passed one of the airport bars. Wait a minute. What was she doing there? Her face was turned away from me, but the maroon blouse had stopped me. I thought she was in a rush to get to baggage?

Mrs. Busybody was talking to a man in an agitated manner, arms flailing and mouth moving quickly. Odd. I thought she was the calm and relaxed one. The man stood too close to her, a handsome man with black hair, a mustache, and an arrogant expression. He looked familiar.

Over the airport intercom, a nasally voice announced my flight. I was going to miss it. I forgot the restroom as I continued my way to the gate. Where did I know that man? Why would I know him? It wasn't until I had settled into my narrow seat in the frighteningly small plane that it came to me.

He was the stranger in Telford's Pipe Shop.

CHAPTER TWENTY-FOUR

"But why would I want to add more illustrations to the book?" Barbara asked. We were sitting on the yacht. Virgin Island sun illuminated her manuscript, which was strewn about the table on the top deck. I picked up the large glass of iced tea her husband had given me and tried to smile, masking my sincere wish to kill her with a nearby fishing pole.

"Because our reader surveys, and all relevant research on medical textbooks like yours, have stressed that illustrations are valued. Highly valued," I answered.

"If my book is written well enough, we don't need illustrations for a reader to understand what I'm explaining," Barbara insisted.

"That's not the point." I looked up at the sun, wishing I were back home, sitting on my couch reading a good book. God, this woman could be so frustrating.

"But that's precisely the point," Barbara continued, like a dog with an over chewed rawhide. "I thought you said this was the best written O.T. book in the country."

"It will be. I mean, it is," I stammered.

"It will be?"

"When we add more illustrations," I answered.

Barbara sat back in her chair, looking at me with eyes slit, one leg crossed with the ankle leaning on top of her other knee. "Roger!" she shouted suddenly. "Come here." Nice Roger, the beleaguered husband, came up from below deck where I'm sure he was hiding from his wife's frequent requests. "Sit down," she demanded, and of course he did.

"Meredith is young. You and I have discussed this." Barbara spoke to Roger as if I weren't there. "She's got a good degree from Boston College, some nice experience with publishing houses, but overall, she's still young. She thinks she knows it all, and she's not mature enough to realize yet that she doesn't."

I wanted to stand up and leave. Looking around, I knew there was no way to escape. I was surrounded by water. I was half tempted to just leap off the side of the yacht. But did sharks cruise the Caribbean water? As I watched Barbara talking to Roger, I questioned if it was any safer here on the boat. A huge shark was sitting across from me, and she was trying to bite.

I stood up and stretched as if I was in the middle of the beach on a hot summer day. Looked pointedly to my right and my left. "Barbara, I've come a long way to discover you're not pleased with my editing skills. But I can assure you that Arthur Flack will be happy to find you an older, more mature editor." This was a lie. I was the oldest editor currently working for the company.

I turned to Roger. "Perhaps you could take me into town now, and I can spend the night at my hotel before I leave." He hopped up.

Barbara rolled her eyes. "Sit down, Roger," she demanded. "No one is going anywhere. Meredith, stop being so sensitive. Now, let's consider who is doing these illustrations you want so badly."

Okay, I'd won that round. Knowing Barbara, several more would arise during my four-day stay in St. Thomas. Four days too many, as far as I was concerned. I had dreaded this trip and so far Barbara hadn't given me reason to feel otherwise. However, I couldn't complain about my off-work time.

When I arrived in St. Thomas the day before, a taxi driver dropped me off at a surprisingly good-looking hotel. As I had told Gregory, I expected a little room in a dingy motel with no water view. Instead, Arthur had outdone himself; I had a newly renovated room with a king-sized bed, a private balcony, and a view of the picturesque harbor of Charlotte Amalie.

The hotel was just across the street from the inter-island ferries and seaplane (and access to Barbara's yacht) and within walking distance of nice restaurants and local sites. Perfect. If I could only ignore my overwrought imagination regarding dark strangers, and if I could just tolerate Barbara and her shenanigans, the four days could be quick and productive.

Barbara was a highly respected woman in her field, and I decided it had gone to her head. She hadn't actually practiced occupational therapy in over ten years, but her books, thanks to Flack, Inc., were extremely successful. She earned nice royalties from them, but the better she did, the more she asserted her powerful personality. I looked at her closely. She was an attractive 60-year-old, tall and lean, brown from her time on the yacht. Her husband, on the other hand, was a bit paunchy, shorter than Barbara by a few inches, balding, and completely in her control. I wondered briefly how he had done so well in business, but obviously he had.

I took a deep breath. "I have the perfect illustrator in mind. And I happen to have some examples," I said as I riffled through my heavy leather briefcase, which fit in nicely at the office, but seemed out-of-place in this warm oasis. As I pulled my head back up to the table, the horizon moved crazily, as if I were watching a mirage. "Whoa."

"Are you okay?" Roger asked. He quickly came to my side. "Ah, a little bit of seasickness?"

I nodded my head and was immediately sorry.

"Let's get you on land. You and Barbara have done enough for today."

I couldn't agree with him more. Faster than I thought possible, Roger had me on his speedboat, and we were back on land in ten minutes. After I assured him that I was okay and could get to my hotel on my own, he returned to the yacht. I breathed a sigh of relief. Alone! I began to walk the winding, up-hill streets. The exercise felt good to my legs, and my stomach. As advertised, the hills of the island were emerald and dazzling. I walked at a good pace, passing droves of sightseers. But after about five minutes, I felt a chill cross my back. I shivered in the 80-degree late afternoon heat and turned my head swiftly. I was sure I saw a pair of dark brown eyes stare into mine, but when I looked again, more closely, I only saw tourists enjoying the scenery. I continued toward my hotel, not feeling as content, nor as alone, as I'd like.

Needing some sense of safety, I called Gregory, who was still in his office. See? I thought. There he was, just where he should be, available when needed.

"I can't believe how much I miss you," he said. "When are you coming back?"

"I've just been here a day." I hesitated. "I miss you too Gregory." But I wasn't sure that was true. I missed home. I missed work and my early morning runs and my 10 a.m. blueberry muffin. I missed the slight chill of early fall, and the way the sun slanted on the deep green leaves as they prepared to turn color. I missed my bed, and the smell of lavender on my pillows. Did I miss Gregory? God, I hoped so.

"Your dad called. He lost your cell phone number again." We both laughed. "He sounded odd, though. Something up with him?"

I nodded my head, forgetting for a second that Gregory couldn't see me. "Yes, but he's not divulging much, that's for sure. I don't know, Gregory, weird things are happening to the people I love."

"What do you mean? Who?"

"Well, Shannon has met a guy, but she's not talking about it. Dad's afraid to introduce me to the woman he's dating. Par..." Oh my god, I almost mentioned Parker and his problems.

"Par?" Gregory said. "Par what?"

"Par for the course," I said. "Dad never talks about his life – work or personal. I wouldn't have even known that he was finally dating if he hadn't brought it up the other day." I held my breath.

"Oh."

The rest of the conversation was desultory and short. Was Gregory upset with me? He was just as bad as everyone else. Did everyone have secrets?

.

CHAPTER TWENTY-FIVE

I had a vision of the Caribbean – sunny, bright, warm every day. I woke up with my illusions shattered. The sky threatened rain, the air was as moist as a wet towel, and my mood somberly played along with the weather.

But I had a job to do, so I wore a bright yellow top over my jean skirt and walked swiftly to the harbor. I was early. No sign of Roger yet, so I figured this was a good time to check in with Mom.

"Hey you," she answered cheerfully. "How's that sweet Caribbean island? Do you have a tan yet?"

"Well, actually, it's cloudy and humid," I answered, "And..."

"Hmmm, well that's too bad. Did I ever tell you about the time George took me to St. Croix? That's the island south of St. Thomas, you know. George was quite the romantic. You remember him? He was the one before Larry. Well he..."

"Mom, yes, I remember. But sorry, I can't talk now. My ride has just arrived." That was true; Roger's motor boat was easing against the mooring. "I just wanted you to know I'm here, safe and sound."

"Oh, you never have time to talk. Call me later tonight, when you have more time, okay? In the meantime, enjoy the island!"

She acted as if I was here on a holiday. I sighed, promised I'd call later, and then stepped gingerly into Roger's boat.

"Gonna be a fun day," he said cryptically.

I looked out at the gray horizon, spotted with blue-black clouds.

"You mean because of the weather?" I asked.

"Sure."

"Are we expecting heavy rain?" What else could I talk about with my author's husband but the weather? I didn't understand what he did for work, and I had no idea what he did for pleasure.

"Thunder and lightening, for starters." Roger looked at me then, his squinty eyes surveying me. Had I dressed wrong for a rainy Caribbean day? Or was he thinking of something else? I checked him out as he steered the motorboat toward his yacht; he wore red and green plaid shorts with a dark brown shirt. I laughed to myself. Roger dressed like a hick from the country, yet he was a wealthy investor and lived on a yacht. Who did we really know, I mused as Barbara threw the rope ladder over to Roger and we climbed on board. Like life, each of us was a mystery.

~~~~~~~~~~~~~~~~~~~~~~~

An hour later I was sitting uncomfortably below deck, listening to Barbara defend her overuse of the word 'handicapped' in the manuscript. Her voice had a tendency to move up and down, like a pianist playing scales; in self-defense, I tuned out. The rain snapped me out of it; a hard rain that hit against the yacht's windows like birds pecking at an empty birdfeeder. The noise startled me, and Barbara, in her annoying singsong voice, intoned, "Earth calling Mars. Earth calling Mars."

"Whoops, sorry Barbara," I answered, perking up as much as one can in a rolling, rollicking boat anchored in an angry Caribbean bay.

"Where were you, on the moon? Or were you just mooning, my young friend?" Barbara was fishing for personal information, information that I never planned to give her. No matter how troubled I was by my phone conversation with Gregory last night, and by the fact that I was unable to reach him this morning, I was not going to get personal with her.

Sweat dotted my forehead. "Just feeling a little claustrophobic." In truth, I felt like hell. From what I could see, hell right now was pouring hot spikes of water down on us, just daring us to try to get a breath of fresh air on this machine of motion.

"How about a little lunch? I could make us a tuna sandwich."

My stomach roiled in anguish, and I tried to remember where the bathroom was.

"You're turning yellow, my dear. Was it my question, or are you getting sea sick?"

"It's the latter. I don't do well on objects that move – boats, planes, cars, even restaurants."

Barbara snickered.

"Well," I said defensively. "Restaurants were not meant to move, nor were we humans meant to fly, or sit on rocking boats. We're supposed to be earth-bound creatures." The churning in my stomach increased, and I wondered if I was about to lose my breakfast. Barbara's manuscript was strewn on the cabin's table in front of me, red editing marks swimming in front of my watery eyes. I was about to soil it unforgivingly. Barbara handed me a warm glass of dark liquid.

"Here, drink this. Strong coke. Can't buy it in the stores. Roger gets it for me. Works every time."

I looked at her out of two bleary eyes and swallowed. If she'd told me it was poison, I would have downed it happily. Nothing was worse than motion sickness. However, like a miracle, on my last swallow the sun beamed through the dark clouds and brightened what had been an ominous scene. I ran up the little staircase to the open deck, breathing in the fresh air like a miner returning from a long day down in the caverns. "Much better!" I exclaimed as Barbara followed me, picking up her binoculars and looking out toward the open sea.

"Oh no," Barbara groaned. "Where is Roger? Why isn't Roger here?" Her short gray hair looked wired, as if she'd just been electrocuted.

"He went to the main land. You asked him to go grocery shopping," I reminded her. I was still in awe of a woman who told her man to get the groceries. I'd never seen Parker enter a grocery store; Gregory was nice enough to sit outside in his car while I raced around the supermarket, throwing whatever I needed into the basket so I could be finished as quickly as possible. But Barbara had given Roger a list as long as a snake, and... I looked over. What ever was the matter with Barbara? Her eyes were wide and wild, even though the sun was peeking through the sky.

I ignored the woman as I gulped in the sweet Caribbean air. I would not go back down into that cabin if my life depended on it. My stomach was still threatening to heave, so I held on to the railing and looked out to the horizon. Always look straight ahead when you get motion sick, my father told me as a child. I tried not to move my eyes, but Barbara was leaning close to me, eyes scanning the sky above.

"Barbara, relax," I managed, rubbing my hand along my stomach. "Heaven is winning; hell is losing. Look, the sky is gorgeous. The sun is peeking through those immense clouds." I pointed. "That one looks like a beaver. And look up over there! That one looks just like ..."

"Meredith, you're going to have to go back down in the galley. Both of us are. We'll have to batten down the hatches. I think that's what Roger calls it. Oh shit. Why isn't he here? Oh damn. Move, Meredith, move!"

No way was I moving back down into the depths of sickness and despair. I was just beginning to feel human again, now that the water was calming and the air was as still as a sleeping giant. No way, no how.

"Barbara – the storm has passed! Listen. There's no wind at all, which is rather strange, isn't it, since it was so stormy just a few minutes ago."

"Now, Meredith. Don't you know a wind funnel when you see one?"

"A what?"

"A wind funnel. Otherwise known as a tornado, only this is on the water. Look."

I moved my eyes to where she pointed, and sure enough, in the distance I could see a long dark funnel, wider at the top, narrow where it seemed to just touch the ocean.

"Looks like a cone of dark gray cotton candy," I said to Barbara.

"Nothing sweet about a wind funnel. It's extremely dangerous, and by the looks of it, will hit here within five to ten minutes. The yacht will be bouncing around like a ball in a pinball machine in half that time. Get downstairs now!"

I still didn't budge. I'd rather die out here, in wind-swept fury, then go through that nausea again. But I looked around me, at the other yachts, bigger and stronger than this one. Not a sailor was in sight, not even a pretty woman in a tiny bikini enjoying the newfound sun. They were all entombed in their boats, waiting for the rage of the ocean. I looked at the author, the one I'd edited for over two years, the one the publishing company was banking on to make big bucks for the medical division, and I knew I had to placate her in some way.

"If it's that dangerous, we better get off the boat," I suggested.

I thought Barbara was going to hit me. She pressed her lips together, hard, and then said, slowly, as if to a child, "Roger has the small boat. We don't have a way to get off this thing. And we wouldn't have time anyway. Now, Meredith. Downstairs."

"You go down, Barbara. I'll make sure everything is secured tightly. Don't worry about me."

She glared, made a noise like a mad goose, grabbed my arms, and we lunged together down into the doom of the cabin. I immediately felt like a tiger encased in a tiny cage. Barbara closed the hatch, or whatever it was called, and locked it. The only noise was our breathing – short and fast. Then the yacht began to shake, and we were both on the floor of the cabin.

I was petrified. I hated motion and I hated small spaces, yet here I was. Panic boiled up in me as if I was full teakettle on a hot stovetop. My stomach heaved, and I was thankful I'd only had a small breakfast. The less in, the less I could vomit out. My body trembled, and within minutes I was soaked with sweat.

I tried to stand up. "Barbara, I don't care what happens. I have to get out of here!" I screamed. But the noise from the storm, or tornado, or whatever she called it, overpowered my voice and took over the cabin.

"Get down!" Barbara yelled. At least, that's what I thought she said. I was pushed back down on the hard floor, though nobody was near me. Barbara braced herself on the floor, legs straight out against the seating area, arms around the legs of the bolted table, and I did the same.

The boat rocked so hard we both shrieked. Manuscript pages flew around the cabin like large confetti, and Barbara's coffee pot landed inches from her head.

"Be careful!" she shouted. How the hell was I supposed to be careful? I was too scared to even be sick. Then I saw motion in the back bedroom area; the drawers from the built-in dresser were opening and closing as if by invisible hands. I nodded my head toward it, clinging onto the secured table legs as hard as I could, while both Barbara and I watched one of the drawers tear loose from the dresser and bang hard onto the floor.

Barbara's eyes were larger than pancakes, and I knew we were in big trouble. This woman was not the type to scare easily. I wanted to ask her if she'd ever done this before, survived a wind funnel, but my attention was diverted by the contents of the dresser drawer. Small brown wrapped objects were scattering all over the floor, released from that drawer. What were they? I looked closely as the yacht heaved again, and one of the objects rolled right next to me. I picked it up.

A cigar.

CHAPTER TWENTY-SIX

Barbara ignored me as I grabbed for another cigar rolling my way.

"Let the stupid thing go and hang on!" she shouted.

"But they're cigars!" I yelled back. "Why do you have dozens of cigars in your dresser?"

The yacht jerked, and I banged my head against the table.

"Hold on!" Barbara screamed at me unnecessarily. The cigars rolled to the other side of the cabin as I curled my arm around the leg of the secured table. I closed my eyes, imagining the immense waves that were rocking us so haphazardly from side to side. I almost retched, and quickly re-opened my eyes. Just in time to see Barbara looking at the cigars with a huge question mark in her eyes. So, she didn't know about them.

But I couldn't worry about that now. A bolt of lightning added theatrics to our already scary show. I clamped my teeth tight to hold back a scream. Instead, I thought of Parker. Why? I tried to erase his image out of my mind -- the image of Parker in his faded jeans, chambray shirt, and crooked grin as he said goodbye to me just off the Longfellow Bridge.

Then I thought of his secret message to me. T R M F Y. Trying to figure out what it meant kept me from thinking about imminent death. T R M F Y. I intoned it to myself silently. TRMFY. TRMFY. Trimfy, it sounded like.

"What?" Barbara shouted. A roar surrounded us, and the yacht seemed to be hiccupping convulsively.

"Trimfy, Trimfy," I kept repeating.

"What the hell does that mean?" Barbara asked loudly. She looked at me as if I were scaring her. I laughed out loud.

"I don't know what it means," I shouted back. "T R M F Y. What's that mean to you?"

Barbara just shook her head and held on tight. I followed her example, still whispering "trimfy, trimfy," which for some reason I found comforting. Hours later, although Barbara assured me it was only ten minutes, the shaking slowed down, the roaring lightened to a sharp hiss as rain pelted the yacht, and my chanting stopped.

The yacht still moved, but now in a softer, rolling pattern. Up and down, up and down. If I wasn't about to puke, it would have been comforting, like a rocking chair.

"We made it," Barbara said triumphantly, standing up with legs wide apart, a conqueror's smile on her thin lips. I raced up the stairs, opened the hatch, and scurried into the open air. I didn't care if I got wet. In fact, the rain would feel good. But the storm had completely passed as if it had never occurred. The sun shone brightly, and birds swooped overhead. I wondered briefly where they'd been while we were all shuttered up like bugs. I think I would have preferred to have been with the birds.

Barbara came over and stood by me. She was breathing hard, as if she'd just run up a steep hill.

"That was the scariest thing I've ever gone through," she said confidentially.

I looked at Barbara, saying nothing.

"You did great," she added. Huge compliment from a woman who gives out criticism like some people give out hugs.

"I was scared shitless," I responded.

Barbara laughed. The sun shone so brightly I needed my sunglasses.

"Look!" I pointed halfway between the harbor and the yacht. "Roger's on his way."

"Thank God," Barbara said. "I need a good stiff drink. I hope he stopped at the liquor store."

I looked at her, wanting to ask, but wondering how. "So, those cigars were a surprise, huh?"

"What cigars?"

"You know, when the drawer burst open. Wasn't that odd? All those cigars rolling all over the place?"

Barbara looked at me blankly. "Why shouldn't Roger have cigars?"

My turn to look blank. "Oh. Roger smokes cigars?"

"No, I didn't say that." Barbara turned toward the motorboat and waved her long, skinny arm as if it was a flag. Then she turned back to me. "We have parties here. Lots of Roger's friends smoke," she added.

I nodded my head as if that made sense. At this point, nothing made sense, since my stomach was still queasy, and my head felt like it was stuffed with wads of cotton. As Roger pulled up and began to hand Barbara bags of groceries, I massaged my temples, as if that simple act would help me feel better. Barbara talked swiftly, telling her husband about our recent adventure. She didn't mention the cigars.

"Let me help," I offered as she turned to bring the bags downstairs.

"No way, my friend. You need to get off this boat and feel better."

I was immensely relieved, but also felt a bit guilty. "But I should help with the mess downstairs..." I began.

"Roger, this young lady is suffering. She hasn't thrown up on our teak floors yet, but I wouldn't give her another second."

Roger practically saluted her. "Yes ma'am. Meredith, back to land! You have been commanded."

I didn't argue. I couldn't wait to get off the boat.

~~~~~~~~~~~~~~~~~~~~~~~~

Twenty minutes later I was back on the ground, walking the safe, steady streets again. But were they safe? Roger had looked at me oddly when he dropped me off at the dock, as if he wanted to say something. I wondered what Barbara had whispered to him right before we left the yacht. Had she mentioned the cigars? And now as I walked, I had the feeling that I was being watched. This time, a dark-haired, deeply tanned man wearing a Hawaiian shirt strolled near me, almost side by side amidst the other tourists. He tried to act like he was part of the crowd, but I saw him steal glances my way every few minutes. Was I being paranoid?

I tried to shake him as I walked up and down the narrow, still-wet streets, stretching my legs and enjoying the smell of sun drying the moisture off the trees and flowering bushes. I thought back to Gregory's voice last night, so deep and lonely, and of my attempts to reach him this morning. But thoughts of phone calls crashed into silence as I saw the man again, following me into a flower store. When I turned around, he wasn't there. I bought a couple of orchid stems to brighten my room and hastily walked back to the hotel. I needed to talk to someone. Once in my room, I called Shannon.

"There you are," she exclaimed. "How's paradise?"

"Ha, if you only knew." I described my experience with the wind funnel, and she sounded duly impressed. But I could tell her mind was on something else.

"Hey Merry, can I pick your brain for a minute?"

"Sure." I laid back on my bed facing the big window that overlooked the harbor. The sun was fading, and the dark blue sky changed to lavender and light rose. "But first, let me ask you something. Were you at that neat new Boston restaurant the other night? Um, what night was it?" Seemed like ages ago, but I realized I'd only been here for two days. "Wednesday night. At the bar?"

There was a definite hesitation before Shannon answered. "Oh yeah! I meant to talk to you about that. I was there briefly. Saw you, but you looked pretty busy, with your mom and Gregory and some other man. Who was he?"

"Nice deflection, my friend. He was, is, my mom's new boyfriend. Donald. And who were you with? I couldn't see, but my mom thought she recognized him."

"She did? That's strange. I'm sorry I didn't come over and say hello to her. And to Gregory. But we were late for a dinner reservation someplace else. Anyway, ready for my question?"

Wow. Now I was getting suspicious. Had Shannon and Parker been together at the restaurant? How could that be? No. She'd tell me. Wouldn't she? Of course she would. She was my best friend. But why was she being so evasive? "Shoot," I said, wanting to ask a lot more, but not wanting to be like my mom, pushing for information that didn't want to be given.

"If you were dating a man who had children, grown children, how soon do you think you should meet them, in the course of the relationship?"

I sat up straighter. "Wow. Shannon. You didn't tell me you were getting that serious about this guy. He has grown children? How old is he?" I realized immediately that my question was probing. "Don't answer that. If you and he have dated long enough to know that you want to continue seriously, I think it would be nice to meet his kids. Kind of scary though, huh?"

As I talked with Shannon, I walked over to the window and watched the sunset while musing. Shannon was actually in a serious relationship. I was pleased for her and couldn't wait to meet her new man. Shannon's voice was whispery, higher-pitched than usual, as she talked about him. I smiled. A sure sign of love. But movement below on the hotel grounds caught my attention.

"Hold on, Shannon." I put the phone down and hid behind the blinds, looking at the place where I thought I saw someone. Yes, definitely a man was standing by a large bush, looking up toward my room. And he was wearing a Hawaiian shirt like the one I saw earlier in the flower shop. I returned to the phone.

"You know what Shannon? I'm ready to come home. I am not getting good vibes from this place." I told her about my misgivings, the feelings of being followed, the man in the bushes below.

"Call hotel security first," Shannon suggested. "Then tomorrow, go to the police."

"What am I going to say? 'Oh, excuse me, I looked out my window and someone was standing outside.' It's a park, Shannon. They'll tell me there's no law against standing in the park."

"They could get him for loitering."

"Give me a break. I'm sorry. I don't mean to be short with you. How about if it's all in my imagination? I still might just be shell-shocked, or whatever, spooked, from that mugging a few nights ago in Cambridge."

"Merry, you really need to go to the police," Shannon insisted. "That's why they're there. You're a tourist. Tell them you're being followed. At least let them know where you are during the day, and where you're staying. They'll keep an eye on you."

"I don't have any proof!"

"Meredith, I'm serious. Go to the police. Or I'll call them."

Funny thing was, I didn't doubt that she would.

We hung up, dissatisfied. I hadn't learned more about the mystery man Shannon was dating, and she'd only gotten a vague, 'okay, I'll try' from me regarding the police.

Little did I know that by the end of the next day, the police would be the least of my problems.

CHAPTER TWENTY-SEVEN

I had no idea where the police station was in St. Thomas, but I didn't want to ask Barbara for directions. She'd wonder why I needed to know. If I told her I thought I was being followed, she'd think I was off my rocker and tell me to get a life. That was Barbara. I could understand why she was never a mother – she had not one ounce of compassion or empathy or even the ability to have any sympathy within her tall, upright body. Hell of an occupational therapist though.

So I waited the next day until we had finished Chapter 7. It was 3:30. The sun was hot as we sat out on the topside of the yacht. We had gone through three pitchers of iced tea, and I said quite sincerely, "Barbara, that's enough. The sun has wiped me out. Let's call it a day, and we'll continue tomorrow."

"Just as well," she said. "I'm planning a surprise cocktail party here in your honor tonight, starting at 6."

I looked at her, amazed. She just assumed that I'd be available for her whenever she snapped her fingers. Unfortunately, she was right.

"I don't have anything to wear," I lied.

"Sure you do," she answered, "That pink sundress you wore the first day will do just fine. See you at 6."

I was dismissed, and Roger shuttled me toward the island in his little motorboat. How he put up with Commander Barbara I didn't know. I was almost fed up enough to ask him, but he seemed to read my mind.

"You know, she's all bluster, no bite," Roger offered a few minutes after we left the yacht.

I looked at him. "There would be plenty of bite if I didn't go to her little party tonight," I blurted, immediately angry with myself for saying anything.

Roger just laughed. "Oh, you'll do fine at the cocktail party. Just a bunch of retired wannabes with too much money and no brains."

"Are they the friends who smoke all those cigars?" I asked.

Roger's narrow eyes widened for a fraction of a second, then he chuckled. "Is that what Barbara told you? That we store cigars for our friends?" He shook his head, obviously amused. "She's quite a woman, my Barbara."

"Yes she is," I responded. He still hadn't explained why they had all those cigars.

"You know, Meredith, you handle Barbara just fine. She's very impressed with you, and she's not impressed with many people."

I stared ahead, not sure how to respond.

"She's not an easy woman to get along with. She has high expectations of people, and usually she's disappointed." He looked at me and waited for my reaction. But I just nodded.

"Yesterday was a test, and you passed with flying colors," he added.

"A test? When?"

"During the wind funnel."

"What, Barbara conjured that up with a flick of her hand? She has more power than I realized!" I said, kidding.

Roger leaned back, legs stretched out in front of him, obviously enjoying the conversation.

"No. No, it was your reactions, and the way you kept yourself together during the godawful time below deck, that impressed her. She thinks you're terrific, Meredith. That says a lot."

"Thanks, I guess," I said. I was still mad about Barbara's demand that I attend her party without even asking me about it beforehand. And the way Roger stuck up for his wife was a little arrogant and very self-assured. I still didn't 'get' this couple, and I was feeling uncomfortable.

"Funny, how a crisis can bring out the true character of a person, isn't it?" Roger mused.

Again, I didn't know how to respond.

He leaned forward and touched my knee with his hand. I looked up at him, startled. "Don't mind me," he said. "Socrates once said, 'By all means marry: if you get a good wife, you'll be happy; if you get a bad one, you'll become a philosopher.' "

Just at that moment we reached the dock. I jumped up to throw the rope over the pier banister. "Thank you, Roger. It's nice of you to keep taxiing me back and forth every day."

"My pleasure, Meredith." He paused. "Barbara may have told you that I'm the one who insisted that she ask you to come here and edit on her turf."

I was surprised. "No, she didn't mention that."

"Oh. Well, I figured it would be good for the editorial bond between you and Barbara. And I was right!"

I wagged my head up and down slowly.

"You must be tired, Meredith. Let me get you a cab this time." With a flap of his arm, he hailed one. I thanked him again and entered the car.

Roger thought I was going back to my hotel, but instead once I got in I said, "Police Station, please." A short time later, the cabbie stopped in front of an attractive yellow building. I had planned on a casual conversation with a friendly police officer, but instead, I got a stiffly uniformed man checking everyone who approached the front door of the building.

"Ya? What's your business?" the man asked, his eyes staring into mine as if I was about to commit a crime.

"I need to talk to a police officer."

"Ya?"

Well, as far as I knew it was none of his business why I needed to talk to the police, so I walked past him into a too well air-conditioned lobby empty of people. I hated not knowing where I was. Another reason I didn't like to travel. But the man I had just talked to came in, shook his head, and took my elbow gently, leading me up the stairs, down the hall, and into a brightly lit office with five desks full of ringing phones, boxes of donuts, uniformed men, and loud talk.

"Hey man. She's here to talk to a 'police officer.'"

The room silenced faster than a gunshot, and
half a dozen dark eyes suddenly were focused on me. I
gulped. More silence. Finally an older official, gray
streaked in his black curly hair, spectacles leaning
precariously on his nose, walked up to me and asked,
"Yes, how can I help you?"

"I'd like to talk about my concerns. What I
mean is that I want to talk about. Well, I mean. I think
someone is following me."

His large gloomy eyes rolled up in his head and
then he turned to everyone and said, "She thinks
someone is following her."

"Ya, ya," I heard, as well as a snicker or two.
Then they all went back to their desks, and the phones
began to ring again.

The officer took pity on me and offered his
hand. "Captain Bill Flores. Come, sit down. I'm sorry.
We don't mean to be rude. But we don't often have the
pleasure of such an attractive woman here." The
Captain paused as if deciding what to say next. "In
other words, we don't find it unlikely that you are
being followed. Yes?"

"No," I answered. I wondered if they ever heard
of sex discrimination here. Or sexual harassment. I
couldn't believe I wasn't being taken seriously just
because of my appearance. I felt my hair rise, as if a
bird with ruffled feathers, and I opened my mouth to

speak, then closed it. Perhaps I'd better watch which words I used.

"What I mean, Captain, is that you don't know me. I am not the kind of woman who gets paranoid. Before I came to St. Thomas, I was accosted in a city street, and someone smashed a window in my house. Both times I knew that someone was following me...." I stopped, frustrated.

The Captain's dark brown eyes were unexpressive. Finally he said, "You think the same person who followed you in ...?"

"Boston," I finished for him.

"In Boston flew all the way down here to follow you in St. Thomas?"

When he said it that way, it sounded ridiculous.

"Well, no, I didn't say the same person. I just..."

"I'll tell you what I think, Miss..." Again, the Captain waited for me to help him out.

"Ms. Powers. Meredith Powers."

"Yes, well, Miss Powers. I think you got, how's the expression go, freaked out in Boston, and you've brought your fright with you here."

I stood up and looked at him, thinking of turning on my heels and leaving. Then I sat down and faced Captain Flores again. "No, I don't think that's true. In fact, I waited a while before I came here with my misgivings, just in case what you've just said was true. But I trust my instincts, and I don't think I should ignore them."

"Why were you being followed in Boston, Miss Powers?"

Stymied again. Should I say, for a chubby brown cigar? I blew out a breath in exasperation. "I don't really know. Someone is trying to scare me, but I can't say why."

"And now they want to scare you in St. Thomas, also." Captain Flores took my elbow and led me away from the room toward the stairs. "Miss Powers. Go back to your hotel. Enjoy your stay here in beautiful St. Thomas. Sit out in the sun. Dance in the nightclubs. Relax." Then he dismissed me by turning away.

"Captain!" I said loudly. He turned back toward me, slowly. "I came to this office because I was encouraged by friends who told me I'd be safer by relaying my fears to you. They told me that the police in St. Thomas care about the welfare of the island's guests. I see that they were wrong." I started to turn my back on him, but he stopped me by shouting my name.

"Miss Powers. Wait. Please."

I faced him, feeling my face redden.

"We have a safe island here. There are troubles. We are not immune to them. But they are not your troubles. I ..." He paused, selecting his words carefully.

"At this moment, I do not have the manpower to send an officer to watch over a pretty woman. We're in the middle of ... well, never mind. Please. Relax. Enjoy our lovely island."

I stared into his earnest eyes, then shrugged him off and walked quickly down the stairs.

~~~~~~~~~~~~~~~~~~~~~~~~~

I didn't hail a cab because I needed to walk and think. Maybe Captain Flores was right. I needed to leave my troubles and fears in Boston, shake them all loose. But did I truly believe that the shadows and roving eyes I had seen were a consequence of my own mixed up emotions? I shook my head in disgust and almost missed the ringing of my cell phone. Was it Gregory? Jill with some work question? To hell with work. I should take the Captain's advice and put on my bathing suit and relax in the sun. Except for the fact that I had a stupid yacht party to attend in two hours, thanks to the illustrious Barbara Browning.

I checked the name on my phone and then quickly opened it. "Dad?"

"Hi sweetie."

"Everything alright?"

"Well, yes. But I have a proposition for you."

"Okay." I drew out the word in two long syllables. This did not sound like my father. He never 'had a proposition' for me. He was a research scientist. He spoke in straight, short, to-the-point sentences.

"I've decided to come visit you in St. Thomas."

I stopped in my tracks. WHAT? My father was going to fly, to see me, in a Caribbean island that was known for its beaches and its sun? People came here to vacation. To rest. My father hadn't taken a vacation since, well, since I'd known him. And he only flew on emergencies. Work emergencies.

"What's wrong?" I asked.

Dad cleared his throat. "Since you're down there anyway, I thought it might be a good idea to bring my friend down, for a little break. And then we could meet you when you're not busy. Well, meet isn't the right word, but you know what I mean. And the three of us can get used to this relationship in a relaxed setting."

I allowed silence to settle between Caribbean and East Coast satellites as I pondered his little speech. Finally I said, "I repeat. What's wrong?"

He sighed. "Merry, just give me a little room here, will you? I'm trying to do the right thing. I want you to meet my friend, and I want it to be fun. Is it okay if we come down or not?"

I sighed this time. "Of course, Dad. I'm sorry. It sounds like a lovely idea. I have one or two more days of editing with my author, and then I'm scheduled to come home. Maybe I could stay an extra day."

Inwardly, I groaned. My relationship with Gregory was doomed. He would not be happy if I lengthened my stay away from him. Maybe I should tell him to come down after all. Heck, might as well have the whole family here. I'd invite Mom too, and Donald. At that thought, I laughed out loud.

"What?" Dad asked.

"Oh. Nothing. Do you think you could get plane tickets this quickly? Come down in two days?"

"Already done. We arrive tomorrow at 11 a.m."

Now it was my turn. "What?"

Dad chuckled. He chuckled! Who was this man? But as I listened to him explain that he had been so excited about the idea, he'd already talked to a travel agent and worked out an itinerary, I decided I liked it. This new father. He sounded happy. What a wonderful thing. When he finished, I blurted out, "Maybe I should invite Gregory too."

"Sure!" Dad said. "Great idea! See you tomorrow. We're going to stay at a hotel a few miles away from town. I'll call you when we get in."

I immediately dialed Gregory at work, because he still wasn't answering his cell. But his secretary picked up the phone instead. When she told me where he was, I stopped in the middle of the sidewalk.

Gregory had rushed out of the office to catch a plane to Miami, and she had no idea why.

CHAPTER TWENTY-EIGHT

The yacht was dressed up for the occasion. Small white lights sparkled from the masts and around the perimeter of the boat. Music drifted up from below deck: Frank Sinatra, Tony Bennett, and Ella Fitzgerald.

Classics, I thought, pleased despite my misgivings about attending this shindig. I'd much prefer to be in my hotel room with the windows open, listening to the soft Caribbean breeze as I read the latest romance I'd optimistically packed in the overnight bag. But no, I was here at Barbara's request – demand, actually - on a clear, moon-full night, gearing myself up to greet a bunch of people I'd never met before, and most likely would never meet again.

"Meredith! Just in time," Barbara chortled as Roger helped me up from the motorboat onto the yacht. He had been quiet on the ride over; I guessed his afternoon chattiness had been an anomaly.

After climbing up the ladder, I quickly perused the party and saw at least a dozen people chatting with wine glasses in hand. Just in time for what?

"Roger's brother's wife's step-brother is here," she continued. "He just happened to be visiting St. Thomas on business. Roger ran into him in town this morning. Like you, he knows no one here. Come say hello."

I groaned inwardly. His brother's wife's step-brother? How far removed was that? Maybe we could play 'six degrees of separation' for the next hour. Otherwise, what would I talk to him about? Barbara led me, her hand on my back, to a tall, dark man leaning against the railing, looking out toward the harbor. Not a particularly friendly fellow, I surmised. He held a small glass of what looked like scotch on the rocks. That dated him, since no one I knew in his thirties drank scotch.

At Barbara's greeting the man turned around, and I gasped. Ignoring Barbara, he stared directly into my eyes as if daring me to say something.

I knew this man, but I didn't know his name or where he was from. I had last seen him in Miami, and before that, at Telford's Pipe Shop.

"Meredith, this is Mr. Carlos Medina. Carlos, Meredith Powers," Barbara introduced.

"Ah, Meredith Powers. Yes, I've heard about you. So nice to meet the real person – the accolades, I see, were not exaggerated." His voice was soft and silky, like marshmallows melting on a hot stick. His chocolate eyes were inscrutable, but under his mustache his lips were curved in a welcoming smile. His wavy hair curled over the collar of a pressed powder blue polo. He took my hand as if it were a butterfly and kissed it.

"And what have you heard?" I asked, really wanting to say, what are you doing here? He opened his mouth to speak but Barbara quickly interrupted.

"I'll leave you two to get acquainted. Must see to my guests!" No! I wanted to shout. This man followed me here all the way from Boston. But how could I prove any of that? Carlos grabbed my attention with a quick cough.

"You're in publishing, as I am, Ms. Powers," he began. "I can't wait to hear about your business. I have my own newsletter, you know, printed and distributed nationally."

"Oh," I said. What was he talking about? I was sure this was the same guy I'd seen at Telford's. Wasn't he? But how could he be connected to Roger and Barbara, in a distant family kind of way? To keep the conversation going, I added, "What's the newsletter about?"

"Drugs," he said. I got the feeling he was waiting for my reaction.

"Drugs?"

"You know. Pharmaceutical drugs. My newsletter keeps pharmacists informed of the latest developments in medicines – what's out there, what's being researched, what's popular with patients, etc. It's indispensable to good pharmacists."

"Ah," I responded. My mind was racing. Drugs. Parker. Cigar shop. This guy was connected to Parker somehow. I knew it. "What's the name?"

"New Century Pharmaceuticals," Carlos answered almost apologetically. "Not a very imaginative name, but pharmacists prefer things straightforward."

A soft but chilly breeze encouraged me to tug my silk shawl around my shoulders. Carlos gently pulled one end over my arm while whispering in my ear, "It's a tough business, though, no?" His breath was a mixture of pipe tobacco and mint, and his thick mustache tickled my ear.

"What business?" I asked. What was he talking about? So he knew Parker was with the D.E.A.? Was Parker in trouble? With this guy?

"The publishing business, of course. What else did you think I was talking about?" Carlos responded with a small smile. He looked at me quizzically as he took a sip of his scotch. "I'm impressed with what you do, Ms. Powers. Not only do you contend with the day-to-day drudgery of editing, but you also manage high-strung authors." He nodded toward Barbara, who was chatting with some of the other guests. "A high stress combination."

I nodded noncommittally. "Do you find editing stressful?"

Carlos laughed. "Oh, I'm not that involved with the day-to-day production, Meredith. May I call you Meredith?"

I smiled sweetly but didn't answer.

He moved his hand up to my neck and fingered my necklace. "What a beautiful string of pearls," he commented, stroking them and sending a shiver down my back. This man was smooth. And darkly handsome. He almost made me forget that I should be scared of him. But that sense of ease made me uncomfortable enough to search for an excuse to leave. Roger arrived as if reading my thoughts.

"Hey, you look like someone who needs a drink," he said cheerfully. Giving Carlos a backward glance, Roger led me toward the booze.

"Hey, sorry Barbara stuck you with Carlos. He's harmless. Likes to flirt with the ladies, but in actuality, he's very married, if you know what I mean."

"No, what do you mean?" I asked, tired and cranky. I was also terribly confused about Carlos and frustrated at Barbara and her little party social games. Would it be too much to expect Roger to act like a normal human being and tell me what was going on?

Roger looked at me sideways as we reached the booze table. "What's your pleasure?' he asked, ignoring my question.

"Just a glass of white wine will be fine."

Roger poured from a bottle of Chardonnay. "I know it's been a long day for you, Meredith. Tonight means a lot to Barbara, though. You may not realize it, but she's showing you off. 'Her' editor, that's how she talks about you. Most of these people are yachtsmen – wealthy Americans and some Brits – whom we've gotten to know over the past few years. No one of any significance, but Barbara wants to feel like she's part of the group."

"The St. Thomas group?"

"Well, the group of people who have 'made' it." Roger nodded his head to one white-haired man. "He's a venture capitalist." He nodded at a younger man.

"That one made his millions during the Silicon Valley dot.com days." Roger pointed to a well dressed, highly coiffed middle-aged woman. "Her husband was an oil man in Houston until he retired here with his millions." Roger leaned against the railing and looked at me earnestly. "Barbara grew up poor in Baltimore. She feels a need to belong."

"Uh huh. And how did you make your millions?" I asked, hiding my impertinence by taking another sip of wine.

"Drugs, of course."

I gasped.

"Pharmaceuticals, Meredith. I played the market very well. Johnson and Johnson, Chiron, Pfizer, their stocks all helped buy this yacht."

"Oh." I suppressed a yawn. I was so tired. I just wanted to go home. To Boston. I opened my purse and checked my cell phone. Still no word from Gregory.

"Expecting a call?" Roger smiled hello to a guest, but waited for my reply.

"My boyfriend," I admitted. "I think he may be coming here to surprise me."

Roger stiffened. "To St. Thomas?"

"Maybe. I don't know. Just a feeling." I put the phone back in my purse.

"Hmmm."

"Roger, I understand the reason Barbara is having this party, and who the guests are. But why is your relative here?"

"My relative?" Roger looked around as if expecting his mother to show up.

"You know, Carlos, your brother's step-wife's something or other. Oh yeah, brother's wife's step-brother. I think."

"Oh, Carlos!" Roger looked befuddled for an instant, then regained his nonchalant stance, not an easy feat when wearing tan pants an inch too short and a pink-striped seersucker jacket. "He just happened to be in town. I invited him to join us."

"Really?" I was putting two and two together, but it seemed to add up to 22. "Did he help you with your investments?"

"What?" He seemed truly puzzled by my question.

"You know, since he publishes a newsletter on pharmaceutical research, and you invest in pharmaceuticals, I figured maybe..."

"No, no. What a thought." Roger stepped closer to me and opened his mouth to say something. I was sure it would have been important, too, but just at that moment Barbara blew into a small captain's horn and announced in a loud voice, "Ladies and gentleman, I'd like to make a proper, formal introduction of my editor. Meredith, where are you?"

Damn. I smiled as Roger pushed me gently toward his wife, and then he began to clap. Good heavens. Could this evening get any worse? I gritted my teeth, hoping my lips still looked like they were smiling, and walked over to Barbara, standing fore on the yacht, as others joined in with the clapping.

Barbara hugged me, the first time she'd shown any kind of affection toward me in the three years I'd worked with her.

"Meredith Powers, everyone. She flew all the way from Boston to our small island just to make sure I dot my i's properly, and cross my t's." Everyone laughed politely. "I won't say I couldn't have published my books without her, because I could. I had already published two tomes before I connected with Flack, Inc. But I'll admit, Meredith has changed the look of my books - they're cleaner, peppier, if you will, since she came on board, so to speak."

A few smiles. My hands were sweating; I tightened my fingers around my wine glass, slippery in my fingers. Unfortunately, Barbara kept going.

"My last book sold thousands more than we expected, and my new one, out by early next year, will sell more than the last one." Cheers and clapping at that humungous stretch of the truth. We at Flack had no idea how well the book would do. We only produced what the market needed, then promoted the hell out of it.

Barbara nodded toward me. "Your turn, Meredith."

Obviously I was now supposed to gush over Barbara the author. I couldn't think of one nice thing to say, but then I thought back to Roger's earlier conversation with me. Okay, so she was showing off. I supposed this was part of my job, too.

As I spoke of Barbara's esteemed role in the field of occupational therapy, and how thrilled I was to work with her, I kept my eyes on Carlos, who had walked to the back of the yacht, away from the group. Rude, but not surprising. However, by the time I extolled Barbara's writing skills, Roger had joined Carlos, and the two whispered conspiratorially.

I finished my little speech with a raised glass and wishes of good luck for Barbara's next publishing achievement, heard a round of 'here, here,' and finally I was free. Barbara turned her back to me as she accepted congratulations from the Houston millionaire, and I walked to the other side of the yacht, where only a few congregated. After checking my cell phone for messages – none – I called my dad.

"Everything okay, sweetie? You haven't changed your mind about tomorrow?" he asked.

"Of course not, Dad. Just a quick business question. Have you ever heard of a pharmaceutical newsletter called 'New Century Pharmaceuticals'?"

He paused. "Sounds familiar. There are so many, you know."

"You mean there's more than one newsletter about new drug research?"

"Meredith, dozens. Of course each pharmaceutical company promotes drugs it's working on, and then there are government newsletters, and independent ones."

"Oh." I hadn't thought of that, but it made sense. "Okay, thanks Dad."

"That's it? That was easy. See you tomorrow then. I'll call after we arrive and get settled."

I closed the phone with a snap. So maybe Carlos' story checked out. That still didn't explain why, after seeing me in Cambridge, Carlos was here, and how he was connected to Parker. It didn't explain...

My cell phone rang. I had just placed it back in my purse, so I fumbled as I tried to retrieve it. Had Dad thought of something else?

I looked at the Caller ID.

It was Gregory.

CHAPTER TWENTY-NINE

Finally! I didn't even say hello when I answered. "Where are you?"

"Meredith. I'm sorry. I made a ------ decision. Listen, I'm in Miami, on my way to St. -------. I'll explain when I see you. Are ---- in your hotel?"

"No, I'm ..."

"Get to ----- hotel. Just stay ----- until I get there. Please?"

"Gregory, I can barely hear you."

No response.

"Gregory? Greg?" I was talking too loud. I'd lost him anyway. As I snapped my phone shut, Roger sidled up to me.

"Problems?"

"No. But I need to get back to my hotel."

"So something is wrong," Roger said.

"No, nothing is wrong. I just have some personal things to take care of. It's been a lovely party, but Barbara and I still have a lot of work to do. I'll be back tomorrow morning, 8:30 sharp."

"And you need a good night's sleep. Okay. I'll explain to Barbara later. She'll be disappointed you didn't stay longer, but...listen. Could you do me a huge favor? Carlos is leaving now too. Do you mind if I escort you both back to shore? That way I only have to go back once, and not miss too much here."

"Oh." The last thing I wanted was to spend more time with Carlos. But I couldn't reject Roger's suggestion; he'd already ferried me back and forth from the harbor twice today. "Um, sure. Is he ready to leave now?"

"Definitely." Roger pointed his index finger toward Carlos and curled it twice. As if waiting for the signal, Carlos put his drink down and walked swiftly toward us.

"Meredith needs to go back to shore now too, Carlos, so I'll take you both at the same time."

"Perfect." Carlos bowed to me. "Young lady," he said, then he followed Roger, and I followed him. I hadn't been called a young lady since eighth grade. Carlos was full of 'old world charm,' but it was lost on me. Roger, on the other hand, wasn't worried about manners or charm, since we left without any goodbyes to Barbara. Maybe he figured she'd just give us a bad time for leaving so soon, so it was better this way.

As we approached the dock, Carlos asked me, "Where are you staying?"

"The Diamond Harbor Hotel."

"How convenient. My hotel is a block away. Please, allow my driver to drop you off."

"You have a driver?" I didn't realize that publishing a newsletter could be so lucrative.

"I have business on the other side of the island, so I find it useful," Carlos responded.

"Well, thank you for the offer, but I prefer to walk back."

Carlos looked disappointed. Roger docked the boat and offered me his hand. Then I remembered – Gregory did ask me to get back to my hotel as soon as possible. "On second thought, I am a bit tired. I guess I will take that ride."

"Marvelous." Carlos shook Roger's hand, and a sleek black limousine drove up. Carlos opened one of the doors. "After you, Meredith."

I stepped in to a dark interior. I briefly wondered why the light didn't go on when the car door opened. Then someone grabbed my arm.

"What?" I exclaimed.

A sharp prick, and a masked face in front of me blurred.

That was the last thing I remembered.

~~~~~~~~~~~~~~~~~~~~~~

I woke up some time later. That same night? An hour later, or days? I couldn't tell. My head throbbed as if a helicopter had landed inside my brain. Thump Thump Thump. I tried to sit up. I was crouched in the fetal position on something hard. Where was I?

"She's waking up," a man said. I couldn't see anything. When I tried to open my eyes, my lashes blinked against something soft, a blindfold.

"What's your name?" he asked.

I didn't answer. My heart was now thumping as hard as the throbbing in my head.

The man asked again, more insistent now. "What's your name?"

"Cleopatra," I tried to say, but my mouth was so dry, I could barely open my lips.

"Give her a class of water," I heard. Someone lifted me up to a chair and pressed a glass into my hands. One sip made me nauseous.

"Drink some more," he suggested. Instead, I held my hand out with the glass, and it was taken away.

The chair was soft, comfortable. I just wanted to curl up and go to sleep, but the man kept talking to me. Asking me questions.

"Go away," I said.

"Just answer the question."

"What question?"

"She's not with it yet. Let her wake up," a different man said.

"She's awake. She knows the answer. Try again."

A cool cloth moved across my forehead, over my nose, and around my cheeks. My mind slowly unwound, like film in an old camera. The party. Gregory's phone call. Roger. Carlos. The car. A pinprick.

"Where am I?" My voice was hoarse, raspy.

"Just answer the questions, Meredith, and then you'll be fine."

"What questions?" I was waking up. I was scared. Had I been kidnapped? What were they going to do to me? What did they want?

"Just tell us where Parker is."

I groaned. I didn't mean to. The sound just rose from deep in my stomach and jumped out my throat. Parker? This was all about Parker?

"I don't know," I replied honestly.

One of the voices said, "Told you."

"She's lying," said the other.

"Shhh. Meredith, we're sorry. If there were any other way to do this, we'd do it. But we have to find Parker. Just tell us where Parker is, and we'll let you go."

"Who are you?" I asked. "Where am I?"

I heard the swoosh of fabric, and then my eyes blinked from the sudden light.

I tried to stand up, but the room kept spinning. I sat back down. My eyes focused on the wall in front of me, with two identical pictures of a ship. I blinked. No, three pictures. I blinked again. Now there was only one.

I turned my head to the left, where some diffused light shone through a gauzy white curtain. To my right, a half open door, and the corridor beyond. Someone coughed, and I turned to look behind me. Three men. I recognized only one of them.

Carlos Medina.

I looked carefully at the man who had kidnapped me. He walked to the front of my chair and leaned toward me, intense brown eyes searching my face as if for the clue to life's mystery. His high cheekbones accentuated a full, masculine mouth that was curved in a small smile, no longer topped with a thick black mustache. His full head of black hair was worn in perfect GQ style.

"Meredith, this will all make sense soon, I assure you. If there had been any other way..." Carlos nodded his head, and a man brought him a chair. He sat down in front of me. "You just need to answer my questions."

I stared at him. I was so scared I thought I would wet myself, but I did not want this man to know that. My head was groggy, and I could throw up at any minute. "What do you want?"

"We just need to know where your boyfriend is."

"My boyfriend's name is Gregory. He's an accountant, for God's sake." Why were they asking about Gregory?

Carlos shook his head in frustration. "Parker, Meredith. We need to know where Parker is."

"Parker's not my boyfriend, Mr. Medina."

"Just forget it," a voice behind me said. Carlos' eyes looked into mine as if he was trying to read my mind.

"We will find out, Meredith. The sooner the better. For you. For Parker. You don't understand." He stood up, looking down at me as if I'd disappointed him.

Another man came in from the corridor. "Boat's ready. We need to go."

"You're not helping anyone by keeping quiet, Meredith," Carlos began.

A man interrupted. "It doesn't matter. We'll find him soon enough. Let's finish this up."

Carlos nodded his head. Someone grabbed my arm.

I screamed. "Let me go! HELP!"

"Shut up!" a brusque voice said. I felt a prick, again, and then blackness enveloped me like a dark, angry cloud.

CHAPTER THIRTY

I woke in a room that was swaying back and forth. I belched.

"I have to get up," I tried to say, but it sounded like "Mmm ffwith ppf."

"I'm going to throw up!" I said, loudly, but again, my words came out muffled.

I lay there, allowing my brain to slowly register where I was, who I was. I looked down at my body. I was lying in a bunk, a blanket pulled up to my chin. I pulled myself up with my arms, feeling weak as a baby.

I was alive. I quickly realized how amazing this fact was, and how crucial. I was alive! I almost shouted out, but then it all came back to me, starting with my name (Meredith Powers, I whispered), my occupation, where I worked, where I lived, who I loved (Dad...Mom...Gregory...Shannon). Parker. Then I thought of the yacht, the party, a limousine, and a sharp prick.

"Help!" I cried out.

Then I shut my mouth tight. Stupid. Stupid, stupid. I couldn't let them know I was awake! I slunk back down in the blanket, closing my eyes. No one came.

I sat up again. The interrogation rushed back to me. They wanted to know about Parker. This was all about Parker! Did I say anything? I couldn't remember. Did I say he was hiding? Did I say he worked for the D.E.A.? Oh God. What did I say?

Why me? Why did they want me? Until this week, I hadn't seen Parker in six months. I didn't have anything to do with Parker anymore.

Yet, he had come back to me. He had been in trouble, and he needed me.

Had I betrayed him? Did I say anything that would give my kidnappers a clue about how to find him? Because of me, Parker might die.

Actually, because of Parker, I might die.

I heard voices. Male, and gruff. I hid under the scratchy blanket. Maybe if I pretended I was asleep, the voices would go away. Silence again, but it was the kind of silence that made me suspicious. Then footsteps only inches from my bed.

"Stop pretending, Meredith."

I kept my eyes shut.

"Acting as if you're asleep won't make me go away. I'll stand here until you sit up. We have a lot to talk about."

I sighed and threw the blanket away from my head. Now I was mad. I'd been taken against my will, thrown in the backseat of a car, told to shut up (a crime in itself), drugged, and thrown onto a boat. Enough was enough.

"You're damn right we have things to talk about, Mr. Medina," I said loudly as I sat up against the wall. I looked at Carlos, standing in front of the bunk bed, arms crossed, legs spread. "Get me out of here," I began, but then I shut my mouth. I was going to throw up, damn it.

"Where's the bathroom?" I asked through clenched teeth. Carlos pointed to a door on the other side of the room, and I stood up, wobbly. He quickly held on to me as I tried to walk toward the door. As he opened it, I felt my stomach unclench, and I vomited a foot from the toilet, not minding that Carlos' shoes got soiled in the process.

Carlos seemed unperturbed. "Sorry, Meredith. I heard you weren't a sailor." He cleaned his shoes off with some toilet paper, then walked me back to the bunk, and I sank down, miserable.

"Just get me out of here," I pleaded. I wanted to lie back down on the bed, but I knew I needed to stay awake and figure out what was happening.

"Let's go, I'll take you topside," he said as if doing me a huge favor.

I stood up, swaying, and we walked out of the room and up narrow stairs, me the invalid, Carlos the helpful nurse.

Millions of stars dotted the huge expanse of black sky.

"Night," I said. I breathed deeply and took in the salty, sweet Caribbean air. Looking straight ahead to the horizon. I saw the darker form of land ahead.

"Where are we going?" I asked Carlos, as I looked straight out at the sea and not at him.

"To a place where it's safe – for you, for Parker, for all of us," he answered.

I faced the man. My strength was returning, and my anger. "Who the hell are you? What do you want from me?"

Carlos did a strange thing then. He placed his hand lightly on top of my head and patted it, as if anointing me. Then he whispered, "I am so sorry, Meredith. If there was any other way..." He looked at me tenderly. I blinked, and stepped back.

"But there isn't," he said in a full voice. "We need you to convince Parker to return."

"Return?" I asked. "Return to what? Who are you?" I was tired. Tired, scared, worried, and still sick to my stomach.

"Return to us," Carlos said. Then he closed his mouth, looking as if he'd said too much. "I'm going to get someone to clean up your room, then you'll need to remain there until we arrive. Stay here. Don't move." He called out and a man, almost invisible in his black clothes, waved back. "Don't move," Carlos said again, and then he left.

I kept my eye on the dark shape of land that loomed larger minute by minute.

Carlos was using me as bait. I was the worm. He was the fisherman. Parker was the fish. I thought about worms, and how they were crushed, alive, onto the sharp hook. I thought about the tiny room he was about to put me back in, and I thought about the water and the approaching land.

I looked over at the man who was standing on the other side of the boat, and slowly, slowly, I unzipped my sundress. I was shoeless; God knew what they'd done with my sandals. I took in a deep breath, pulled off my dress, climbed over the railing, and jumped into the water.

CHAPTER THIRTY-ONE

Even though the ocean was warm, my body reacted with shock as I splashed straight down, immediately kicking my legs underwater to get away from the boat. Ten years of swim team practice and competitive meets came back to me as I stroked under water, waiting as long as I could before I surfaced and gulped in air. Unfortunately, I swallowed some of the ocean too. Coughing and swimming for your life at the same time was not an easy feat. Nor was swimming while still under the influence of a sedative.

I tried to ignore my sore lungs and heavy limbs as I began to swim toward the shore. While on the boat, the distance hadn't looked so far; here, from the water, the distance seemed insurmountable. I stretched my arms straight in front of me and pulled through the water hard, stroke after stroke. When I looked up, land seemed just as far away as it had a hundred strokes earlier.

But I had to be getting closer, because suddenly the water was swelling – smaller waves at first, then large breakers as I swam harder and harder. I tried to guess how long I'd been out in the ocean – fifteen minutes? Twenty? I knew I was tiring. My muscles stung. My lungs wheezed out air with every exhale.

I stopped and doggy paddled as I tried to get my bearings. Land was in front of me. But I couldn't see any lights indicating hotels or homes or a harbor. I didn't want to look behind me, but finally I turned around, still treading water, hoping that the boat was where I'd left it.

But no, the boat was following me and stood less than fifty yards away. I couldn't hear them, but I saw two men pointing my way. I restrained the impulse to stretch my arm out of the water and give them the finger. Not only would that be juvenile, it would also be a waste of energy. Right now, energy leaked out of me like air from an old balloon.

I turned my head away from the boat and concentrated on the shore. It was there. The tide was helping me along, finally. A wave lifted me up, higher and higher. I panicked. I'd never swum this far out in an ocean. I had never been a body surfer, and now I was in the middle of surf heaven. If only I had a surfboard. But I didn't. A wave crashed on top of me, sending me down into the salty water. I screamed.

My panic increased as the waves continued to unfold, one after the other after the other. Just as my head rose up out of a wave to guzzle in air, water pushed me back down. I didn't have time to see if I was getting closer to shore. Instead, I fought for my life.

I took in another mouthful of air, but instead, I swallowed water. Lots of water. Enough water to nauseate me. I tried to vomit, but another wave knocked me back down into the depths of the sea. I swallowed more water. I tried to move my arms to pull me up, but they were suddenly as heavy as anchors. My legs moved with the tide like seaweed.

I was lucid enough to say to myself, I'm drowning! But I didn't panic. I stayed calm. So this was it. I wasn't happy. I wasn't sad. I dropped to the bottom, feeling the water soothe me, like a bathtub filled with bubbles. Soft. Gentle. Cool. The noise of the surf stopped. Instead, it was as silent as a winter's night. I closed my eyes and felt the lightness of being. I was one with the sea. I was...

Something grabbed me. Hard. Mean. I pulled against the pressure, but it continued. My lungs screamed, and my ears roared. I felt the force of water drag against me as something nearly pulled my arm out of its socket. I would have cried out, but I didn't have the energy. I heard water rush through my ears, stuffing my head with fluid. Then my brain shut down.

~~~~~~~~~~~~~~~~~

I woke up coughing and vomiting water. The pain in my stomach was excruciating. I couldn't stop the heaving, though. I sounded like an animal. A wounded, angry animal. Finally, tears poured from my eyes.

Eventually everything stopped. No more convulsing, no more tears. I was spent, down to the tiniest bone in my body. I laid flat on my back, still sucking in air, and finally looked around me. I was on sand. Dawn was breaking somber gray skies. And a man's face peered down at me, looking as if he wasn't sure he was glad or mad that I was alive.

Carlos.

"You stupid damn fool," were the first words out of his mouth.

I shut my eyes, but he continued anyway.

"If I hadn't ordered them to drive that boat closer to the shore...." Carlos moved his glare from me to the sea, where I assumed the boat was anchored nearby. "We could have wrecked the boat....," he added. His voice rose, "If I hadn't jumped in when I did..."

I cleared my throat, unsure if what I was thinking would come out. "If you hadn't kidnapped me..." I said scratchily. Ha! My voice still worked. But saying just those few words exhausted me. I closed my eyes, and fell asleep.

~~~~~~~~~~~~~~~~~~~~~~~~

When I woke up, I'd been transported to a different place, a different universe. I was floating in a sky that was filled with white clouds. As my head cleared, I realized I was lying on a white four-poster bed covered with white eyelet sheets and canopy overhead. The white lamp and white dresser looked like clouds against a pale blue wall. From my vantage point, I could tell that the large window overlooked an expanse of white sand.

Maybe I had drowned and this was heaven.

But then I saw a man standing in the doorway. I didn't recognize him, but he peered into the room, then disappeared. I shut my eyes and breathed deeply, then re-opened them. Nope, the room wasn't a figment of my imagination. I was lying in between soft cool sheets, still dressed in my underwear, I noticed, head comfortable on a soft full pillow. I reached up to my neck; amazingly, my pearls were still there.

But where the hell was I, and why? Then I remembered. I was the worm. Well, right now I was more a half-drowned rat. A rat who was not willing to be sequestered in a lab, part of some experiment to entrap Parker.

Carlos walked casually into my room. "Feeling better?" he asked as if we'd just returned from a relaxing stroll.

I didn't reply.

"Well, you can thank me later," he said. "I imagine you'll feel more human after a warm shower and lots of soap." He nodded his head toward the back corner. "Your private bathroom awaits. Then we'll talk."

I stayed in the shower forever trying to rinse the smell of salt water, brine, and sand out of every pore of my skin. First I scrubbed with soap – a pale pink bar with a floral scent – but still I could smell the sea. Then I used gobs of a rose shower gel that stood in the corner of the stall. But still, I couldn't erase the smell, not so much of ocean and jellyfish, but of fear.

I sank down to the bottom of the tub, naked and shivering while the hot water beat down on me. I thought back to the near drowning and the attempt of the waves to smack me down into the sandy pit of the ocean's bottom. I gulped in deep breaths of air, sprinkled with the shower's spray, as I remembered the heavy feeling in my lungs and the desperate attempt to suck oxygen into my body as I struggled to reach the top of a wave's crest.

I heard a knock at the door.

"Meredith, are you okay?"

It was Carlos. Sounding concerned. I couldn't answer him, even though I tried to swallow my sobs. I stood back up in the shower and pressed my head against the tile wall.

"Meredith?"

Carlos. A man I despised, now my rescuer.

"I'm fine. Thank you," I mumbled loud enough for him to hear.

"You don't sound okay. I'm coming in."

God, he was presumptuous.

"No!" I shouted, too loudly, too fearfully. I turned off the shower and pulled a towel around me. "No," I said again, shuddering at the thought of needing to thank this man before finding a way to escape.

"I only want to help you, Meredith. That's all. If you don't believe me, ask..." He stopped then, as if rethinking his comment.

"Ask whom?" I now stood against the bathroom door, shivering, trying to hear every nuance in his voice.

"If I told you, you'd never believe me." His mysterious comment came out low and husky, sounding

like a little boy who feared he'd be misunderstood. I
didn't want to be taken in by his words, yet I was in no
condition to ignore him.

"Give me a second," I told him through the door
as I quickly dried myself and looked around for some
clothes. My soaking bra and underpants lay in a heap
on the floor. "I don't have anything to wear," I said,
assuming he was still waiting by the door.

"That's why I'm standing here with my arm
extended," Carlos replied smoothly. I opened the door
two inches and peered through the crack. Yes, he was
there, holding a bundle of clothes. I opened the door
another inch and put my hand out as if testing the chill
in the air. Carlos chuckled, which infuriated me, and
then he placed the clothes in my hand. I withdrew my
arm and closed the door. I had to get out of here.

The soft, silk shorts and white linen top fit
beautifully over the lacy bra and panties he had
provided. The sizes were exactly correct. How did he
do that? I pulled my fingers through my wet, curling
hair, opened the bathroom door, and took in a breath.
He was gone.

I walked past the bed and opened the bedroom
door, looking up and down the empty corridor. Music
floated down the hall, wistful and eerie and sexy. I bit
my lip, took in a deep breath, and headed toward the
sound.

CHAPTER THIRTY-TWO

Luxury surrounded me. Wherever Carlos and his entourage had stashed me, they did it in style. The high-ceilinged hallway outside my bedroom was lit by delicate chandeliers, which cast a warm glow on walls decorated with original oil paintings of seascapes and birds. My feet sunk into a thick, soft blue carpet. I passed a half dozen closed doors, cherry chair-side desks standing by each door with a newspaper, a crystal decanter and a silver bucket of ice cubes. Three doors down, I heard a phone ring. I paused outside the door; the phone rang eight more times before it stopped. Since I heard no voices, I decided the room must be empty. Breathing deeply, I turned the doorknob, then pushed the door open.

Unlike my beautifully appointed bedroom, this room was sparsely furnished: a desk with a computer, phone, and fax machine; two straight-backed chairs, and a small table holding a coffee machine. A half full cup of steaming coffee sat on top of the desk, waiting for its master. Whoops. Not wanting to be discovered snooping, I turned back toward the door, jumping when I heard the whir of a fax. Sure enough, a piece of paper printed out of the machine.

I stood still, feet pointed back toward the hallway. But no door opened. No secretary or guard came running toward the noise. Gingerly, I placed one foot in front of the other toward the desk. Two pages had printed, and then the machine stopped. Glancing over my shoulder, I picked them up and looked at the first page briefly. It seemed to be a copy of a newspaper article. The headline read:

Caribbean Assassination

I looked left and right, then walked swiftly back to my room, holding the papers as if I'd just stolen a diamond necklace from an upscale jewelry store.

After closing the door and locking it, surprised that I could lock myself in, I sat back on the bed, pulled the bedsheet over me, and read.

> Police said it was unclear whether the
> assassination of a senior police officer in St.
> Thomas was connected to similar killings in
> other Caribbean islands, where drug cartels
> have been battling security forces.
> St. Thomas police captain William Flores, 61,
> and his bodyguard were shot dead in a
> department vehicle Sunday night. They were
> driving home on a busy avenue near the harbor.
> Flores was a former army colonel.

Oh, my God! I leaped up off the bed and began
to pace. Captain Flores. The police officer I had talked
to just, what, yesterday? He had been killed. Why? I
had just talked to him! My heart began to race as if I
was at the end of a 10-mile run. I sat back down on the
bed. My hands grew clammy, and I wiped them on the
bed sheets. Read, Meredith, read the rest of the article,
I told myself.

> Police had made no arrests and were still
> investigating.
> 'We don't know how many gunmen, or who
> they were,' a police spokesman said.
> Flores 'had 15 bullet wounds, mainly in his
> head and neck. We can't see a motive. He
> works in an office planning public security. He's

not on operations and has nothing to do with
investigating drug cartels.'

Drug cartels? Drugs? There was that word
again. Drugs. Parker was hiding from some drug lord
or something. What had he said? His 'cover had been
blown.' He didn't get the main 'operative,' or
something like that. So the bad guys were after Parker.
So now they were after me? But what did Captain
Flores have to do with it? I went back to the article.

> The spokesman added that the assassination
> 'has the markings of a narco-killing.'
> Last weekend, kidnappers killed four policemen
> in the Pacific coast state of Guerrero; three
> were gagged and shot and one was beheaded.
> Last week, police in Puerto Rico found the
> severed heads of police officers and a fourth
> man. At least five police officials have been
> gunned down this year in the coastal cities of
> Columbia. The D.E.A. believes that these
> killings may be related.

I began to shiver. Parker was in deep, deep
trouble. These people were ruthless. Even though he
never told me specifically where he traveled when we
lived together, I knew that over the year and a half we
were a couple he had visited Mexico, Columbia, Texas,

California, Guatemala. The list went on and on. I knew now that he was following a huge raid – the largest of its kind. Well, this sounded huge – Guerrero, Tijuana, Puerto Rico. Horrible killings everywhere.

> Police killings are more rare in the Virgin Islands, although the resort area has seen a few civilian murders in recent months. 'We believe the increased violence in the Caribbean is related to the other drug-related deaths we've seen worldwide,' said U.S. Customs spokesman Floyd Denton.

Denton again! He had worked with Parker and was quoted in the Boston Globe article I read less than a week ago. God, it seemed like it had been months since I had that interrupted lunch with Parker at Antonio's.

> 'Drug-related violence has claimed the lives of more than 600 people this year in Mexico alone. In 2012, more than 1,500 died in gang-related drug violence. The cartels are now spreading into meth usage, and....'

A knock on the door almost threw me off the bed. I thrust the fax under the pillow as I heard Carlos. "Meredith? Meredith, are you in there?"

My heart jumped so hard I put a hand on my chest to settle it down. Suddenly, I was more scared than I'd ever been in my life. More scared than when I'd been in the middle of a wind funnel. More scared than when I'd been drugged and dragged onto a boat. More scared than when I almost drowned. Finally, I realized the situation I was in - stuck on some island in the middle of nowhere with horrible, violent, ruthless men.

I sucked in air, breathing too fast and too deep. I started to hyperventilate, and the room began to swirl. Think! Think! I looked around and noticed a closet in the back corner. Smiling as if I had found the answer to all my problems, I dashed over, opened the door, and hurled myself inside, closing myself into a small stuffy dark space.

Carlos' calls were muffled. But I could still hear "Meredith!" and pounding on the bedroom door. I was dead, I decided. If Parker didn't show up, I was dead. But why would he? He didn't even know where I was. And worse, Parker may have already 'disappeared' in the protection program. I hadn't heard from him since before I left for St. Thomas. Did someone already hide him, for good?

My fears and questions suddenly stopped. What the hell was I doing in a closet, the only closet in a room with nowhere else to hide? I ran out and faced the door as I heard some kind of scraping. Any minute now, Carlos would open this door. I was going to be ready for him. I looked around the room and spotted the perfect weapon. Without bothering to pull the cord out of the wall socket, I yanked the heavy pewter lamp and hiked it up above my head just as the door swung open.

I flung the lamp down. Crash! The noise of heavy metal on thick skull was sickening. I saw the body fall, then gasped. His body was much too big and broad to be Carlos'. I hesitated for one second, then tried to sprint over the man to reach the hallway.

But Carlos stood solidly on the other side of the door. He pulled my arm and led me back into the room. "Meredith?" His voice was surprisingly gentle, though reproving. "What do you think you're doing?"

CHAPTER THIRTY-THREE

I looked down at the lifeless body at my feet.

"Meredith, whatever are you doing?" Carlos repeated, looking at me as if I were addled.

"Did I kill him?" I whispered.

The downed man whimpered.

"No, but I think he's going to have a huge headache tonight," Carlos answered. He turned toward another man looming in the hallway, who walked around the lamp and helped the moaning man stand up.

"You need three men to open a bedroom door?" I asked, regaining my composure. I marched past them, toward the window, and looked out at the view of garden below, then sand, ocean, and skyline further out.

The two men backed out of the room, at Carlos' instruction. "We need to talk," he said. "Follow me." We walked past the same closed doors to the end of the hallway and a well-hidden staircase. Two flights down, we exited a heavy door, and I felt warm sunshine on my body. Involuntarily, my muscles relaxed.

I walked slowly but moved my head left and right, trying to size up my location. Where were we? The building we just left looked like a high-end resort with white-stuccoed walls and lush landscaping, but it was noticeably empty. No cars, no bell hops or guests. Had Carlos commandeered it?

My shoeless feet felt massaged by the crystal white sand. The air was warm, probably mid 80s, and normally I would have raised my face toward the sun like a flower. But this wasn't a normal situation. I was being held against my will on a nameless Caribbean island so beautiful my eyes hurt. The sky was as blue as my favorite chambray shirt. The sea sparkled like millions of tiny sapphires bobbing in a humongous bucket.

I stopped in my tracks, and turned to face my captor.

"That's far enough. Just spit it out, Mr. Medina. Why did you bring me here? What do you want?" I tried not to look into his eyes when I asked the question. Carlos' eyes were too full of... something. Instead, I stared at his forehead. I needed to concentrate on my purpose. To escape. I didn't want to be diverted by this man's agenda, whatever it was.

"Carlos," he answered softly.

'What?" I looked straight into those coffee eyes, which were searching mine with humor, compassion, and something sexy I didn't want to see.

"Please call me Carlos." He placed his hand lightly on my elbow, encouraging us to continue walking on the beach. I moved my arm just as lightly to get away from his hand. He had us walking like a couple. I wanted to walk like a woman who was there against her will. But there was no passerby to ask for help, to explain that the scene was a pretense, and that this courtly man had kidnapped me.

"I don't want to call you Carlos," I said tightly. "I want you to tell me who you are, and when you intend to let me go." Then I kicked him in the shin.

He was fast. Somehow, he saw it coming and backed up so my foot barely touched him. He smiled slightly, not a scary smile, not even a patronizing one. He smiled as if I was a child, and he was the father trying to help me solve a difficult math equation.

"We're going to see a lot of each other, Ms. Meredith Powers. That's how I'm going to protect you. By sticking by your side, 24/7." His accented voice was so mannerly, so proper, that his words sounded less ridiculous than they were. Instead of protesting, I kept my mouth closed and walked a few steps. The waves were only a foot away. The sound was soothing, unlike the thoughts roiling around in my brain.

"Protect me from what?" I asked.

"Why from your boyfriend, of course. Parker Webb."

"I don't know a Parker Webb," I replied. "My boyfriend's name is Gregory."

"Now, now, Ms. Powers. Let's strip the facade and be honest. I have a lot to tell you. That's why I brought you out here for this delightful walk on one of the most beautiful beaches in the world. You need protection from a double agent who has changed allegiances so many times that even he's confused. I don't know what he's told you, but Parker Webb is a dangerous man. A lot of people want to kill him. Now, are you ready for the real story of Mr. Parker Webb? Or are you too afraid to hear the truth?"

I turned my head from the man. He pulled my shoulder and made me look into his face. I pushed him away.

"Adlibbing the words of an old Scottish proverb," I said to him, "your absence would be good company." Then I began to walk back toward the resort, ignoring his presence beside me.

Until he began to laugh. Loudly and with obvious delight.

"Oh, you are a kick!" Carlos said. "He warned me that you wouldn't be easy. That..."

"Who warned you? What do you mean?" I turned toward Carlos, my hands bunched into fists. The waves were crashing hard enough against the sand that I had to raise my voice to be heard. Carlos ignored my question.

"Okay, here's another question, Mr. Carlos Medina. Who are you, really? Roger Browning introduced you as his brother's wife's step-brother, or something like that. Is that true? Back in the yacht, you claimed you published pharmaceutical newsletters. Was that all a lie?"

Carlos stood mute, a tiny smile on his lips. I watched the expression on his face change from one of aloofness to thoughtfulness. "Let's just say I was being economical with the truth."

I shook my head in disgust. "My yoga instructor once told us an old Ashanti Proverb: 'One falsehood spoils a thousand truths.'"

When Carlos laughed again, his head fell back as if he didn't have a care in the world. "You're full of proverbs, aren't you Meredith? The sign of a well-educated woman with little experience. Well, I return your quotes with one of my favorites. 'Good judgment comes from experience, which comes from poor judgment.' " His face, intent on my reaction, turned from an expression of mirth to sincerity, as if he were teaching me something of grave importance. But he was no professor, and I was certainly not his student. I didn't want to hear a thing he was saying, yet I was his captive audience, all pun intended. We continued to walk on the sand, the crashing blue waves accentuating the conversation.

"You think Parker is a good man, an honorable man," he continued. "I'm telling you through my experience that he is not honorable."

"And you are?" I interrupted. The man was a pompous ass. A handsome, charming one, but an ass, nonetheless.

"Oh, Meredith, you have no idea how honorable I am." His voice softened into a caress, and I turned my head away from his lingering stare.

"Let's get one thing out of the way, Meredith, so we understand each other better. We know about you and Parker."

"There is no 'me and Parker,' " I interrupted.

Carlos continued as if I hadn't said a word. "You lived together for 16 months. You were the first woman, are the only woman, he cared about. For some reason, you kicked him out. He tried to keep you out of his life, but he couldn't do it. Just last week, he returned to you. He asked you to get back together again. He loves you."

Inadvertently, I placed my hand on my stomach, which began to twist into a hard knot.

"Sorry to put it so succinctly, Meredith, but it's only fair to let you know what cards are on the table."

"Why the hell should you care?" I asked, frightened by what this stranger was telling me about my life.

"Because Parker has to be stopped, and you are the best way we can do that."

I didn't want the conversation to carry on, but then again, I knew I should find out what he knew. "Stopped? What's that mean?"

"Parker thought he could play both sides. He started with the C.I.A., transferred to the D.E.A., and then switched hats and played on the side of the cartel. Just as he was succeeding, he got caught, another example of bad judgment, and now he is trying to switch yet again back to the D.E.A. But it's too late. He's a wanted man, and he doesn't have the good judgment to turn himself in."

"First, I don't believe a word you're saying," I responded. "Second, you don't know the Parker Webb I know, a man who would never, ever turn on his government, or the people he worked with. Parker is loyal to a fault." I didn't even want to think about how hard I was defending a man I thought I didn't care about any more.

"Ah ha, you admit Parker has faults. That's a beginning. Meredith, you are so over your head here. You think you know Parker Webb, but you don't. Why do you think you stopped the relationship? Just because he traveled so much? No. Admit it. Deep down. Deep deep down in your gut, you knew something was wrong. You knew he was deceiving you."

I didn't want to listen. Carlos was purposely confusing me, trying to make me doubt myself and my relationship with Parker. As he talked, I began to surreptitiously look at my surroundings. How to escape? During this walk, we hadn't passed any other buildings or resorts, surfers or sunbathers. Nothing. So my only recourse would be to escape by water, or inland, where some human activity would have to crop up, hopefully sooner rather than later.

Carlos mumbled something else about Parker, something about him giving up. My mind continued to race – how to escape. How?

Carlos stopped short, and I walked one step ahead of him. He grabbed my arm and squeezed it lightly, possessively. "Did you hear that, Meredith? He doesn't want to give himself up, yet he must."

"Yes?" I replied noncommittally.

"That, my dear, is where you come in."

CHAPTER THIRTY-FOUR

Carlos led me back to the seemingly deserted resort, through a maze of hallways, until we reached an opulent office set in the bowels of the building. The room was majestic and intimidating. On the further end was a sumptuous-looking couch bordered on each side with well-cushioned armchairs and a side table topped with a silver tray holding glass carafes of port or sherry. On the other side of the room, two large leather chairs faced a desk that must have been at least ten feet long and five feet wide. Carlos' hand, touching the back of my spine lightly, led me to the front of the desk, and then he walked smoothly behind it. Now I truly did feel like the student in for a lecture from her professor.

"I have a letter for you to read, Meredith. I wasn't planning to show it to you. It's government property, for one, and it's confidential and probably illegal to be read by anyone not in the auspices of the top echelon of the D.E.A." Carlos stopped, moving his facial features to show concern for his impropriety. I shut my mind at his overuse of words, wishing he would just shut up. I just wanted to get out of there. I was exhausted, emotionally even more than physically. I wanted to crawl into my bed and escape into sleep until this entire nightmare ended.

"Meredith." I jumped at Carlos' sharp tone and peered up at him. The disapproving look almost made me laugh, except I was scared to death of what Carlos wanted to show me. Could it be true? Could Parker have really messed up, big time? Gotten over his head with counterespionage until he had lost the trust of the people he needed most? Because that was the only kind of trouble I could imagine. I could not believe that Parker had truly turned. But what if he had played his role so convincingly that now even the Feds were after him?

Carlos handed me an envelope that had already been opened. I took it from him and held it gingerly as if it was a grenade.

"Open it," Carlos insisted. "Read it."

Even before I opened the letter, I knew what it was going to say. In some way, it was going to incriminate Parker. I didn't want to read it. I put my hands by my side and looked down at the rug. Nice wool – tan Berber with hints of silvery thread woven throughout.

"Meredith. I expected more from you than this." Carlos took the envelope back from me and opened it quickly. "See? It has the seal of the D.E.A. on the front. It's addressed to me, Carlos Medina, head of Operatives in Secret Affairs."

"They really have a title like that?" I asked, dumbfounded. " 'Head of operatives in secret affairs'? That sounds like something from a 1950s movie." I shook my head in disgust. I was not going to make this easy for Carlos. He sat down in his tufted leather chair behind the desk, unperturbed, and waved his hand for me to do the same. I did.

Carlos continued, "I won't go into the introductory parts of the letter. We'll just get to the meat. 'We have determined that Parker Webb had a strategic role in the release of Miguel Rodriquez from the Bogotá prison. Rodriquez, who once controlled the Cali drug cartel, responsible over the last half dozen years for hundreds of shipments of cocaine and methamphetamine to areas across the globe, immediately disappeared. He and his brother-in-law,

Gilberto, had been arrested in 1999 and sentenced to prison until 2020. Judge Pedro Suarez released him with no comment last Monday. As the government investigated the judge to determine when a bribe occurred, another judge upheld the decision.' "

Carlos looked up at me. "The Cali drug cartel, by the way, once controlled 80 per cent of the world's cocaine trade. It was the world's most powerful drug gang after the demise of the Medellin cartel."

"What happened to that cartel?" I asked, not wanting to be part of this conversation, but drawn into it, nonetheless.

"Their leader, Pablo Escobar, was killed by police." Carlos paused as if wondering whether to continue. "That activity was possible because of the undercover work of Operatives of Secret Affairs, the title you find so funny. The top undercover agent then was a man named Parker Webb."

I stood up. "See? Parker has devoted his life catching drug leaders like Escobar...and Rodriquez. He didn't turn. What is wrong with you people? Parker is obviously in trouble. He's in deep, but why do you immediately believe the worse, that he's working for the cartel now? That's just plain stupid." I turned on my heel and walked out the door. I was more convinced than ever of Parker's innocence.

I turned toward the exit door, planning on running out to the beach. I needed to listen to the waves, let that rhythmic sound drown out Carlos' words. But I felt a light touch on my elbow, and a tall, muscular man was standing by my side, directing me the opposite direction.

"Carlos asked me to see you to your room," he said softly.

"What, I have a bodyguard?" I answered.

He looked at me sideways. "I'm sorry, Ms. Powers, but we need to keep you under house arrest, so to speak."

"What right do you have to do that?" I asked loudly.

"By the authority of the U.S. Government," he answered solemnly. He quickly flashed a badge that he wore beneath his navy jacket. "D.E.A. agent, ma'am."

I held back my tears until he escorted me to my room, where I noticed immediately that the doorknob was missing. They couldn't lock me in or out. I sank onto the bed, then wept until I fell into a fitful sleep.

~~~~~~~~~~~~~~~~~

I woke up in the dark some time later. I hadn't meant to fall asleep, but a woman can cry only so long without collapsing in fatigue. My head felt as heavy as a rock. As I stood up, I noticed that a small nightlight shone from the bathroom, and when I turned on the

lamp (a replacement already), saw a negligee and silky
bathrobe positioned at the end of my bed. My stomach
complained of hunger, but I didn't care. I was too
worried to eat, anyway.

After washing my face with cold water,
undressing, and putting on the robe – a perfect fit, of
course – I walked toward the floor-to-ceiling-window,
which I now realized opened onto a large deck. I
wandered out into the sweet night air, the smell of
hibiscus and bougainvillea waking me up faster than
any cup of coffee. The sky was illuminated by
thousands of sparkling stars. I couldn't see the ocean,
but its nearby soft rumble soothed me. I could think
now.

Escape seemed out of the question. Rescue
unlikely. By this time, Dad was in St. Thomas,
wondering where I was. Would he have any way of
discovering what had happened to me? And Mom. I had
promised to call her last night. Would she be worried?
Would she call the police? Most likely she'd call
Gregory, but he was just as clueless, probably also
waiting in St. Thomas, maybe with my father.

The waiting game was the diagnosis, but I
didn't even know who or what I was waiting for. Parker
was lost to me, if I ever had him in the first place. I still
found Carlos' explanation implausible. The Parker I
knew was loyal and driven, sincere almost to a fault and
always, always against the bad guys. He hated drugs

and what they were doing to our country. To become a double agent, to turn his back against all he once believed in.... No, Carlos was wrong. He had to be wrong.

"Sad thoughts on such a beautiful, star-filled night, Meredith?" I heard his low rhythmic voice before I saw him. Where had he come from? Had he been standing there, on the deck, while I was sleeping? Undressing? I looked around to find another entrance, but the darkness of the evening only created shadows, not answers.

Carlos appeared out of those shadows, as cool and composed as always. He was a handsome man, but tonight he even looked untouchable, a mirage in the middle of a desert. His image flickered in front of me, which I quickly ascribed to the starlight's glow and soft breeze that seductively blew his silk shirt around his chest and arms. His face grew closer to me, more in focus but pale, like the sheen of moonlight brightening slowly against the lowering sun.

"I'm sorry you're hurting, Meredith," Carlos said softly. "I don't like to be the bearer of bad news. But this day was a necessity, not one that I savored."

"You work for the United States Government. You say you're the head of some secret branch of the D.E.A. Yet you kidnapped me, a U.S. citizen." I spoke to Carlos in a soft voice. I was so tired, so confused about all that had happened. "You drugged me and brought me here, away from my family, my job. How could you do that?" I felt tears running down my cheeks. I couldn't stop them.

Carlos took a step closer and wiped my face with his handkerchief. "I know. I'm sorry. I tried to tell you. We didn't want to do it, but we had no choice."

"No choice?" I protested. "You had lots of choices. The wrong choice is standing in front of you now."

Carlos put his hands on my shoulders. I didn't try to stop him. I didn't have the strength for it. He leaned down and planted a soft kiss on my lips, pressing ever so lightly, as if to make the hurt go away. I should have pushed him at once. But I stood there and felt the soft crush of his lips and, surprisingly, the responsive opening of my own lips against his. Carlos took his cue and squeezed me even closer to him, chest to breasts, hips to hips. I felt my body curve into his, the seduction of solace and need and, yes, sex, tempting me.

God help me, I kissed back. His arms wrapped tightly around me, and I felt warm, inside and out, as his own need stretched against my pelvis. For one minute I forgot who I was and what I was doing. I just wanted the comfort of someone's touch. For a second, my fear was replaced by a man's heat and passion.

I could feel his heart beating hard and fast as he kissed me deeper, pulling his fingers through my hair.

His pounding heartbeat roused me. He was a man, just a man who right now, at this second, was under my power. I moved my hand to his chest and pulled away hard. He stepped back with the look of lust on his face that he quickly changed to shocked concern. "Meredith. I'm sorry. I was just trying to comfort you and...."

"Right. I don't need that kind of comfort right now, Carlos." I didn't want him to know how unsettled I was by our kiss, nor how much my knees were shaking. "The best comfort would be for me to get back to St. Thomas and my hotel and my work. Back to my life. You have warned me away from Parker. I got the message. Thank you. Now let me go."

Carlos smiled slightly. "So anxious to leave my company? I find that hard to believe, Meredith. No, now, more than ever, I'm convinced that you can help us solve this problem. Before it gets out of hand."

"It? Before it gets out of hand? Don't you mean he?"

Carlos nodded his head in acknowledgement. "Yes, you're right. Parker is already out of control. Before more damage is done," and here Carlos stared at me intently. "Before more people are killed, we need to stop him."

"Before more people are killed? Are you saying that Parker is responsible for murder? Like the murder of...." I stopped. I didn't want Carlos to think I knew about Captain Flores' death. "I can't talk about this any more..." I pressed my fingers on my forehead. The low-level headache I'd been ignoring was starting to thrum like a bad song played repeatedly. The last thing I needed now was a migraine. "Look, I'm not the right bait for you. I know nothing about Parker and where he is and what he's doing."

"Go to bed, Meredith. Get a good night's sleep. Then we'll talk more in the morning."

"But..." He moved away from me and walked toward the door, self-assured, confident that he had the upper hand. Damn! "Carlos, wait!"

He turned at the panic in my voice.

"I think I'm getting a migraine. My pills. They were in my pocketbook when you..."

"Relax. We brought them here," Carlos interrupted. He picked up the phone next to my bed and hit a couple of buttons, mumbling low enough that I couldn't hear him. Seconds later, a man knocked on the door, holding my bottle of pills.

"How many?" Carlos asked, reading the prescription taped on the outside.

"Um, one should do it," I answered, feeling silly talking about something so normal as pills and dosage in the middle of this surreal night. "If I take a pill soon enough, I can stop the headache from turning into something worse."

Carlos handed me a pill, then gave the bottle back to the man. "We'll store these somewhere safe for you, Meredith." As he turned to go, he seemed to have forgotten something, and faced me again. "You haven't always had migraines, have you Meredith? Didn't they start soon after you met Mr. Parker Webb?" Then he strolled out of my room.

Double damn! Who did this man think he was? I was going to get hold of the situation one way or another, and if it meant another kiss, another fondle, so be it. I paced around my luxurious jail, finally landing on the bed.

As I fought the exhaustion that forced my eyes to close after I settled under the sheets, my mind continued a silent discussion. Carlos thought he had me under his control. Perhaps his self-confidence could be just the weapon I needed.

CHAPTER THIRTY-FIVE

Soft light entered the window stealthily, awakening me to a sky tinged with deep dark blue, a blue as fathomless as the ocean. A new morning. The lull of the sea's waves talked me out of a nightmare I couldn't remember, but the terror remained. Seconds later, I realized that the nightmare was my reality. I stood up from my prison, a beautiful bedroom, determined to escape, one way or another.

I looked out the window. It was still dark enough that I could see lights twinkling in the distance. Were they from a cruise ship out at sea? Another island? People were out there. People who could help me. But how could I contact them? My room was high enough to give me magnificent views of the ocean; it was also high enough that if I tried to jump into the garden below, I'd break my legs.

The blue sky became more distinctive, and the lights twinkled less vibrantly as the sun made its slow ascent. Lavender, peachy pink, and tangerine filled the sky until its normal light blue appeared with just a few puffs of white interrupting the sameness of it.

The day began quiet and peaceful, except for a knock on my door at 7. When I opened it, a silver tray of hot tea, warm croissants, and a bowl of fruit awaited me. I wanted to ignore the food, but the hunger pangs wouldn't let me.

I stood out on the deck as I savored the sweet taste of a perfectly ripe peach. I watched a few lizards crawl slowly out from under the bushes beneath me, like the munchkins after the wicked witch had died. They flitted from underbrush to underbrush. But I saw no human presence for almost an hour, an hour that passed quickly as I surveyed the sky for answers to an unfathomable question.

Had my own government imprisoned me? What else could I believe? Carlos said that the men surrounding me were D.E.A. agents. If this was true, I had to decide what to believe in most: a government agency that thought the ends justified the means, or an honorable man I once loved who may have gone bad.

Once loved? I moved my gaze from the enormous ocean just hundreds of yards away inward to my own ocean of emotions. Parker was deep inside there, silent but stirring. I thought I had erased him from my memories, from my feelings, but with his return a week ago, and now, with his name ever present on the lips of my captor, I knew that I had been lying to myself.

An older man appeared suddenly in the garden directly below me. I couldn't tell his age; he might have been 50, or 80, but he was bent over as if arthritic. He wore a light long-sleeved shirt, ragged baggy pants, and well-used brown sandals. A large straw hat protected his face. The lizards ignored him, and he ignored the lizards. He held a large woven basket while he slowly, patiently weeded, placing dead exotic flowers in the basket. He worked methodically, looking neither right nor left. I willed him to look two stories up, and when, long minutes later, he did, his face was hidden by the shadow of his floppy woven hat. I felt, rather than saw, his eyes rove up and down my body as if he just saw an outline of someone once living. His eyes never met mine, and after a minute, he shrugged and continued with his gardening.

I wanted to scream and shout at the old man, but I figured it would be useless. Being an eternal optimist, I tried anyway.

"Psst. Sir. Hello! Hello?" I spoke each word louder, but the man ignored me. Just as I suspected. He knew what he had to do to keep his job. The sun was up now, bright and clean and promising. I heard another knock on the door. As I considered disregarding it, the door opened wide.

A maid stared at me as if afraid to speak.

"Yes?" I prompted.

"Please, ma'am. Clothes. In the closet. Please dress and join Mr. Medina downstairs in the garden." She spoke with a charming accent, much like the policeman, Flores, in St. Thomas. Before I could respond, the woman began to back out.

"Wait!"

She stopped, looking at me with veiled eyes. I returned her gaze as honestly and openly as I could.

"I'm a prisoner. I don't know where I am. Can you tell..."

A large, unpleasant looking man barged into the room. "Solana. What are you doing? Leave right now. You know you're not supposed to..."

I laughed out loud. "I didn't know it was a crime to ask for a toothbrush. Solana was just about to tell me where I might secure one before you interrupted."

The maid kept her gaze to the floor. "In the cabinet above the sink, ma'am," she said softly. She walked quietly past the man, who looked at me briefly, then closed the door behind him.

I checked out the closet. Sure enough, several sundresses hung cheerfully in the once empty closet, two pairs of sandals, running shoes, and a pair of black heels. I guessed that underwear and other essentials would be neatly folded in the drawers. I didn't have to look for the toothbrush, since I'd found it in the cabinet the night before.

As I dressed, I wondered what would happen if I refused Carlos' invitation and stayed in my room. But I didn't have the luxury to wait and see.

~~~~~~~~~~~~~~~~~

I walked toward the garden wearing one of the sundresses. The tight waist accentuated my breasts, and the skirt fell right above my knees. The bright red fabric was not a color I'd have picked for myself. Well, nothing of the outfit was what I'd have worn, including the red-heeled sandals. I looked around me. Gorgeous landscaping, but the gardener was gone. Carlos stood alone in a bricked walkway set off by a dozen vibrant hibiscus plants.

When I reached him, he nodded formally. "Thank you for joining me, Meredith. You look beautiful."

We stared at each other warily. Or maybe I looked at him warily, and he looked at me like a tiger about to play with a mouse.

"I hope you've had time to reflect on what we talked about last night, Meredith," he continued.

"About which subject?" I asked, deflecting for a moment. "You've told me so much in the short time we've known each other."

Carlos stepped closer to me, eyes on my lips. In a gentle voice he whispered, "The subject of your boyfriend's deception."

I stepped away. "Oh, that subject." I looked out toward the ocean, then back to his dark eyes. The time was now. If I was going to seduce the man to get him off guard, to buy some time and figure out how to escape, I had to begin. "Sorry. I'm a bit confused right now. And it's your fault. I came here under duress, yet I'm standing in a beautiful, fragrant garden, looking at the sparkling waters of the Atlantic Ocean, warmed by this tropical sun, and I can't remember why I don't want to be here." I stepped further away from Carlos. I couldn't let this seem too easy.

"At first I thought you were the bad guy," I continued. "But yesterday you tried to prove to me that everything I thought I knew.... People I thought were good...." I paused. "Then last night, when you kissed me...."

"I apologized for that Meredith. A mistake. Professionally."

"Was it?" I turned to face the ocean. I found it difficult to look at the man while I flirted. Taking in a deep breath, I turned back to find him less than a foot away. "Was it a mistake, Carlos?" I stared into his eyes, then down at his mouth. "If that's all it was, a chance to take advantage of me...."

"No, that's not what I said," Carlos interjected quickly. "That's just the point. I don't want you thinking that I'm doing that. Taking advantage. This isn't what I expected."

"What's not what you expected?" I looked around me, then up toward my room. "It seems to me that this was all planned out pretty well."

Carlos looked at me as if I'd surprised him. Then he exhaled loudly. "Meredith, you are much smarter, and more beautiful, than I had anticipated."

"Thanks for the compliment. I think," I answered, smiling just a little. "I'm a bit out of my element, you know. I'm a medical editor. Besides being kidnapped by my government just to catch an agent gone bad...."

"More than that," Carlos interrupted.

I broke in quickly, "to finish my sentence, besides finding myself in a gorgeous tropical island while being told that an old boyfriend is the enemy, I'm kissed by a handsome James Bond-type who says he's on my side. Do you blame me for being a bit bewildered? I need some time to sort this out."

Carlos stretched like a lean, lazy cat, then strolled to a wicker chair by the bougainvillea and sat down. "I wish we had all the time in the world, Meredith. I'm here to catch a stray agent; instead, I'm distracted by a stunning woman." His eyes swung over to the other chair, asking me silently to join him. "This 'bewilderment' is getting in the way."

Just what I wanted to hear. If my little distractions helped sidetrack the situation, all the better. I sat in the chair near him and crossed my legs, trying to look confused and sexy at the same time.

"But," he continued, pulling his linen sleeves down over his wrists one arm at a time, "I'm willing to let today's plans take a little hiatus, while you and I, to use a cliché, 'get to know each other better.' Anything to put you at ease."

I leaned my head back and turned my eyes skyward. "Thank you." I paused. "You know, you were right yesterday, when you challenged me on why I had broken up with Parker a year ago. I knew something was wrong. I kept telling myself that I just didn't like how much he traveled, but it was more than that. I'm pretty good at telling when people are lying to me, and Parker, I felt, wasn't telling me the truth."

Carlos looked at me intently. I could tell he was loving every word I said.

"However, I still don't believe that he's become part of a cartel. That he's changed sides. That doesn't make sense."

I sat up stiffly as Carlos leaned toward me. "No, you wouldn't understand that, Meredith. One of the things I like about you." He placed his hand lightly on my arm. His touch was warm. "You can't imagine how seductive money can be. Or power."

"Parker never cared about that either," I argued. I sat back on the lounger, trying to look relaxed.

"Meredith." Carlos' voice sounded like the low hum of a bell after it's rung. Soothing. Enticing. "Excuse me for saying this, but you have no idea who Parker is, or what he's like."

I rested my head on the chair, speaking more to myself than to Carlos. "My best friend tells me repeatedly that I don't know how to judge men."

In a nanosecond, Carlos pushed his chair closer to mine so we were face to face, his lips cocked in a gentle smile. He pressed two fingers against the loose tendrils of my hair and moved them behind my ear. I barely breathed until his hands were back at his sides.

"I'm new at this," he said quietly.

"At what?" I asked. I bit my tongue so I wouldn't blurt out 'new at kidnapping? Or at trying to seduce your prisoner?'

"At falling for someone. I'm always in control." He moved a little closer, as if he'd seen another piece of my hair that needed tending. I moved further back against my chair.

"You're tenacious, I'll give you that."

"And is that such a bad thing?" he asked calmly. No doubt about it, this guy was smooth. And he used his words to his advantage, their meaning could be stretched in many directions, but behind it all was a message of determination. I just needed to figure out exactly what he was determined to do.

"Carlos, I'm feeling a little uncomfortable," I said matter-of-factly.

He just stared at me, warm brown eyes full of questions I had no intention of answering. I moved my legs slowly away from his, which were suddenly pressing mine.

"Give me a chance. You may be surprised." He put one hand across his chest, as if making a vow. "I am a gentleman. I would like to show you."

"Show me what?" I asked before realizing that was just the opening Carlos was looking for. He leaned over, lips touching mine.

I closed my eyes as I felt his touch. I had to admit, he was a good kisser. A great one. I realized how an actress must feel, kissing a handsome co-star whom she can't stand. The body responds as the mind recoils.

He opened my mouth with his tongue and pushed it inside. My mouth opened slightly, while my brain started to scream Stop! What the hell was I doing? I didn't know how to play these games. I was afraid I'd lose, particularly as his hands began to move onto my waist, and up. I opened my eyes. Carlos released me, sitting as still as a lizard, waiting for my reaction. Beyond him, I saw movement. What was it? Just as I saw the gardener's straw hat move behind the shrubs, Carlos turned to see what had caught my attention.

My expression innocent, I placed my hands on his face and moved it back in front of me. "I'm afraid your bodyguard is getting a front row seat, Carlos. I'm embarrassed." I don't know why I fibbed, but at that moment, I felt as if I had just saved the gardener from some terrible fate.

I stood up. "I need to leave. You're not helping. You're just confusing me even more."

CHAPTER THIRTY-SIX

"Meredith, where are you going?" Carlos jumped up, seemingly shocked that I would leave him mid-kiss.

"Listen, Carlos, I...." Fortunately I didn't have to make up my excuse for getting away from him, since a tall, sinewy man arrived from the building and sidled up to Carlos, whispering in his ear. Didn't they have walkie-talkies or some kind of spy equipment for this kind of thing? In cool secret agent movies, the security guys and bodyguards have neat little earpieces that help them communicate with each other. What was wrong with the D.E.A.? Did they overspend their budget?

Carlos' eyes flung toward me halfway in the whispering. He nodded at the man, indicated five with his outstretched hand, then meandered toward me as if he wasn't concerned about the interruption.

"Some business has come up," Carlos said. I wondered why he couldn't be a little more imaginative than that.

"Someone else to kidnap?" I quipped before remembering I was trying to seduce my captor.

Carlos just laughed.

I rearranged my face to look earnest. "I'm going crazy in my room. I'm a runner. Could I change and get some exercise?"

Carlos thought about it, then shook his head. "Running's not a good idea. I'm not sure any of my guys could keep up with you." He smiled as if that was a joke. Or as if he'd read my mind. "But you can stay out here and go for a walk." With the flick of his hand, one of the D.E.A. agents ran over. Where had he been hiding? In the bushes? With the gardener?

"Ray, Ms. Powers wants to stretch her legs. Give her a little room, but keep an eye on her."

Ray nodded his head and moved five paces away from me. Well, that was a start.

I casually waved goodbye to Carlos, who was looking nervously toward the building, and then I kicked off my shoes and walked near the water. While listening to the soothing call of the ocean, watching the shorebirds race back and forth from the surf, and walking mindlessly on the sand, I could almost forget that I was a prisoner.

I marveled at the colors displayed in front of me, where the sun illuminated the whiteness of the sand, the blueness of the sea, and the soft pearliness of the horizon. The warmth mesmerized me for a minute. Only a minute. Then I directed my mind away from the beauty surrounding me. Back to Carlos.

Carlos wanted to trick me, confuse me into forgetting who I was and what, or whom, I believed in. Even knowing that, I felt pulled into his seductive lair. What was the truth? What was real, and what was pretend? In this environment, I could no longer be sure. Maybe even this gem-like sky was a lie. At that thought, I quickly averted my gaze from above me and moved it to my bare feet, watching them march quickly and purposely, as if they really had some place to go. I walked away from the sea and toward the end of the sandbank, where dainty bushes dotted the landscape.

Beyond the small dunes, the island seemed to spread out into nothingness. No homes. No humans to reach out to for a rescue. The frustration inside me began to bubble and boil. Claustrophobic, I felt ready to scream and dash for the ocean.

But then I saw it.

A dollar bill, flapping in the tropical breeze. Maybe it escaped from the pocket of one of the bodyguards, or even from the wallet of a gardener or maid. As I walked closer to the bill, fluttering from the frowsy branches of a small, mimosa-type bush, I did so nonchalantly, so my bodyguard wouldn't get suspicious.

I bent over as if looking at a particularly beautiful flower and plucked the money away from the thorny branch. It was a twenty dollar bill! A lot to escape a pocket or wallet and go unnoticed. For the sake of the large, overly muscled man following me twenty feet away, I stopped casually to put it in my pocket. That's when I saw the letters on the bill.

Along the forehead of Andrew Jackson were the initials – TRMFY.

Parker!

He had to be here. The only other times I'd seen those initials were when he tried to get my attention back at home on the note in the bottom of my china figurine, and on the restaurant menu in Boston. I still didn't know what the letters meant, but at least I knew whom they were from.

At that point, seeing evidence of Parker's presence, of him, I knew that I'd been lying to myself for way too long. I breathed in deeply, patted the bill in the pocket of my sundress, and walked on as leisurely as possible with a heart thumping so loudly it could be heard in Las Vegas.

Parker. Here. Let the games begin.

CHAPTER THIRTY-SEVEN

"Hey, where are you going?"

I kept walking fast, almost running, which wasn't easy wearing no shoes on the sand.

"Hey, miss. Uh, Miss Powers. Hold on."

I ignored Ray, Carlos' D.E.A. chump, and kept trotting back to the hotel. Seeing the sign from Parker renewed me and gave me the energy to be more courageous. I knew what I had to do: find Carlos and continue my game of seduction. See what I could discover, what his weaknesses were, and what he was really up to. He might be a government agent, but I didn't agree with the way he was running his operation. Time to call a few shots of my own.

"Meredith Powers, hold up."

Since I didn't want to wait, but I also didn't want the secret agent man to follow me, I turned around and shouted to him, "I have to go to the bathroom. I'll be right back." Sure enough, that stopped him in his tracks. I continued down the path into the building and followed the hallway to the stairs and Carlos' office.

I heard the shouting before I reached the top of the staircase.

"You're full of shit! I want to know where she is. This was not part of the deal!"

I recognized the voice, but it didn't compute in my brain. It couldn't be.

"Shut up and sit down." Carlos' voice was harsh. I didn't have to see his face to figure out what it looked like. Scary.

I slowed down and walked quietly on the carpet toward the conversation, glad now that I wasn't wearing shoes.

"You knew what you were getting into. You have no leverage here. We blackmailed you. You delivered the product, or at least helped in its delivery. Now go back to Boston and leave it alone." Carlos' voice had softened, but it didn't sound any less scary. In fact, I began to tremble, and I held one hand with the other to try and calm myself.

"Look, all you want is Parker Webb," the other man responded. "I get that. I want him too. Remember, he's the one who busted me. But what's his girlfriend have to do with it? She doesn't know anything."

"She says Parker's not her boyfriend. She says you are." Carlos' sarcastic words stopped me faster than a punch.

"Well, that was the plan, wasn't it?"

I gasped loudly, realizing what he just said. My reaction immediately alerted two of Carlos' goons to my presence: they were out of Carlos' office and on top of me within seconds. They dragged me, completely humiliated, in front of the two men I least wanted to see. I stared down at the tan carpet.

"Meredith, look up," Carlos commanded.

I lifted my eyes, turning toward the other man first. He stood there, eyes glinting like granite, fists tight at his side. He avoided my glare. Tears started spilling down my face.

"Gregory?" I finally said.

"I'm sorry you had to see this," Carlos said. "Meredith, look at me."

I refused. I turned my back on both of them.

"Meredith." Gregory pleaded. "It's not like it seems."

"Shut up," Carlos barked. Nodding to the two men standing at the doorway, he continued, "Take her back to her room." I ignored him and Gregory, and walked slowly out of the office and down the hall. Once I reached the stairs, I heard a thump, then a muted scream.

~~~~~~~~~~~~~~~~~

I walked around my bedroom in a daze. The realization of what I had just encountered hit me like a fist.

It couldn't be.

But it was.

How did I miss the signs? But what signs, really? Why would I suspect Gregory of being anything other than what he professed to be? A mid-level accountant looking for love.

I sat down on the edge of the bed and saw my life flash in front of me, or at least the past two years.

Parker's absences. The abrupt end of the relationship. My need for security and love. A man I could depend on.

Yes, Gregory sneaked in through the back door because he knew my vulnerabilities. He knew what kind of man I needed. Calm, docile, boring. And I fell for him! Hook, line and ...

Sinking further into the mattress I cradled my head in my hands and shook it back and forth.

Was Gregory really one of them? So who, then, was I? Someone to be fooled so easily, so successfully. I groaned as the tears continued to fall.

But the crying stopped when I heard shouting, roaring actually, from somewhere in the hotel. The sounds of a man angry enough to kill. Was it Gregory? I stood up and opened the door. I couldn't describe the noise – chaos in the midst of violent crunching and groans. Ugly sounds that convinced me that I had to scheme my way out of this place.

Then I heard Gregory call my name.

"Meredith! "Mere---" And the smack of what sounded like a shovel hitting concrete.

Oh my God! Sickened, I ran to the bathroom and fell to the floor, sweat streaming down my face. What just happened to Gregory?

~~~~~~~~~~~~~~~~

Minutes turned into a half hour, and I heard no more sounds. Unable to stay cooped up in my room, I opened the door and looked out. No one. I raced down the stairs to the outside door, walking swiftly away from the hotel and straight toward the ocean. One of the men was probably following me, but I didn't care. The air was hot and heavy; just three minutes away from the air-conditioned rooms, I felt tiny beads of perspiration trickle down the sides of my face and back. I hadn't thought to put on shoes, and now I was glad I hadn't. The white hot sand massaged my feet, and I felt comforted by the contact.

I walked faster. The sun was overhead, a faceless nameless observer, unable to help. I kept my gaze straight ahead as if waiting for someone, or something, to appear on the horizon between sea and space. A ship? A sailboat? But only a flock of flying seagulls filled the seascape.

I heard a high, light squeal ahead of me and walked even faster. People! Real people. I saw three of them, afraid at first that the sun, fatigue, and stress had caused a mirage. But no, as I reached the shrieks, I saw two small children running toward the waves, their skinny brown bodies moving like shorebirds, back and forth, back and forth. Their small-boned mother, late teens maybe, looked up at me with gentle brown eyes, then dismissed me as if I was just another pretty shell found on the beach. She called her children in a high sweet voice, and they all scurried away.

I stood, amazed, until Ray appeared.

"People," I said stupidly.

"Sure," he answered. Maybe he felt sorry for me. Maybe he was unsettled by what had just happened in the hotel, because he continued to talk. "This island is full of them. On the other side, mostly."

"So this isn't a remote island?"

He shook his head slowly. "Well, remote enough for me. But no, there's a town on the other side. A couple of first class resorts, the kind that only the rich know about. Some nice restaurants." He closed his mouth tightly then, as if just figuring something out.

"No place you can get to. Come on, back to your room."

His words helped me. As we walked back to the hotel and my room, I remembered the twenty dollar bill. TRMFY. Now, the news that we weren't alone. I regained some of my strength and resolve. Then, I came up with a plan to escape. It wasn't brilliant. But if it worked, that didn't matter.

"God, I have a horrible headache," I moaned as we entered my room.

Ray turned to me sympathetically.

"Look, I get migraines. Carlos knows. He stored my prescription bottle somewhere. Could you have the maid get it for me?" I looked at my bodyguard, whose face was noncommittal.

I rubbed my fingers up and down my forehead. "Ray, if I don't stop this headache in time, I'm going to get really sick. I don't think Carlos would be too pleased."

He shrugged, not responding. He left me sitting on my bed, holding my head in my hands. I looked out the window at the ocean, hoping against hope, and sure enough, ten minutes later, I heard a light knock on the door.

"Miss? Something for your headache?"

The same maid, Solana, who had been here this morning, handed me my bottle of migraine pills. I almost kissed her, but instead thanked her profusely. She opened her mouth as if to say something, but only blinked slowly, then retreated.

CHAPTER THIRTY-EIGHT

Thirty minutes later, I left my room and bumped into Ray, standing guard.

"Back in the room," he mumbled.

"But Ray, I have to see Carlos. I really really really need to talk to him. Please?" I hated to plead, but it usually worked.

"No."

"Just ask him. I bet he'll see me. Tell him it's important."

The man sighed and spoke in his little walkie-talkie. "Stay here. We're watching you. I'll be right back."

"I won't move."

And I didn't. Seven and a half minutes later, Ray was back. "Okay, let's go."

I sashayed in my sundress, a new one I had discovered in the bedroom closet, azure blue with dainty white lace on the bodice, hem, and two large pockets on the either side of the billowing skirt. Demure and sexy at the same time. That was me. I tried to walk confidently down the hall, but my hands trembled in the pockets. Could I pull this off?

~~~~~~~~~~~~~~~

Carlos was not alone, much to my disappointment. Three men, agents I presumed, stood at the other side of his desk while Carlos pointed to something on top of it. "You follow the route – see if the boxes are getting to their destination as planned." When one of the men turned to go, Carlos added, "and talk to that nitwit Roger. Make sure he's keeping his mouth shut." Then Carlos caught sight of me.

"Roger?" I asked. My voice cracked. "Roger is in on this too?"

Carlos shooed the other men away with the wave of his fingertips; they walked out, avoiding me in the doorway.

"I'm not talking about any Roger you know," Carlos said. "Now, I'm glad you asked to see me. We have a lot to talk about."

"Damn right we do," I spat out. Whoops. I wanted to be seductive, sexy. Not the right approach. I walked further into the room, unable to keep my mouth shut. "Carlos, you want my cooperation, yet you haven't been honest with me. You're a representative of the United States Government. I'm a civilian. I've done nothing incorrect except once date the wrong man. Not only have you..." I had to stop because Carlos had walked around his desk and approached me with a soft, unfocused expression on his face. Had he listened to a word I said? He placed his hands gently on my shoulders.

"Go on," Carlos said kindly. He looked into my eyes as if he was about to kiss me. I felt as comfortable as a woman about to leap off a six-story building. "You were saying? Not only have I what?" His hands caressed my arms as playfully as a kitten with a soft ball of yarn.

I stood still, afraid to breathe. Talking more slowly, I continued. "Not only have you kidnapped me to catch this 'drug dealer,' or whatever it is you think Parker is, but you purposely sent an agent to seduce me, so you could catch this ex-boyfriend of mine. Why couldn't you have just been honest with me from the very first? Just knocked on my front door in Cambridge, explained the problem, and asked for my help? Why all the subterfuge?"

All breath gone, I moved away from Carlos and sat heavily in the large leather couch at the other end of the room. The skirt of my blue sundress puffed out around me, and as I attempted to pull it below my knees, Carlos followed me and sat down.

"It's not as simple as that," he said softly, looking at me with dark eyes. "Gregory Dunne had a direct link to Parker Webb. If he could have stopped Parker in Cambridge, none of this..." and here Carlos nodded his head to include the room and the island "would have been necessary. Gregory failed."

To be truthful, I stopped listening to Carlos' explanation. I knew that I didn't have much time to get moving with my escape plan. I nodded my head as if I believed everything Carlos said. I took a deep breath, to show him that I was calming down.

"I'm absolutely exhausted. This cloak and dagger stuff is too much for me," I sighed. Then I turned my eyes to the right and acted surprised to see the silver tray with port and sherry sitting on the side table next to the couch. "God, I could use a glass of whatever you have there."

Carlos sprang up. "Excellent idea! Are you hungry, Meredith? Why don't I call someone to fix you a little sandwich?"

I stood up next to him, laying my hand on his arm. "I have a better idea. Could we just relax here and have an uninterrupted conversation for a little while?

You call off your guys, I'll pour a little port, and maybe then we can sit here and relax, and you can explain exactly what you need me to do."

Carlos stood still, staring at me. "Okay," he finally said. He walked toward the telephone, and I moved to the table and picked up a bottle of "Porto," a deep, red port. Perfect. As I listened to him talk on the phone in a subdued voice, asking that no one disturb him, I poured two glasses. In one of them, I added the tiny specks of migraine pills that I'd pummeled with the end of my hairbrush and then hidden in the pocket of my dress a few minutes earlier in my room.

I looked up as Carlos walked to the office door and locked it, at the same time swirling my pinky in the dark liquid, willing the pills to dissolve. As the solution swirled, he turned and walked back toward me with a sexy grin. I gulped and took my gaze away from the two small glasses.

Would it work? Only my life depended on it.

CHAPTER THIRTY-NINE

Just as Carlos sat down next to me on the couch, the telephone rang.

"Damn," he said. "I told them not to disturb us." He looked at me; I smiled innocently, watching him get up and walk toward the phone on the desk. As he spoke, back turned toward me, I frantically swirled my finger in the port again. Most of the grains had dissolved, but a few still floated at the top.

"I really don't care where he is. I'm busy now. Don't disturb me again. No. Wait!"

I stopped, scared that Carlos was speaking to me, but he was still facing away, talking on the phone.

"I do want to know when Rog...um, when he arrives," Carlos said.

I swirled one more time, then sucked the liquid off my pinky.

"Just ring twice, then hang up. Right." Carlos let the phone bang as he hung up. "Okay, now we should have some peace, Meredith. But first, how about that port."

Elegantly, I handed Carlos his tumbler while raising mine up toward him. "Your toast."

"To communication, in more ways than one." He moved his eyes from my glass to my lips.

I smiled with all the warmth I could muster, and then took a dainty sip. Carlos, I was happy to see, took a more lusty gulp, swallowed, and then drank a bit more.

"Now to answer some of your well-thought-out questions," he began. He handed me his port to place on the table beside me, but I held up my hand.

"One more toast," I said, encouraging Carlos to keep his glass. He nodded his head and sat on the edge of the couch next to me. "To honesty," I said. Carlos clicked his glass lightly against mine, and we drank. I put my port down on the table, and then Carlos'. It was almost empty.

He leaned back against the couch and moved his arm around my shoulders. "So, where should we start, Meredith?"

"Well, how about from the beginning?" I said. "When did you first realize that Parker had become a double agent? Is that what you call it? When an agent goes against the government that he was first working for?"

Carlos smiled, looking contented and a bit sleepy. I remembered reading the sheet of warnings when I first got the prescription. If you experience vomiting, extreme fatigue, or muscle weakness, call your doctor immediately.

"Parker made his mistake when he left me," he said, words slurring a little. Carlos bent over and picked up the bottle of port from the table, squinting as he read the label. "Strong stuff. But good."

"Um," I agreed. "What do you mean, when he left you?"

Carlos replaced the bottle on the table and leaned against the side of the couch, looking directly at me. "He was good. I believed in him. Believed he was one of us. Then the raid. A lot of my men were killed. Or captured. The guys who were taken into custody gave me up, but of course I had disappeared by then. But the operation was over. All because of Parker. He ruined everything."

"Which operation are you talking about?" I asked, confused. "And why did you have to disappear?

Carlos' eyes closed halfway, but he watched me attentively. "I haven't felt this relaxed in months. Must be you, huh?" He lunged toward me, his body covering mine as I leaned back. "You, my lovely woman, are hard to resist."

I jumped up off the couch. "I'm flattered, Carlos. But could we take things a little more slowly?" I chuckled softly. "Wow. Warm in here, isn't it? I wonder if the air conditioning is working." Inane, I told myself. How much more idiotic could I sound? How much longer for these drugs to knock him out? Will they knock him out?

Carlos patted the seat next to him. "Come on, Meredith. I won't bite. I promise. We were just getting to the good part."

"The good part?" I asked, still standing.

"You know, about Parker. Why he defected. Why he thought he could get away with it, I should say. He underestimated me. That was his big mistake. Among many." Carlos yawned. "God, I'm sleepy." He slapped the leather next to him. "Come on. We don't have much time."

I took one step back. Carlos' eyes closed, then reopened, like he was forcing himself to look at me. "Just give me a few minutes." He closed his eyes as he spoke. "I need you to sit next to me while I take a fast nap. Not that I don't trust you, but I'll sleep better. Come on, Meredith. Take a seat."

I sat far enough away that he would know I was there, but he couldn't reach me without moving. And I could tell that the man was not going to move. In fact, he opened his mouth to speak, but all that came out was a long, slow sigh. Then silence.

I wondered briefly if I'd killed him. Looking closely, I saw his chest move up and down. Okay, he was down, but not dead. Now I just had to get up and...

"Hey, where are you going?" Carlos' hand snapped out and grabbed me, pulling me down on top of him. His arm wrapped me against him, and he whispered softly in my ear. "Ah, now I have you where I want you."

I struggled to get free. "I thought we were taking it a little slower," I managed, trying not to show how terrified I was.

"Ah, you like it slow. I'm not surprised. You're a classy lady, Meredith. Knew that from the first time I saw you." Although his words came out as slow as honey on a hot day, his grip did not loosen. In fact, his body became harder, in every place that counted.

I panicked. "Leave me alone!" I blurted, unlike the seductress I was supposed to be. As I jumped out of his embrace, I felt my hand rise to slap him, stopping just in time.

The man was sound asleep. He had not reacted when I escaped his grip. In fact, he lay on the couch like a large lifeless lump. A slap might have disturbed his sleep, but he probably wouldn't have even felt it.

For a minute I stood listening to his breathing, wondering if I dared believe that my ruse had worked. Then Carlos' breathing stopped. I held my breath until his chest began to move again, up and down, and the soft whistling snores resumed.

In the next instance I shocked myself by picking up a pillow. Could I do it? Could I smother him in his sleep? I closed my eyes and envisioned the fantasy. In his condition, he wouldn't have time to struggle.

I dropped the pillow as if it had just burned my hands. How could I think of doing such a thing? Yes, he'd lied to me, kidnapped me, confused me and maybe hurt two men I thought I loved. But I was not a killer. I shuttered, sickened by my impulse.

I tiptoed toward the door and peeked out. Amazingly, his bodyguards/agents, or whatever the hell they were, had taken him literally. They had left us alone. Completely. I walked a little faster away from the office and down the hall, intending to leave the building and run for miles, if I had to, and find the other side of the island. I'd find a phone, a friendly face, maybe even an ex-boyfriend.

"Miss. Shhhhhhhhh. Miss."

Damn. The maid was practically racing toward me, knees and head bent as if afraid of getting hit by something, while beseeching me with her eyes.

I put my finger to my lips. "Solana, I'm just going out for a walk," I whispered as she got closer. The poor woman looked like she was going to faint. The way she shook her head back and forth, it was no wonder she was dizzy.

"No, no, no," she whispered back. "Follow me. A man. He asks for you. Come."

A man? Parker? Parker was hidden somewhere here? I didn't even stop to question her further. I followed the uniformed woman down the hall, to another staircase that led us further into a lower level I hadn't known existed. The light dimmed, the concrete floor had never seen carpeting, and the walls were institutional white.

"Where are we going?" I whispered. This place spooked me. The only noise I heard was the buzzing of florescent lights above us, and a clanking within the walls.

"Shhhhhhhhh," Solana answered. Her face broke into a sweat, and her eyes widened like a frightened pony. "Dangerous. But he begged me. He told me...."

"What?" I asked, but she only waved her hand down, as in 'shut up,' I surmised.

She stopped in front of a door, took out a set of keys from her uniform pocket, and turned the lock. "You go in," she said. "Fast. Can't stay long. I'll keep watch."

Parker, here, locked up? Hopes dashed, I walked swiftly into the low-lit room, which was empty. But another doorway led to another room. I inhaled deeply, and stepped into the second room, smaller, and even darker. A cot sat in the corner, and as my eyes adjusted, I saw a prone figure slowly attempt to sit up.

When he turned his face toward me, I gasped.

CHAPTER FORTY

"Gregory! What have they done to you?" I hurried toward him, but he held his hand out to stop me.

"Get away." He retched and held his head over a bowl by the side of the cot. It was full of a reddish fluid. Blood.

"Gregory!" Lord help me, for one instant I wanted to turn around and leave. Then I tamped down my anger at the man. He'd been worst than dishonest with me. Our entire relationship had been a lie. Yet I would never have wished this on him, no matter how hurt I was.

Gregory looked up at me as if wondering who I was. One eye was swollen half shut. His chest was black with bruises, some of them open and oozing blood.

I sat down next to him on the cot and placed my fingers lightly over his beaten face. "Oh, God. Gregory."

"Meredith? How did you find me?" His voice sounded strained, as if he'd been shouting for a long time.

"The maid."

At first he looked confused, and I wondered if they'd beaten him senseless. But then he nodded his head as if he remembered and grabbed my hands, trying to smile. One tooth was missing.

"I'm sorry," he said. "I want you to understand that I didn't know in the beginning. Didn't know."

"Didn't know what, Gregory?" I asked.

"I didn't know how much I'd care for you," he said.

"But how could you fool me like that? How could you act like you wanted to be with me, love me?"

He didn't answer.

"Wait. Gregory. When did it start? How did you...?"

"I tripped you, purposely, on the running trail." At least he looked ashamed, but he still avoided my eyes.

"The morning we first met?" Even though it made sense now, I still couldn't believe it.

"It was my assignment. Meet you, get you to open up. Talk. Date. Bring Parker out." His voice weakened. "All to get Parker."

I stood up. "You scum." I wished I could have come up with something better, what with a degree in English and years of editing behind me. But that was the first word that came to mind. "You used me? You flirted with me, asked me out, slept with me, all to get Parker's attention?"

Gregory nodded. "At first, yes. But then I made a mistake. I started thinking about you all the time, worrying about you and wondering if you were in any danger. That's why I asked to move in with you. That's why I wouldn't let you run alone."

I released a sharp harrumph.

"No, Meredith. Listen to me. At first it was all about Parker, but then..."

I interrupted. "Why? I don't understand. Why was it so important to get Parker?"

"I was hoping to warn Parker. He needed to know..." Gregory stopped talking, folding his head below his knees and taking in deep breaths.

"What are you talking about? You and Carlos planned this to get him. You think Parker is crooked. You think..."

"Stop!" Gregory grimaced as the word flew out of his mouth. "It's all about following the drugs. D.E.A. officials have been following a U.S.-based drug operation that imports and then sells large quantities of methamphetamine."

"Okay. Methamphetamine. It's called 'meth,' right? But what...."

"On the streets, it's knows as 'ice' or 'crystal meth.' Popular stuff with the kids, who either inject or smoke it."

"Uh huh." I nodded my head. I should have known all this. Parker had been working to stop drugs from entering the U.S., drugs like this meth, and yet I had remained clueless about what his job really entailed. I realized now that I hadn't been much of a girlfriend. "Go on," I encouraged. Talking seemed to calm Gregory. He was resting his back against the wall, and his eyes looked heavy. All was quiet.

"The D.E.A. discovered that this U.S. drug ring sends the proceeds from the meth sales to Middle East accounts that have been connected to terrorist groups." Gregory stood up as he finished his last sentence, bending a bit as if it hurt to stand up straight.

"Whoa." I said after a minute's silence. The conversation had just moved from a lying boyfriend to drug operations and terrorists. I didn't know what to ask next. What was Gregory's role in all this? Was Carlos investigating the drug ring also, and what did that have to do with Parker? I had a hundred more questions for Gregory.

"So you and Carlos are part of a D.E.A. operation to stop the American-based drug ring? Or maybe to follow the organization and see if it leads to terrorists?"

"Meredith, I've already told you too much. The less you know, the better, but..."

We both heard soft shoes running on concrete.

Gregory grabbed my arm. His fingers felt like claws. "You have to get away." He began to cough, long, shattering hacks that led to more spit-up blood.

"But why did the D.E.A. do this to you?" My brain was crammed full of bewildering uncertainties.

"Not the D.E.A.," Gregory managed. As his coughing worsened, Solana burst in.

"Miss. Someone coming. We must leave. Now."

"I can't leave him like this. Gregory!"

He pushed me toward the door. "Go. Get out of here!"

~~~~~~~~~~~~~~~~~~~~~~~~

I raced after Solana, who closed and locked Gregory's prison door and then ran down the hallway toward the staircase. She wore sneakers. My heeled sandals smacked against the concrete floor like a flat palm on a face.

The maid uttered a muffled scream a second before I ran straight into the hard chest of one of Carlos' men. "Up to his office. Now."

Another man held the maid roughly by her arms.

"Let the woman go. I asked her to bring me down here," I said.

The men ignored me.

I didn't budge. "I am happy to go back upstairs and see Carlos. We haven't finished our conversation. But I don't want to be treated like I'm a criminal. Carlos has assured me many times that I am not a prisoner."

The two men looked at each other. One shrugged at the other one, who released Solana.

"Thank you. Now, this woman has brought me towels, meals, and fresh clothes. I don't think you want to punish her for doing her job." I nodded my head toward her, my eyes expressing what my voice could not: get away from here now. She backed out, avoiding the glares from the two men, and then dashed away. I breathed a sigh of relief. Solana, I hoped, would prove helpful in the not too distant future.

~~~~~~~~~~~~~~~~~~~~~~~~~

Within minutes, we were back upstairs. As we headed to Carlos' office, I bit my tongue so I wouldn't ask the men if he was alive. Did they even know that I'd drugged him?

When we walked through the door, I stared in disbelief.

"What were you thinking?" Carlos asked silkily from the couch, one knee bent with his right arm draped casually over it.

How could he possibly be awake and lucid? I gave him enough migraine pills to shut down the brain of a one-ton whale.

Carlos leaned over and picked up a cup of steaming brown liquid. A long lingering chill crept up my spine despite the island's tropical heat. Then I realized that the temperature in the room was frosty.

Seeing me rub my arms with my hands, Carlos motioned to one of his men. "Okay, we can put the room temp back to normal. And I'd like more coffee. Black and hot." He dismissed them with a nod.

"How was your nap?" I asked.

Carlos sent me a fearsome smile. "I don't usually fall asleep before consummation," he said matter-of-factly. "And I would never choose to fall asleep in front of such a lovely companion."

He glanced over toward the bottle of port, then back at me. He smiled again, looking like a tiger. A small glint of teeth, lips thinned, eyes dark and dead.

"You're good," he finally said. "But not good enough. I want you to go back to your room. I don't trust you. And I know you certainly don't trust me."

"But..."

He waved away my protest, half heartedly, I was happy to note. "I don't know what Gregory told you...."

My eyes widened. So Carlos knew I found him?

".....but you really should wonder about the words of a man who deceived you the way he did. Now, go away. I'm tired of your games."

The telephone rang as I opened my mouth. Carlos picked up the nearest phone, listened for a few seconds, nodded, then looked at me with deep satisfaction. "Sure, bring him in."

I turned when the office door opened again. One of the 'agents' walked in and then a man wearing green and yellow plaid shorts and a black t-shirt.

Roger.

He looked shocked when he saw me standing beside an obviously relaxed Carlos, still flopped on the couch.

Roger spun toward Carlos. "What's she doing here? I thought you said...."

Carlos shut him down with a look. "We'll talk business after the lady leaves. Meredith?"

"I don't understand," I said, looking only at Roger. "Are you also with the D.E.A.?"

Roger's face paled. "The D.E.A.?"

"Shut up!" Carlos commanded. "Get her out of here!"

I stood my ground, but the agent took me by the arm to lead me away.

I should have used the pillow when I had the chance.

CHAPTER FORTY-ONE

Could this day get any worse? I walked out to my balcony and gazed out toward the ocean. I needed to figure out what the puzzle looked like once I put together all the little pieces.

Parker. Gregory. Barbara and Roger. Carlos.

I played the sequence of events from the last half year in my mind over and over while pacing back and forth, stopping when I saw activity below me. Tables were being set up on the patio. Solana, now dressed in a black and white uniform, smoothed white linen tablecloths over the round tables, then added silverware and goblets. What was happening now?

I paced some more.

Parker. Gregory. Barbara and Roger. Carlos.

Who created the scenario in which I was now imprisoned in a beautiful isolated hotel?

I jumped when the door opened with no warning knock or greeting.

I gasped when I saw who strode into the room, face fierce.

"Gregory!"

"Shhh," he admonished.

"But how did you....?" I took a step back. This was not the Gregory I knew.

"The guards were too busy with some new prisoners to realize that my door was unlocked."

"How did..."

"The maid." Gregory seemed to anticipate my questions before they slipped out of my mouth.

"Solana? Why is she helping?"

"I told her I'd help her get off the island."

"How can you promise that?"

"I just can," he said.

I didn't know how to respond to that. This Gregory was not dull or quiet; this Gregory seemed quite sure of himself.

"Well, at least we have someone on our side," I finally said.

"We?"

The expression on Gregory's face turned hopeful so quickly I corrected myself immediately. "Me, I mean."

He opened his mouth to retort, then stopped, as still as stone. "Quiet," he whispered.

"I don't hear...." Then I shut my mouth. Gregory stood by the door with the lamp in his hand. I could have told him that it was a perfect device to knock someone out, but I figured he already knew that. Besides, he alarmed me, with his beat up face, torn jeans and blood on his t-shirt. This wasn't the boring accountant I thought I had fallen in love with eons ago back in the safety of my normal life in Boston. This man, who had pretended to care for me, worked for Carlos. And now, he stood here with me, alone, in my room.

"What do you want?" I hissed. Then his words hit me like a tub of cold water. "Wait! Prisoners? What prisoners? Did Carlos...? Is Parker....?"

Gregory moved away from the door, placing the lamp back on the table, and walked toward the balcony, carefully looking at what was going on below. "No, Meredith, your precious Parker has not been captured."

"Then who?"

Gregory moved closer, his bruised face looking at me intently. "This isn't just about you and Parker, you know, Meredith. What's going down here is a lot bigger than your missing boyfriend."

I stepped back, surprised at his venom. "What a minute, you're the one who faked a romance with me just to get Parker. How should I know what's going on besides what I see? Damn it, what the hell is going on?"

"Quiet!" Gregory raised his hand, and I thought he was going to cover my mouth. "Instead, he touched his cheek, as if checking for a broken bone, then took a deep breath. "I'm sorry. You're in the middle of a big mess, and none of it is your fault."

"Right," I whispered. "And the prisoners are?"

Gregory sat on the bed, obviously exhausted, and I sat down beside him. He talked in a low voice. "A photographer from Los Angeles and a British reporter."

My eyes widened.

"They were kidnapped a week ago, while following a lead about those drug sales in the United States that support terrorist organizations. Obviously, they got too close to the truth. Their disappearance made the papers a few days ago. That's one of the reasons..." Gregory stopped, looking as if he wondered if he could trust me. "The D.E.A. has been secretly investigating the same lead. Notice the word 'secretly,' Meredith."

"I'm still lost," I confessed. How did all this connect him, Carlos, Parker, and this island?

"Meredith, I've already divulged more than I should. You must know as little as possible. That way, if Carlos..."

"Damn it! I'm the one whose former boyfriend suddenly reappeared in my life, saying he had to hide because his cover was blown. I'm the one whose new boyfriend just pretended to love me so he could hang around and find the first boyfriend. I'm the one who's been kidnapped to some remote island so that the D.E.A. could capture my first boyfriend. Don't you think I deserve to know what the hell is going on?" My voice had risen into a whispered shout by the time I finished, and I could feel the blood pounding in my head. I would be in trouble if I got a migraine, because all my pills had gone into Carlos' port.

Gregory stood up and walked to the balcony, once again looking out at the activities below. Then he walked over to the door and opened it to survey the hallway. I held my breath until he came toward me on the bed, pulling me up by the arms so I was standing in front of him, face to face.

"Yes, you do deserve to know what's going on," he replied quietly. His brown eyes stared at me so directly, and with so much respect, I felt my heart curl in response. "But we don't have time for that now. Whatever you do, don't trust Carlos. Don't believe a word he says. If at all possible, stay away from him."

"But he's got D.E.A. agents all over the place. He..."

Gregory shook his head impatiently. A noise startled us both, and he jumped as if hit by electricity. Neither of us moved until Gregory said, "I'm leaving."

"Why? If Carlos is...."

Gregory grabbed me by the shoulders, standing me inches from his face, and spoke to me in a soft, stern voice. "Carlos is not D.E.A. And he's dangerous, Meredith. Just stay here, don't try to leave. I'm going to escape. I need you to create a distraction. Anything. Scream. But don't do it until you count to forty after I'm gone."

I stepped away from him. "But what about the prisoners? What about me?"

Gregory touched my face with the back of his fingers. "That's why I need to escape. Damn you. Meredith. Whatever you think of me, know this." Gregory took in a deep breath before saying his next words. "I love you."

Before I could reply, he opened the door, looked both ways, and ran down the hallway. I could still feel his fingerprints on my arms. 'I love you,' he said. So I wasn't totally delusional, back in Cambridge, in my other life. Gregory loved me. But who the hell was Gregory?

I counted softly to forty-two, and then I screamed loud enough for the entire island to hear.

CHAPTER FORTY-TWO

Three men appeared, breathless and ruby-faced, just seconds after my scream ended. They barged into the room as if ready to face a three-headed dragon. Instead, I pointed to the corner of the room next to the balcony doors.

"A tarantula," I said in the most frightened female voice I could muster.

If it had been a different situation, I would have laughed at the expression on their faces. Finally one of them spoke, "You screamed because of a spider?"

I nodded, speechless, still pointing. The three men walked toward where my finger indicated, obviously not happy with me, or the spider. Unfortunately, they couldn't find anything.

"It was there," I insisted. "Huge. And black. With a red stripe down its back."

Suddenly, a real tarantula walked into the room.

Carlos.

I stared at him, amazed. Dressed in an impeccable black tuxedo, the man looked like a Hollywood A-list star, not like the villain I knew him to be.

"We don't have tarantulas here," he stated.

I muttered, "Oh yes we do. I'm looking at one."

"Excuse me?" Carlos stared me down with laser-like eyes.

"I said, 'yes we do, it had a stripe on him.' "

Carlos ignored me and looked toward the three men, who were still trying to find a non-existent bug. "Tarantulas don't have stripes. Most are black or brown; only a few exotic ones have bright-red markings...on their legs."

"How do you know?" I retorted.

"They're called the Mexican-Red-legged Tarantula. And I've seen one."

That shut me up. But just for a second.

"I don't care what color it is, I don't want it to bite me," I stated.

"Tarantulas are harmless to human beings," Carlos returned.

"That's what you say..."

"Enough!" Carlos' calm seemed to be evaporating. "Meredith, dinner will be served downstairs in half an hour. Dress appropriately." He looked down at his own formal wear as if giving me a clue.

"I'm not hungry," I said.

"It's not a choice," he replied.

"I'm not going downstairs for dinner. That is my choice..." I began until Carlos started to laugh lightly, as if he was in the middle of a conversation during a cocktail party.

"Something funny?" I snapped.

"I haven't been around a young child in a long, long time. And that is what you are acting like. A 3-year-old who isn't getting her way."

I closed my mouth tightly.

"I repeat, Meredith. It is not a choice. This is the night we catch a fallen man. I have an entertaining evening planned, including gourmet food and a surprise visitor."

"Who's the surprise visitor?" I asked, despite my determination to seem uninterested.

"Parker Webb."

I froze, fingers clenched into a fist.

"Yes, I'm sure he'll arrive tonight," Carlos continued. "He will be unable to resist all the temptations I've provided. You. Gregory. Me. A few other juicy morsels. He'll show up, I have no doubt."

"Even more reason for me not to join you."

Carlos looked at me, measuring my words. "I see." He walked to my closet and picked a black dress with a plunging neckline. Then he pulled out a necklace from his pocket. The thin gold choker displayed a shimmering diamond at its center. "I was going to present this to you later tonight, to thank you for your help. I see that I need to express my thanks sooner rather than later."

I shook my head. "No, Carlos."

He threw the dress on the bed and stood in front of me, still wearing a genial smile. "Meredith, your friend Gregory is in quite a lot of pain. Would you like us to increase it?"

"What?" I clenched my hands, panicking. Had Gregory been re-captured?

Carlos continued to talk in a matter-of-fact tone. "Gregory's in bad shape. He should be seen by a doctor. Still coughing up blood, you know. Now we can leave him alone, or we could increase his medical problems. It's all up to you."

I didn't move, but my stomach constricted and I tamped down a moan. I stared at the nice-looking, seemingly civilized man who was blackmailing me into setting a trap for Parker. As he promised, Carlos was giving me no choice. Maybe Gregory had escaped, and Carlos had no idea that he was not in his 'jail' downstairs. Or, Gregory had been re-captured. Either way, I couldn't take the chance.

I thrust my arm toward him, and he pressed the diamond necklace into my hand.

"We've wasted time, Meredith. Be downstairs in 20 minutes." He spun around and left the room.

~~~~~~~~~~~~~~~~~~~~~~

In the first tiny act of defiance, I refused to wear the black dress. I did try it on; my breasts spilled out of it like melons stuffed in a too-small barrel. I tore it off and selected a more sedate sundress – this one light lime green trimmed with tiny pink roses. Not for the first time, I wondered who selected these clothes.

Trembling with trepidation, I walked down the stairs and out the door to the garden. Carlos stood a few yards away, waiting for me. He displayed neither approval nor disapproval as I walked to him, but he did stare at my neck.

"Ah, pearls over diamonds," he observed. Fingering my necklace, I ignored Carlos and looked at the scene ahead of us. The place had been transformed into an upscale, outdoor restaurant; a half dozen lit torches stood like soldiers near each table.

"Relax, Meredith," Carlos whispered in my ear. "You need to act natural, as if you want to be here." He bent his elbow as if I should link my arm with his; instead, I just stood by his side. "The fate of your boyfriend depends on how well you play your part. So far, you're failing."

Wondering which 'boyfriend' he meant, I placed my hand around his arm. Despite his advice that I relax, my arm was as stiff as an ironing board, and his touch as hot as an iron. I tried to move away unobtrusively, but he put two of his fingers on the flesh of my under arm and pinched. I stilled, and we walked serenely to a table that was accessorized by a single pink orchid swimming in a tall slender vase, accented by a glowing candle.

I ignored the seductive setting, more intent on the diners who surrounded us. I couldn't believe it – two other attractive couples were seated around tables, the men also dressed in tuxes, the women in dress slacks and blouses.

"Who are...?" I began, looking straight at Carlos.

"Just sit down, sweetheart," he responded, standing by his chair until I lowered into mine. "Our guests this evening are part of the show. Nothing to concern you."

As a waiter poured water in our goblets and handed us a wine menu, I looked at the couples more closely. I recognized the men now; they were some of Carlos' 'agents' or 'bodyguards.' I hadn't seen the women before, but I noticed the well-defined muscles of their arms, and the bulge on the right side of their blouses. Guns.

The sun was less than an hour away from its descent; the soft blue and pink sky of the early evening was a surreal background to my intense anxiety. Carlos cleared his throat, and I looked up. He'd already ordered our wine – I barely noticed – and he placed an insincere smile on his face. "Talk as if you're fascinated by me."

"Blah blah blah, blah blah, duh duh duh," I said in a sexy, husky voice. His face reddened, and he clenched his jaw. Probably not a good idea to anger the man who was threatening me.

I arranged my face to look pleasant. "I don't understand the subterfuge, Carlos. If you're so sure that Parker will make an appearance because I'm here, and Gregory, and...." I stopped. I didn't want to say anything about the journalists. "Why are you going to all the trouble to make it look like we're having a cozy little dinner?"

Carlos leaned back in his chair, gently moving his glass back and forth so the wine swirled. Then he sniffed it, and took a slow sip. "Wonderful cabernet," he noted before moving his gaze up to my face. "Obviously you don't understand the intricacies of diplomacy."

"Obviously," I agreed, frowning as he pointed to my glass, encouraging me to drink. "Although, I'm confused about something. You're using me as bait, but you also mentioned Gregory. Why would Parker care about Gregory?"

Carlos looked at me thoughtfully. "My guess is that Parker has figured out by now that Gregory works for me."

Confused, I didn't respond. Gregory said that Carlos was not D.E.A. Which would mean that Gregory wasn't either, if he had been working for Carlos. My head began to pound.

"Think, Meredith," Carlos said. "How can Parker get what he wants, and I get what I want, which is him?"

I shrugged my shoulders, sipping my glass of water. The 'couples' around us were ordering off a menu and drinking wine. Perhaps they saw this as time off, and didn't expect much action. I took comfort in that. They didn't seem disturbed with the activity going on in the garden behind them; I saw two gardeners trimming the lavender plants, including the older man with the straw hat. No wonder the place looked like the Garden of Eden.

"I am 'producing' an occasion, you're absolutely right about that, Meredith," Carlos said, regaining my attention. "I'm making it easy, and painless, for Parker to get his way, and for me to get mine."

I wanted to understand what the hell Carlos was saying, but I felt like a 7-year-old in school who just couldn't get her time tables. He sat back, shaking his head as if he was disappointed in me. Then he waved one of the bodyguards over and whispered in his ear. The man reached into the pocket of his jacket and handed something to Carlos.

"You don't mind if I smoke, do you love?" Carlos asked, lighting up a cigar without waiting for my answer.

I closed my eyes and shook my head. Seeing the cigar brought me back to Cambridge and how I first met Carlos, at Telford's Pipe Shop. And then back to Barbara and Roger's yacht, with the boxes of cigars rolling along the floor during the storm.

"Do I need to put it more succinctly?" Carlos asked, pulling me back to the present.

I just stared at him.

The cigar! I kept repeating to myself. It's the cigar!

CHAPTER FORTY-THREE

We were interrupted when the waiter approached, a long lean man in his fifties with a diamond earring on his left ear and a haircut so short it hurt my scalp. I wondered where he came from. The guy did not look like one of Carlos' minions.

Carlos read my mind. "My chef, Jorge. He's been with me for several years. I did him a favor once, and he constantly repays me with superb food."

Jorge bowed. "May I tell you the specials tonight?"

I shrugged. As if I'd taste a bite of anything. Then I waved my hand in front of me as if to disperse the smoke from Carlos' cigar.

Carlos took a drag, then replied for both of us. "Of course."

"First, the catch of the day is fresh mahi mahi sautéed in lemon-ginger and covered lightly with a cornflake and parmesan crust, placed on top of a bed of collared greens. Mashed yellow squash and crisp new potatoes accompany the dish."

I sniffed.

"Meredith?" Carlos said in a question. "Is there a problem?"

"Cornflakes?" I asked. "As in Kellogg's cornflakes? I don't want my mahi mahi covered with cornflakes!"

Carlos sent me a warning glare and said to Jorge. "Sounds delicious to me. Anything else?"

Jorge looked at me as if I might bite him. Then he cleared his throat. "For our second selection, may I recommend the tender flank steak and carmelized Vidalia onions covered with a mushroom and truffle gravy. Asparagus spears complement the dish."

I looked at Jorge in pretend awe. "Truffle gravy? Truffles? Are there pigs on this island?" I leaned back in my chair and looked at Carlos, satisfied that I'd just annoyed the hell out of him.

"Those selections are unsatisfactory," I continued. "Any others?"

"Not funny, Meredith. You seem to be forgetting that you're my guest. Jorge, why don't you give me the steak, and the grumpy one here the mahi mahi." As the chef took a step back, Carlos added, "Oh, and I'll have another glass of the cabernet. Superb." Jorge smiled as if he'd plucked and stomped the grapes himself.

"You seem very sure of yourself," I commented, wanting to continue the conversation we'd started before Jorge arrived. I badly wanted Carlos to be right, that Parker would come to get me out of here. But on the other hand, I didn't want Parker to fall for this 'diplomatic' trap. "You're sure that Parker will show up tonight?"

"Oh, not only that." Fortunately Carlos seemed to have forgotten my bad manners. He looked at his cigar lovingly, like a boy with a favorite toy. "He knows that if he joins us this evening in a civilized performance, you will be allowed to return to your life immediately."

I felt a rush of relief, quickly followed by extreme anxiety. "How does he know that?"

Carlos shook his head as if I were an errant student. "It's just the way things are done, Meredith. Negotiation goes a long way to preventing violence."

I crossed my legs languidly, belying my deep sense of impending disaster. Parker wouldn't just saunter into this garden patio and sit down with me and Carlos. He wouldn't trust Carlos. So why should I?

I breathed in and out, trying to hide my fear. As Jorge placed a crystal dish of shrimp cocktail on the middle of our table, I looked past the patio and armed guards toward the ocean. The sea looked calm and inviting in the dusky light. The soothing sounds of the surf reached us on the patio, and closing my eyes, I invited the soft, repetitive sea murmur to enter my mind.

My eyes popped open when I felt Carlos' hand on my lap. He had moved his chair closer to mine, and his lips tickled my hair as he whispered in my ear. "So let's give Parker a reason to make his appearance sooner rather than later."

I gasped, arms out to push Carlos away.

He grabbed them with his hands as if to embrace me. "Don't, Meredith." The tone of his voice stopped me.

For a moment I had an acute awareness of how we looked, embracing at a candlelit table in the early twilight of a Caribbean nightmare. A person watching would see a romance, with the silhouette of a seductive man leaning over a woman, whispering his undying love.

"I won't stop at murder," Carlos hissed in my ear as I turned my head away. I wished I could shout for help, but I knew I had to go along with the charade. "Don't you think for one instant that I won't sacrifice you, or anyone else on this island, to get my man. Your man," Carlos sneered. He opened his mouth to say more, but the silverware started to roll across the table.

The crash of the shrimp plate falling onto the stone patio caused him to jump away from me. The table shook so hard it seemed to be doing a macabre dance.

Earthquake, I thought immediately, feeling the ground beneath me roil from one side to the other. The sun still softly illuminated the patio, so I had a clear view of the stone floor cracking like ice on a pond – one rip led to another and then another. Lizards scrambled out of their hiding places, leaping between the cracks. The sound of more plates breaking as they fell off trembling tables couldn't mask the thunderous noise from below us.

Then the screams began. Sharp, exclamatory screams. Screams that didn't sound like surprise or shock. Screams that sounded like murder.

CHAPTER FORTY-FOUR

On my left, three bodyguards went down as if in a faint. What? Carlos had grabbed me at the first indication of the earthquake. His fingers dug into my arm, and his face was as intent as a cheetah on the prowl. We both stood up as he snarled, "don't move." The earth moaned, and I lost balance at yet another rocky movement beneath my feet.

Then I laughed.

I laughed! I was stuck with this egomaniacal savage in a tropical land in the midst of an earthquake, and I laughed. I knew then that I was way beyond the Meredith Powers that I had once been, the Merry who loved to clean house on the weekends, cook spaghetti on Friday nights, and drive her car too fast. No, the Merry who worried if her hair was too long, her clothes too tight, and her new boyfriend too dull now seemed like a mirage to me, like a woman who lived long long ago in a faraway land.

Carlos slapped me. "Get a grip." Then he let me go and walked a few feet away, staring at the two men and one woman knocked flat on the ground, unmoving. He brandished a gun, pointing it to the west, and then the east. He had to be thinking what I had begun to surmise. That was no earthquake.

My cheek stung from his slap. My laughter had stopped, but an urge to flee took over. Carlos kept his eyes on me as he surveyed the property, swinging the gun my way every few seconds. I didn't budge. I feared that one tiny move would make him shoot me dead.

I read once that after an earthquake, everything becomes still and silent. The opposite was true here. The island became noisy: muted thumps, the thrashing of palm leaves waving against each other, a humming sound like that of a giant electric lawn mower gone wild. What was going on?

And then everything happened at once. A sound like a speeding arrow whizzed past me. Carlos slumped to the ground just as I saw the gardener with the straw hat lunge toward the patio. I screamed and ran away as fast as I could. My legs seemed stuck in concrete, and I was breathing hard, as if I'd just finished the 100-yard dash.

Someone grabbed me by the ankle, and I fell hard on my knees. "Let me go!" I yelled. Instead, I was pushed into the warm ground. I tasted sand as I twisted to get away. A straw hat obscured my view of the heavy form on top of me.

Then, the voice I most wanted to hear said, "Merry, it's me."

CHAPTER FORTY-FIVE

His grip loosened, and I turned over on the ground to look at him. The hat had fallen off, and his disheveled hair framed a half-crazed face, intent blue eyes beseeching me not to scream. I clamped down the exclamation in my throat and croaked, "Parker."

He squeezed my arm. "We have to get out of here, fast."

I stood up and realized that my knees had become butter. Half carrying me, Parker raced us past the patio and across the sand. Something wet kept hitting my cheeks, and finally I realized it was my own tears, streaming down like a waterfall. I ignored them and ran blindly, hip to hip with Parker, trying not to slow down.

"Here!" Parker pushed me up into a dirty Jeep while frantically fumbling for the keys in his pocket. I sat up straight looking through the filthy front window, fists clenched in my lap. Parker jammed the keys into the ignition; the engine coughed, burped, then started up.

My head swam in questions and confusion.

Parker found me.

Was Carlos alive? Where was Gregory? How could we get off this island?

I turned and looked behind me. The smoke and chaos were moving away from us. I inspected the man beside me, foot pressed down on the accelerator, eyes looking through the rearview mirror.

"Parker."

He looked at me with his little boy expression that made my heart somersault. "Meredith."

I released a sound that was a mixture of wail and whoop, a noise that began in the bottom of my stomach, then up to the chest region, where the sound grew coarser, on to the esophagus, where I choked on it and ended with a quick sob.

Parker drew me close to him, wrapping his arm around me tightly while his left hand steered.

"Meredith," he said again, so softly that his breath tickled my ear.

My eyes closed for a second, then opened to see what was rubbing against my toes. The straw hat. I moved away, slowly putting two and two together.

"You were the gardener?" I asked.

Parker nodded as he put both hands back on the wheel, moving the Jeep off the sand and onto a semi-paved road that led us toward an expanse of trees and marshland.

"I never guessed. He, I mean you, looked so old and weary. So you saw me...?"

"Oh, yeah. Once I got on the island. But wait. Give me a few minutes."

The Jeep sped over the bumpy dirt road, bouncing us so hard my rear end hurt. I turned and looked behind us. Miraculously, no one was following. We were making tracks, as Parker liked to say, the compound at our backs, scrub brush and trees now all around us.

I looked down at myself, pulling my sundress over my bloody knees. What a mess. The dress was ripped at the hem, and my legs and arms were covered in sand and dirt. I wiped some of it off and checked the pearls at my neck. Still there.

Parker slowed down, and the jostling of my joints diminished. I could hear the sweet sound of birds, as well as the peeping of frogs.

"Much better," I noted. "But is it okay? Aren't you worried that someone will find us?" The Jeep had stopped on the side of the road, and Parker turned to look at me.

"We're fine, duchess," he replied. "I think you need time to decompress. Are you okay? You look...well," he stopped as he surveyed me, from top to bottom. "You look absolutely gorgeous."

I snorted. "Right. You, on the other hand, have dirt all over your face. Your eyebrows are singed, and your hair looks hurricane-blown."

"Honest, as always," Parker commented with a smile.

I didn't smile back. "What the hell happened? How did this happen? You left, saying all these enigmatic things about going in hiding and a bad guy after you. I thought I'd never see you again." I stopped, not wanting Parker to hear the emotion in my voice. He picked up my hand and squeezed it. "Then I continued on with my life, or I tried to, until I was kidnapped by that psychopath."

Parker responded grimly, "Carlos is no psychopath. He's smart, and he's smooth, and he knows exactly what he's doing."

I thought of the way Carlos kissed me my first night on this island, and then my attempt to seduce him. "Did you know he wanted you to think that we were a couple? That we..."

Parker slammed his hand on the steering wheel. "That asshole. I wanted to kill him the moment I found you here. Then when I saw him mauling you – you don't know how hard it was for me to wait until I was sure I could get you out of here."

"Who the hell is he? He kept telling me he was with the D.E.A., and that you had become one of the bad guys, and that they needed me to woo you back, to catch you before you killed any more people, and that..."

"Whoa. Calm down. Stop and take a deep breath."

I tamped down my annoyance. Take a deep breath, my ass. I had too many questions to stop and meditate, for God's sake. But Parker looked at me as if scrutinizing a tiger that had just been allowed out of its cage. I breathed in deeply, held my breath to the count of five, then breathed out.

"So, who is Carlos?" I asked.

"The man who wants to kill me."

"Because...?"

"Remember when I talked to you at Antonio's about the good 'catch' I made?"

I thought back to that lunch, which seemed like years ago, but was less than two weeks before. "Yes. You said it would have been a successful operation, but you didn't get the main guy."

"Right. I told you that he got away, and he now knew that I was a D.E.A. agent. My cover was blown. So I had to disappear."

"You're good at that," I interjected.

Parker sighed and looked out the window. I wondered why he didn't seem more worried that we'd be found. The road did look deserted, but still, the resort couldn't be more than five miles away.

"Carlos is that man," Parker said quietly.

My eyes widened. "He's the man who escaped from the botched operation? The man who's after you?"

A crease formed between Parker's eyebrows. "It wasn't a 'botched' operation. We secured tons of methamphetamine. We found out that they were shipping the drug into the U.S., and that the money they made from those sales went to a terrorist organization."

Terrorists. Oh, damn. Finally, my thoughts were coming together. Carlos and the terrorists. Parker and his half-successful operation. The shipment of methamphetamine.

"But we still haven't figured out how they're getting the meth into the U.S.," he continued.

Parker began to drive the Jeep again as my mind swerved. "Where are we going?"

He looked at me, surprised. "We're getting you off this island. You've got a lot of people waiting for you back on St. Thomas."

I ignored his comment. "Look, I'm sure you have a plan. But you're going to have to change it."

"Not on my life, Meredith. Your dad would kill me," he paused. "And your mom would torture me first."

"My dad? My mom?" I had almost forgotten that my father had planned to meet me on St. Thomas, so I could meet his secret someone. How my mom had gotten into the picture, I could only guess. I groaned. "They'll have to wait. Parker, we have to go back."

"What?" Parker asked. The Jeep's coughing fits had eaten up my words.

"WE HAVE TO GO BACK!"

"Exactly. There's a sea plane waiting for us at...."

"No! We have to go back to the resort. Now."

Parker put both hands on the wheel and slowed down. "Why?"

"Two journalists were kidnapped. Carlos is holding the two men back there."

Parker sat up straighter, the Jeep slowing down even more. "You saw them?"

"No, Gregory told me about them."

"Gregory." Parker said the name as if he was saying, "Gangrene."

"Yes! You won't believe it, but Gregory was there. He works for Carlos, or did. I still don't know what happened, but Carlos beat him up and...."

"I know Gregory was there." By now Parker had stopped the Jeep.

"You do?"

"Yes. He helped me with the escape."

"He did?"

Slowly, the Jeep made a ninety degree turn. "Tell me about the reporters."

"Gregory said they were kidnapped because they figured out a link between drugs being sold in the U.S. and a terrorist organization."

"Oh, shit."

"Two men. I guess they found out that the D.E.A. had been secretly monitoring this activity?"

Parker slammed his hand on the steering wheel again. "That's why Gregory told me to just worry about you, and he'd stay to clean up. I knew he had something else up his sleeve, damn him."

I looked at Parker, nonplussed. "You mean Gregory is still back there? 'Cleaning up'?

Parker nodded his head.

This last news made no sense to me. Parker and Gregory were enemies. More questions rose to the surface, like lava in an active volcano.

"How did you make the earth shake? Why'd those agents suddenly collapse? Did you kill Carlos? Why did..."

"Okay, okay. Now I know you're feeling better. One question at a time." The Jeep was traveling faster now, toward the place I least wanted to see.

Parker was right. I felt like myself again, first time in days. My mind was swirling with a hundred questions. I had to pick one to start.

"Why did you trust Gregory to help rescue me? He worked for Carlos." Amazed at my selection, I held my breath for Parker's answer. He looked straight ahead, looking strong and confident at the same time, impressive considering how the Jeep joggled us like dice in a poker game.

"Gregory is one of us," he said.

"One of whom?" I asked.

"He's F.B.I."

CHAPTER FORTY-SIX

I let out a sound between a snort and a gag as the Jeep bounced its way back to the resort. "Gregory worked for Carlos. He pretended he was an accountant. I heard him tell Carlos that you caught him doing something, something to do with drugs. Gregory hates you and to get back at you, worked for Carlos."

"Yeah, that was his cover." Parker kept his eyes trained on the road as if he had to drive between two lines. Or as if he had to watch for a pothole that might explode.

"His cover?" Thoughts swirled in my brain, and although my head ached, I didn't feel a migraine threatening to take over. Why not? Was I experiencing a health miracle while simultaneously finding out that nothing, and I mean nothing, was as it seemed?

"Merry, this gets complicated. We don't have time for explanations now. I'll make it short. Gregory is an F.B.I. agent who's been undercover, working for Carlos."

I opened my mouth.

"No, I didn't know him," he continued, reading my mind. "We worked in two separate locations. I had been Carlos' go-to guy in Columbia, Gregory in the U.S. Like I said, it's complicated."

"Complicated doesn't say the half of it," I muttered. Gregory, sweet boring Gregory, was an F.B.I. agent. Damn. Back in Boston, working undercover with Carlos, Gregory had to get close to me, pretend he liked me, so Carlos could find Parker. Triple damn. But then I thought of something. "But why didn't Gregory tell you who he was when you came looking for me? Why didn't he warn you what Carlos was doing?"

Parker's lips pressed together tightly. "Well, he, um, tried to talk to me, to reach me, but I was pretty unreachable, and even when he succeeded, I didn't believe him."

"You didn't believe Gregory was F.B.I.? Couldn't you have called their headquarters or whatever you call it, and asked them?"

Parker shook his head. "Oh, I realized he was F.B.I. I didn't believe him when he said he hadn't put you in any danger. First, he lied to get close to you; second, he used you to find me. Stupid. Wrong."

I twisted angrily in my seat. "You knew then that Gregory was F.B.I.? Why didn't you tell me?"

Parker moved his hand off the wheel and tried to touch my arm, but I flicked it off. "Merry, I couldn't blow his cover. I couldn't. But I did try to warn you about him."

The Jeep hit a hole and we rocked inside, bumping shoulders. I was so angry I wanted to make him stop and let me out. But that was impossible as we raced back to the resort. I thought, instead, about last week, when Parker told me to watch out for Gregory. I put my head in my hands and shook it back and forth.

Parker drove aggressively, remaining mute.

I removed my hands at the smell of smoke. The resort was probably a mile ahead, but the wind blew gray clouds toward us, darkening the sky even more as the sun continued its descent. "The place is on fire?" I asked.

"Most likely. I set off a bomb near the furnace. I picked a place that would make the most impact, and hurt as few people as possible. Thanks to Gregory, I knew the furnace was on the lower left side, away from the maids' quarters."

"But how about the bodyguards – and Carlos?"

"We hit them with darts."

I gasped.

"The darts were filled with a sleeping agent. Gregory's job was to secure them while we waited for back up. My job was to get you out of there. But I didn't know about the reporters. That complicates things."

The intense expression on Parker's face made me so scared I felt faint. This must be what he was like at work. I mean, work-work, when he wasn't off rescuing me and hiding his identity from the bad guys.

"You think...?"

"I think Gregory may have bitten more than he can chew. If I'd known he had to rescue two civilians, I'd never..." Then he stopped.

"You'd never what?" I asked.

"I'd never agree to rescue you and let him do the rest. That's probably why he didn't tell me. He was too concerned about saving your life."

Parker turned his head and looked at me then, full force. "Exactly what is your relationship with Gregory, Merry?"

~~~~~~~~~~~~~~~~~~~~~~~~~~~~~~~~~~

As he asked the question, more smoke curled toward us from the resort, making it difficult to see ahead. Then a thunderous thump thump thump persuaded me to look overhead. A helicoptor.

I couldn't have answered Parker's question over the cacophony of sound if I'd wanted to, and believe me, I didn't want to.

"Who's that?" I pointed to the sky and screamed the question so he could hear me.

"The Feds. I hope to God Gregory got out of there."

"Why?" I figured rescue was a good thing.

"Because he still needs to work undercover, that's why." Parker's tone was succinct and surly. I was about to retort, but then I saw the figures limping toward us. Parker obviously saw them too; he slowed down and placed his arm across my body protectively. "Don't leave the car," he commanded as he pulled on the emergency brake and jumped out.

Two men clung to the taller man in the middle as he helped them along. As a breeze blew the thick gray smoke away, I recognized the tall one.

Gregory.

CHAPTER FORTY-SEVEN

I moved without thinking, jumping out of the Jeep. By the time I reached the men, Parker was practically carrying one, and Gregory held the other's arm as he limped along. The faces of the two reporters looked scorched, and angry red welts were etched across their cheeks and on their arms.

I stood on the other side of the man Gregory was helping and we walked quickly back toward the Jeep. Parker gently placed the man he held into the back, and the other man joined him. They both looked at us with grateful expressions, but neither spoke a word.

Parker broke the silence. He turned toward Gregory. "Okay, now get back there. You should make it in time."

"In time for what?" I asked, bewildered. "Aren't we driving these men to a clinic or something?"

"They'll get better, faster treatment if we get them on the helicopter," Parker replied. "But before the chopper lands, Gregory needs to get back to the resort." He eyed Gregory with distrust.

"I'm going," Gregory said. "Don't worry; those darts had enough drugs in them to keep those guys asleep for awhile."

"How many?" Parker asked.

"Seven. Including Carlos and the three guards in the patio."

"Any one down?"

"One fatality." Gregory continued his report to Parker. "The bodyguard who found you right after the bomb ignited. I got the prison guards and the Browning guy."

"Roger," Parker stated.

"That's what I said, Roger Browning."

I felt my head turn from one man to the other during the question and answer session. They seemed to have forgotten I was standing there.

"What happened to the chef, Jorge, and his help? And how about the maid, Solana?" I asked, looking at Gregory. "The one you promised to help."

"We got them out before the bomb exploded. They're hidden in the gardener's shed. They'll be fine." Parker turned back to face Gregory. "Thanks for your help. Now go."

"But where is he going?" I asked. "Will someone please tell me what's happening?" I stamped my foot, not an act of a rational adult, but by now I was beyond peeved. We'd rescued the reporters, the Feds were here to clean up, and we all could now breathe a sigh of relief and get back to someplace safe. Like Boston. Now.

Gregory put his hands on my shoulders. "I need to go back and get 'arrested,' along with Carlos and the rest of his gang. The hope is that while we're all incarcerated, I may learn more about their operation." He leaned over and kissed me on the lips.

"Leave her alone!" Parker's face twisted in anger as he pulled Gregory away from me.

Gregory spun away from Parker; I thought he was going to hit him. Instead, he smiled his accountant's smile, the one that looked like a meek and mild Clark Kent. I almost expected him to whip out his wire-rimmed glasses from the torn pocket of his jeans. But he turned and ran toward the resort.

Parker, still in 'he-man' mode, instructed, "Merry, stay here with the reporters. The helicopter will land in a minute."

"Where are you going?" I asked. I didn't want him to follow Gregory. "You should stay here with us."

"I've got to make it look like Gregory tried to fight me," Parker explained.

"What are you going to do?" I asked, suspicious.

"I'm going to tie him up like Carlos and the rest of his buddies," Parker said impatiently. "Stay." And then he ran after Gregory.

Stay. Did Parker think I was a well-trained dog? I hopped into the front seat of the Jeep and looked back over at the two reporters. They were half asleep. I faced front again, my mind whirring like the blades of the helicopter above.

Something kept nagging me. Something that Gregory said. Parker, too. Gregory had to stay undercover so he could get arrested and jailed with Carlos. Gregory was hoping to find out – what? How the drugs were being transported into the U.S.?

"I'll be right back," I shouted to the two men as I jumped out of the Jeep. One of them shook his head; I don't think the other one even heard me as I turned and raced after Parker and Gregory.

CHAPTER FORTY-EIGHT

My lungs labored with the exertion of running in smoky air. My ankle twisted as I tried to sprint wearing my dressy sandals, appropriate for a sunset dinner, not for a race on sand. I lifted one foot at a time and kicked off each shoe.

I caught a glimpse of Parker as he entered the resort. The air cleared once I was inside, and the hallway was bright from fluorescent lighting. Did Parker take the stairs up or down? I listened for footsteps. Down.

I walked noiselessly down the stairs, my still-sandy feet cold on the smooth stairs. Not a body was in sight, and the hallway was eerily silent. Parker and

Gregory, Carlos and his men, had to be somewhere close by, but where? I continued to walk swiftly, turning my head behind me every few steps.

The sound of fist hitting flesh stopped me, and I drew in a shocked breath. Now what? I turned the corner and entered the room that had once been Gregory's prison. There he stood against the wall as Parker punched him in the face.

"What the hell are you doing?" I asked, shocked.

Both of them looked at me angrily. "Quiet," they hissed simultaneously.

Parker strode over and grabbed one of my elbows. "I told you to stay by the Jeep. Damn you, Meredith. Don't you know how dangerous this is?" He stopped himself as if to calm down, then said with more control, "Merry, I'm trying to get you away from all this. Why did you follow me?"

I ignored him as I looked at Gregory's bleeding face. The bruises from his earlier run in with the prison guards had turned deep purple. "Gregory, what ...?"

He sat down on the small bench and looked over at Parker. "Why don't you explain it to her."

Parker closed his mouth as if he didn't want to say anything. He looked at Gregory, then looked back at me. "We have to make it look like Gregory put up a fight. Now I'm going to tie him up and ..."

"And you have to quickly bind up the ones I didn't have time for right after the explosion," Gregory interrupted. "I got them with the dart gun, but didn't stick around. I needed to get the reporters out before the smoke got too thick."

Parker stared at Gregory unhappily. "So I need to tie up Gregory and dump him next to Carlos and his men; when they revive, they'll figure he's in the same shape they are. The Feds will come in and take them all away."

"Wrong," I responded.

Both men looked at me, speechless.

"I don't think it's a good idea," I continued. "Carlos already doesn't trust Gregory. Why else would he beat him up and imprison him, for heaven's sake?" I shook my head. "Anyway, you should be talking to Roger, not Carlos."

"Roger?" Gregory said, his voice lifting as he got to the second syllable.

"Yes, Roger," I confirmed. "You're both too tired to think straight. Haven't you wondered how Roger fits into the equation?"

Parker sat down on the bench next to Gregory. The two men balanced each end – Gregory with his blonde hair and russet eyes, Parker brown-haired and blue-eyed. Two ends on a seesaw.

"Go on," Parker said. "But quickly."

"Roger wasn't a part of Carlos' operation. I mean, he wasn't a drug dealer or thug. He was Carlos' means of transportation."

A pair of brown eyes and a pair of blue stared up at me with sudden understanding.

"The yacht," Gregory whispered.

"The yacht," Parker echoed softly.

"And one more thing," I added, trying not to be smug. "The drugs were hidden in the cigars."

CHAPTER FORTY-NINE

Before either man could react, a bullet sprayed past me and lodged into the wall behind Gregory.

"Down!" Parker shouted.

I dove onto the concrete floor, feeling my knees scrape and bleed again. A figure fell on top of me. Parker? Gregory? Another shot rang out, the sound vibrating in my body. I heard it reach its target with a muted thud. Then a moan.

Parker? Gregory?

I tried to stand up, panicked at the thought of losing one. "Get down," someone hissed as I was pulled back onto the hard floor. That sounded like Parker.

Then silence. No one was moving. No one was breathing. No one said a word.

I couldn't stand it. "Who's hurt?" I called out.

Nothing.

"Parker?"

"I'm fine," came the muffled reply from the body on top of me.

"Gregory?"

"Yeah, I'm okay," he said. Then I heard the rustle of material as he moved.

"So who was hit?"

Parker got off me, still keeping a hand on my back so I had to remain down. But I raised my head enough to see him signal something to Gregory, who rushed out of the room. Then Parker helped me up. I looked around. A hole in the wall. A spot of blood on the floor.

"Who?" I began.

"Carlos," Parker explained. "I shot him in the leg. Gregory will find him."

"He couldn't have gone far," I agreed. Guns. I hadn't thought of the fact that both Gregory and Parker would have them, hidden, probably in their pants or socks or wherever secret agent macho men hid their weapons.

I sank to the floor. Suddenly, my body began to quiver.

"You okay?" Parker asked, looking concerned. I think he realized as soon as he asked that it was a dumb question.

More shots and shouts caused me to stand up fast.

"Don't worry, Merry. That's the FBI." Parker hugged me close to him. "I'm guessing they found Carlos."

The warmth of his chest soothed me almost as much as the touch of his strong legs against my trembling ones. But we pulled apart quickly when a cadre of vest-wearing men jumped into the room, rifles aimed at us.

"Hands up," one of them barked. We both shot our arms up over our heads.

"Parker Webb, D.E.A.," Parker said calmly.

A solid-looking man in his forties, lean and mean-looking, strode toward us. "Right. According to everyone we've seen so far, you all are D.E.A. Where are the bad guys?"

I took a step forward. "Are you being sarcastic? Because if so, it's not appropriate. I've been held here against my will for days. I'd be happy to point out to you who's F.B.I., D.E.A., and the 'bad guys,' as you put it."

"Meredith Powers," the man replied, walking over to me swiftly and putting out his hand for me to shake. "Lieutenant Henry Jamison. Sorry, yes, I was being sarcastic." He did look chagrinned, as he stole a glance at Parker. "Mr. Webb's reputation has preceded him. Just trying to do everything by the book."

Parker smiled tightly. "Meredith, we're in safe hands now. Lieutenant, Gregory Dunne left here chasing a wounded Carlos Medina. Have you found them?"

The Lieutenant nodded. "Everyone should be secure by now, sir. Follow me."

~~~~~~~~~~~~~~~~~~~~~~~~~~~~~~~~~~~

The scene on the patio was almost comical. With a romantic backlight of the six torches, dining chairs had been lined up on one side, and Carlos and his bodyguards, Roger, and Jorge and his cooks, sat facing front, looking beleaguered and angry. Jorge kept insisting that he was a "chef, God damn it, not a drug runner." Roger repeated non-stop, "I must see my lawyer. I must see my lawyer." The bodyguards maintained that their D.E.A. credentials were in the resort office, and their badges were legit. Carlos was the only one who remained silent, blood dripping down a leg that was loosely bandaged.

I sidled over to Gregory, whispering, "I thought you had Carlos drugged and secured."

Gregory looked over at Parker, who had joined us. "Carlos is one of the men I didn't have time to tie up. But I thought he'd stay put. He was nearly comatose when I ran out of there with the reporters."

I nodded. "Carlos has a low reaction to drugs. He recovers quickly."

Gregory and Parker looked at me quizzically.

"Long story," I said. Then I walked over to Roger. There was no time like the present to get some questions answered.

"Ma'am, stay away from the prisoners," Lieutenant Jamison barked.

I ignored him, but I saw the Lieutenant give Parker a warning look.

Parker explained. "We're not allowed to talk to the prisoners, Meredith."

"Maybe you're not," I answered, continuing my stroll toward Roger. When I stood just a few feet away from Barbara's husband, I gave him what Shannon called my 'Power Stare,' disapproving and disdaining at the same time. "So tell me, Rog. How'd you get involved with Carlos?"

Roger shrugged and turned his face away from me. "I need to see my lawyer."

"Uh huh," I said. "You know what? I never took you for a bad guy. I mean, you were so nice to me on the yacht. I usually don't misjudge people. Yet, you made it possible for Carlos to kidnap me."

"Ms. Powers...." The Lieutenant warned. "Stop!"

But Roger turned and looked at me. "I never knew he was going to do that," he began. "I never would have..."

"Shut up!" Carlos growled.

"You never would have what?" I asked, but Roger didn't respond. I continued, "Carlos was blackmailing you, wasn't he?"

Roger's face flooded with color. "How did you know?"

"I said shut up!" Carlos stood, blood still dripping down his leg, and took a menacing step toward Roger.

Parker and Gregory pushed Carlos back down on his chair, picked it up, and moved him to the other side of the patio.

Roger looked at his feet. "I'm really sorry, Meredith. You're a nice girl. I didn't know Carlos was going to kidnap you. He told me I just needed to convince Barbara to get you to the yacht, to work on her book. He said he just needed you out of the way in Boston."

"Well, he lied," I said.

Roger nodded. "But I didn't have a choice anyway. He found out, well, he said that if I didn't transport his cargo, he'd report me to the S.E.C."

Roger was sweating so much his shirt was soaked. Droplets of perspiration dripped down his face and into his collar. The Lieutenant was standing by me now, listening.

"The Securities Exchange Commission? Wow. That was a big threat, huh?" I was trying not to be sarcastic, but losing the battle. "The S.E.C. regulates the stock market, right? Their job is to prevent corporate abuses."

"I know what the S.E.C. is," Roger growled.

"Of course you do." I saw Lieutenant Jamison roll his eyes. At least he wasn't preventing me from grilling Roger. "You had to transport Carlos' cargo so he wouldn't tell the S.E.C. about your illegal activities with the stock market. And the cargo, of course, was cigars."

Roger looked surprised that I had figured it out.

"How many times did you have to take that trip, from St. Thomas to Miami?" I continued.

"It wasn't just me!" Roger blurted out, as if that made him less responsible. "Carlos blackmailed a bunch of us. You met some of them at the party."

"The St. Thomas group?" I asked, amazed. "You mean those rich guys who you said had all 'made it'?"

"Ms. Powers," the Lieutenant said in a warning tone.

I was about to respond, but I heard a commotion above us. Another helicopter.

"Time to get everyone out of here," Jamison shouted as the copter landed near the first one.

"None too soon," I shouted back. I turned to look for Parker and Gregory.

But they were gone.

CHAPTER FIFTY

The journalists had already been helped into the first helicopter as I watched the prisoners lined up, handcuffed, and marched to the second one. Unfortunately, they didn't all fit, so I ended up flying in the first helicopter with Lieutenant Jamison on one side of me, and Carlos directly across from me. Staring straight ahead and looking into those black gleaming eyes sickened me. Staring out the window as we flew over islands and ocean frightened me. By now the sun had vanished and night descended quickly. We flew over small islands that looked like crouching beasts surrounded by dark water.

I tried to look at a neutral spot out the window, hoping my queasy stomach would settle if I found a focal point. But the landscape of water and land kept moving up and down, over and around, until finally I pleaded for an airsick bag.

I discovered that military airplanes and helicopters don't have airsick bags. I supposed military people didn't experience motion sickness. The uniformed agent sitting next to Carlos generously offered me his hat. Right in the nick of time.

Carlos shook his head in mock sympathy. "Reminds me of our first time together," he shouted, "in the boat."

I gagged as Jamison yelled to him, "Shut up."

Thankfully the rest of the ride was conversation-free.

I held onto the hat as if it were a life preserver. When we finally landed in St. Thomas, I wanted to kiss the tarmac. But Jamison had other plans.

"I know your family is waiting to see you," he said after we raced away from the helicopters and entered a long black car. Carlos and the rest of his entourage were pushed into large unmarked vans, the journalists sent to the hospital by ambulance. "But we must debrief you first."

"Debrief me?" My immediate image was of stripping off my dirty, grubby sundress and donning military-issue slacks and blouse. But the image changed as soon as I saw the small, bald-headed man sitting in the back of the stretch.

He nodded hello as if we were back at an embassy party in Washington, D.C.

"Ms. Powers. How do you do? You may not remember me. I'm..."

"Floyd Denton," I finished for him.

"Yes, ma'am."

"We met several years ago. You're with U.S. Customs. But how did you get here so fast?"

Denton smiled, an act his facial muscles seemed unaccustomed to. "We knew Parker and Gregory were closing in on Medina. Between the two of them, I laid odds on them getting him into custody. They did their job. Now I have to do mine."

"Some job," I retorted.

"What do you mean?" Denton asked. His head shone with sweat despite the air-conditioned vehicle.

I just shook my head in answer.

"We need to know everything: when you first saw Carlos; what Roger and Barbara Browning's involvement was; the details of your kidnapping; what Carlos told you ..."

"Okay, okay, I get it." I stared ahead, Denton on my right side, Jamison sitting across from him. The car sped down the same streets I had walked a week ago. I gazed out the window. "Are we going to the police station?"

Lieutenant Jamison looked at me funny. "Yes, ma'am. Why? Have you been there before?"

I didn't answer. I wished I could cross my arms, blink my eyes, and find myself back in Boston, with the debriefing behind me, my life ahead of me. That thought made me ask the next question. "Where's Parker? And Gregory? What about their debriefing?"

Denton squirmed uncomfortably in his seat. "We still don't know where they are," he finally admitted.

~~~~~~~~~~~~~~~~~~~~~~~~~~~~

We walked through the entryway of the police station, up the stairs, past the row of desks where I had met Officer Flores. Then we continued to a larger hallway leading to more rooms. I felt like I was wading against a current, legs straining through thick invisible mud. The police officers stared at me as I marched alongside Jamison and Denton. Sound stopped, except for the ticking of a large clock hanging on the wall. Tick tock. Tick Tock.

Until we entered a large white-walled room.

"Meredith!" A woman's voice screamed my name, and she bounded toward me, red hair flying in all directions.

"Shannon?"

"Oh, honey." My mother strode over more sedately, moving Shannon aside while she hugged me tightly. "We were so worried." She looked over at the man standing next to her. Dad!

"Sweetie." My dad had tears in his eyes.

I noticed the big shape standing outside of the circle, smiling and nodding his head toward me. "Donald!" Then I turned toward Jamison. "Where did they... How did you..."

Jamison laughed. "These people have been on our case since you disappeared. And I mean on our case. I've had a dozen conversations with your dad. Your mom, well, she doesn't take 'no' for an answer."

"But..." I turned to Shannon. "How did you get here so fast? Parker just rescued me, and..."

"Oh, we've been here for two days," Shannon answered. "But forget the questions. We're here. You're here. Thank God!" She squeezed my arm and stared at my dad, as if expecting him to do something.

Instead, mom spoke up. "You're a mess."

"Oh lord." I patted my hair and glanced down at my torn dress. At least I wasn't holding the hat that got me through the helicopter ride.

"You look absolutely wonderful," Dad announced. "Merry, we have been so worried. We thought...," his voice broke, and he looked down at his shoes. Shannon moved over to him and held his hand. What was that all about?

As if in reaction, Donald joined Mom, holding her hand.

"We were all scared silly," Mom said. "What you've gone through is inexcusable. Donald has secured a lawyer for you. He'll be here in a few hours. You're not to say a word until he arrives."

I could see Jamison stiffen in his starched uniform.

"Mom. Donald. Thank you. But that won't be necessary. I'm going to spend a little time with Lieutenant Jamison and Mr. Denton ...after I clean up, that is... and then we'll have lots of time to talk."

Mom examined the diamond watch on her wrist. "Lieutenant, we'll give you thirty minutes with Meredith. Then she's ours."

I had to hand it to her. She had guts. Jamison nodded his head as if he'd just received an order from the attorney general.

"Yes, ma'am. Now if you will excuse us," the Lieutenant began. But a knock at the door brought in a police officer. Jamison turned: "What is it?"

"Excuse me, sir. A woman is here claiming she's Carlos Medina's lawyer."

"Damn," Jamison said loudly. He glanced at Denton, who just nodded noncommittally, and then barked. "Tell her I'll be there in a minute."

"No, sir. I mean, yes, sir, but she followed me and..."

A large woman wearing a conservative charcoal suit and low-heeled shoes walked brazenly into the room. "I want to see my client, now," she demanded.

I looked at her oddly. She seemed vaguely familiar to me, but why? She faced the Lieutenant, so I could only see the side of her face, short gray hair, and dangly silver earrings shaped like sharks.

Oh!

"You!" I said loudly.

She turned toward me, eyes blank as if she'd never seen me in her life.

CHAPTER FIFTY-ONE

"I demand the release of my client," the woman said in a high-pitched voice that confirmed my memory of her.

"You were on the airplane with me!" I pointed at her, then turned to Denton. "She was! She was my seatmate on my flight from Boston to Miami. She asked me all sorts of questions about who I was and where I was going. I thought she was just a busybody." I paused to take a breath. "But she's Carlos' lawyer?"

The woman tried to ignore me, but I saw her cast an anxious glance at Denton. "That's ridiculous. I'm a Miami attorney, hired by Mr. Carlos Medina to secure his freedom from this unlawful arrest."

"Then how'd you get here so soon?" I asked. I could not believe the audacity of this woman. I knew I recognized her from the airplane. I'd also seen her after we landed in Miami, talking to the man from the cigar shop. This was all before I learned that the man was Carlos Medina.

Jamison raised his hand. "Meredith, that's enough. Follow me, please. And Ms..." Jamison stopped, waiting for a name.

"Bella Rodriquez. Attorney at law." She fumbled in her large leather pocketbook, produced a business card, and handed it to Jamison with a huff.

"Um," he said, perusing it quickly. "I'll be with you as soon as possible. Please make yourself comfortable."

I pursed my lips together and held them tightly closed. He couldn't be serious. I watched Rodriquez's eyes roam around the room. My parents, Donald, and Shannon stood away from her, aloof.

"I'll wait in the other room." She turned on her heels and walked out.

"That woman is a fake," I exclaimed. "She pretended she was a wacko passenger on the plane, and then..."

"I believe you," Denton said. "This is perfect. We have you as a witness to her being an accessory to the crime. Airline records will back that up. She's not going to know what hit her."

Lieutenant Jamison nodded in agreement. "There's something about that woman." He handed the business card to the police officer. "Check this out. Look for aliases."

Denton looked at him with a question in his eyes.

The Lieutenant shrugged: "Just a hunch."

Mom came over and pulled me to her. "You okay?"

I studied Mom's ashen face and stricken expression. I had seen the way she had been observing Dad. "I could ask you the same."

She brightened. "Oh, I'm fine! You're back. That's what really matters."

A door opened abruptly and another officer entered and whispered something to Jamison, who nodded slightly. But I saw a gleam of victory in his eyes as he turned to me and Denton. "Seems Bella Rodriquez has another name."

"Don't keep us in suspense," Denton said wryly.

"Bella Medina."

I gasped. "Carlos' wife?"

"His sister. She's been his attorney for years. She married Jose Rodriquez in 1985. Was married to him for five years. Been divorced and single ever since."

"Rodriquez," I said. "That sounds familiar. He's not..."

"You're thinking of Miguel Rodriquez, Jose's brother," Denton said. "Miquel had been head of the Cali drug cartel until he was arrested and disappeared."

"Oh. God." Suddenly I was exhausted. I just wanted to curl up and fall asleep. No, first I wanted to see Parker come through that door, so I could yell at him for disappearing again. Then I wanted to take a hot shower for hours, and collapse in a soft bed.

"The dots are starting to connect," Denton continued. I half listened as the names swirled around me like colors on a kaleidoscope. "Miquel Rodriquez sells tons of cocaine and meth and disappears. His brother's ex-wife is Carlos Medina's sister, Bella. Under Carlos' instructions, Bella makes sure you get on the plane from Logan to Miami, and on to St. Thomas, where Carlos plans to kidnap you and lure Parker to his island. But Parker uses his own bait and switches tactics. Now Carlos needs his sister here to bail him out. Thanks to you, Meredith, Bella Medina is going to have to worry about her own hide."

I acted as if I understood everything the customs agent said. Jamison seemed to realize that he was losing me. "Time for us to start the debriefing." He began to lead me out of the room.

"Wait!" Mom stared the Lieutenant down with her sharp hazel eyes. "Mr. Lieutenant. My daughter is tired and filthy. If you're going to interrogate her, it's going to be in her hotel room. After she's had a shower. And I'm going to be there every step of the way."

Dad shouted out, "Here, here."

Shannon added, "I'll come too, Merry."

Mom opened her mouth to protest, but thought better of it when Jamison looked over again to Denton, who wearily nodded in agreement.

~~~~~~~~~~~~~~~~~~~~~~~~~~~~~~~

Fortunately, the next few hours were a blur. My parents, Shannon, and Donald got to hear about my entire ordeal as Denton grilled me on the when, the where, the who, and the how. Several times Mom shouted out, "Stop pushing her, Floyd!" By this time Mom and Denton were on a first name basis. I used to be annoyed by Mom's pushiness, but this day, I was thankful for it.

We were all sitting in my hotel room. At times Dad and Shannon would walk out on the patio and look at the twinkling lights over the harbor. Mom never left my side as I sat on one of the chairs, now showered and dressed in the hotel's white terry robe, answering Denton's questions. Donald left at one point and came back with food.

"Specialties from the island," he said proudly as he pulled out containers of papaya fritters, fried fish, and coconut rice.

"This all looks great, but what I could really use is a glass of wine," I joked.

"No problem!" Donald said cheerily. And with that, he pulled a bottle of white wine from a third bag. "Believe it or not, even though the Caribbean is known more for its rum, it does produce its own wine too!"

I looked at Denton. "Do you mind?"

"Of course he doesn't," Mom declared. "We're all going to have some." And sure enough, after Donald poured a small amount in the plastic glasses, we all sipped after Shannon toasted, "to Meredith, thank God she's okay."

The wine immediately relaxed me. I ate a bit of food and drank as Denton tried to ask me a few questions. My eyes closed for a second, and I found it difficult to open them again. As I forced myself to stay awake, I watched Dad and Shannon raise their glasses silently to each other and share a secret smile. I looked over at Mom, who watched them wordlessly. I turned my gaze onto Donald, who was watching Mom wistfully.

I shook my head. My imagination was taking over as my brain shut down. I felt someone lead me to the bed, but I never felt my head hit the pillow. Dreams came quickly. Shadows of couples kissing. Soft whisperings. A door closing. A door opening.

And then, lips pressing onto mine.

But I couldn't make myself leave the dreams.

Hours later, maybe days, for all I knew, I awoke, stretched out my arms, and turned my head to the window, which was obscured by closed curtains. Was it night? Day? My cheek grazed something. I sat up and found a piece of white paper on the pillow.

Five large letters were written in black ink:

TRMFY.

CHAPTER FIFTY-TWO

I jumped out of bed and looked around me, but the room was empty. I ran to the window and opened the curtains to discover a bright, sun-filled morning. Boats bobbled in the harbor, a few runners raced on the path below me, and lovers walked hand in hand. Wait. Those 'lovers' looked familiar. What the hell?

I dashed some cold water over my face, brushed my teeth, and quickly changed to a pair of shorts and t-shirt. Just as I approached the door to leave, my mother burst in.

"You're awake!" she exclaimed unnecessarily. She looked me up and down. "And you look a thousand times better. But a little makeup wouldn't hurt."

Some things never change.

"I was about to go out," I stammered. "Um, need some breakfast. I'll be back soon."

Mom held me up with a flip of her hand. "Breakfast has been ordered and it will be here in a few minutes. Why don't you finish getting dressed, and then we'll eat and discuss how soon we can leave this place. I imagine you want to get home."

"But wait. Is the interrogation over? Where's Denton. And Jamison? I don't think I can leave yet." I was desperate to find Parker, but I didn't want Mom to know that. He had to be near. Didn't he? Hadn't he left his calling card?

"Floyd and Henry left as soon as you fell asleep," Mom said, laughing. "Don't you remember? Shannon walked you to the bed. Floyd said he was done with you. That you could go home. They need to 'get all their ducks in a row,' I believe are the exact words the Lieutenant used. Henry said they might need you to fly to Miami sometime – that's where they're going to prosecute Mr. Medina, as soon as they get the official okay from the St. Thomas government."

"But what about..." What? Who? A hundred questions filled my head. The hotel door flung upon, and one of my questions appeared.

"Dad!" A smile enveloped his face. He wore a smart-looking pair of khaki pants and a lime-green short-sleeved shirt. Someone had helped him shop.

"Breakfast!" he exclaimed cheerily, holding up a bag of bakery goods and pulling Shannon into the room with his other hand. Shannon's green eyes sparkled as she laughed out loud, and I knew I finally had it all figured out. Then my friend's eyes peered into mine, asking silently, "Is it okay?"

I nodded. "So, Dad, this is your mystery woman, huh?"

Unfortunately, Mom drowned out my question with a peevish, "But I already ordered breakfast."

Dad's smile leaked a little in the corners. Shannon nudged him, and he said, "Merry, honey, I wonder if I could have a few words with you. Alone."

"She was just about to put on some makeup," Mom responded.

"No, I wasn't," I retorted. "Dad, I noticed this amazing view of a four-sailed vessel from my patio. Care to join me?" He followed me as I pulled open the sliding glass door and shut it behind us.

"Dad, I may be dense, but I finally got it. You and Shannon."

I never in the world expected I'd experience the sight of my dad blush, but he took on the hue of a nearby peach hibiscus. "Weird, huh?" he said.

"Weird? Two caring, loving people who are important in my life discover they like each other and begin a relationship? Much better than weird," I said. "I'd say it's pretty darn perfect."

Dad smiled. "Well, we're not perfect. And we never planned it this way. We bumped into each other in Philadelphia about six months ago. Shannon was visiting a fledgling clothing store, and I was there for business..."

"Don't need the details, Dad. Although I don't know how Shannon kept all this from me for that long."

"Well, she wanted to talk to you about it, particularly after we started seeing each other every week..."

"Every week?" I asked. How'd I miss that?

"But she thought you were pretty engrossed with Gregory, and a little confused about that relationship, so we decided to wait a while longer."

Gregory. I groaned under my breath.

"Merry? You okay?" Dad was by my side in a nanosecond, his arm around my shoulder. He stared at me with such concern that I burst into tears.

"I blew it, Dad. I had the man of my dreams. Then I messed it all up."

Dad hugged me like he used to, back when I was little. "Don't give up," he said. "Don't ever give up."

"But I sent him away, and now, I don't know. Now he may never come back."

Dad looked at me with that sweet, grave expression I had always taken for granted. But now I also saw wisdom in his eyes as he approached his words to me with care. "I think I know who you're talking about, Meredith. And if you've chosen the man I think you have, believe me, he'll find you. He'll be back."

"But how do you know?"

"Because you love him. You've always loved him, Meredith. I knew that. Shannon knew it. He knew it too. He just gave you the time you needed."

"Yeah, well, right now, I just need him."

Dad nodded, then whispered in my ear, "Don't give up."

~~~~~~~~~~~~~~~~~~~~~~~~~~~

The F.B.I. secured first class tickets for me and my parents, Shannon, and Donald, on an early afternoon flight back to Miami, and then Boston. I looked for signs of Parker and Gregory every step of the way. On the limousine ride to the airport I thought the chauffeur might be Parker. At the airport, I listened to every announcement, waiting to hear "Ms. Meredith Powers, you're wanted at the ticket counter." On the flight, I searched the menu – as well as Mom's, Donald's, Dad's, and Shannon's - for any telltale TRMFY's in the margins.

I thought of the report Jamison had asked me to read before we left for the airport. "Don't discuss this with anyone," he said. "If the report helps you remember any other details, please call me, anytime." He gave me a white business card with his name and three different phone numbers.

I mulled over the report now, which had contained not only every aspect of my interview with the two men, but also some follow-up revelations.

Barbara Browning had sought counsel for Roger and herself, but the F.B.I. didn't think she had anything to do with Roger's illegal drug trafficking. Even though the yacht was in her name, as well as Roger's, they wouldn't be filing charges against her.

As much as I didn't like the woman, I was relieved to hear that. I even felt sorry for her. Imagine learning that your husband had been blackmailed, agreed to transport illegal drugs to the United States, and even conspired with someone as evil as Carlos Medina to kidnap me. I shuttered to think how angry, and humiliated, Barbara must be feeling.

I also selfishly wondered what would happen to her book. After all that work!

Putting that disappointment out of my mind, I continued to think about the other disclosures, particularly that they still didn't have enough proof to keep Carlos in jail for years. Kidnapping charges were one thing, and they had the proof for that – ME!

Murder, distributing illegal drugs, and sending the proceeds to terrorists were more serious charges, and charges they couldn't prove without a doubt. How long, the author of the report wondered, before the F.B.I. would decide to plea bargain with Carlos for the right information?

Plea bargain! Did that mean Carlos would be freed?

The rest of the flight, I bundled up inside one of the stale blue airline blankets and stared out of the window, out into nothingness.

CHAPTER FIFTY-THREE

When I finally arrived home, I roamed from the living room, where the window had been replaced while I'd been away, to the kitchen, where I longingly looked at the sink. I made a vow that if Parker returned, unharmed, I'd never use the dishwasher again. Silly.

When I meandered back to the hallway, I stumbled across the shoes I'd tossed off just a few hours earlier. If Gregory reemerged unscathed, full of explanations and apologies, I'd never, ever leave a pair of shoes out of the closet.

I was thankful to be alone in my wanderings. Mom wanted to stay with me when we landed at Logan last night, but I argued my need for privacy. Donald understood, and to help me out, tempted Mom with another night at her favorite Boston hotel - the Four Seasons. I thanked him profusely, and he answered with a wink.

Dad and Shannon left for her place, after the two of them had also tried to persuade me that I needed their company.

As much as I loved my family, they were not who, or what, I needed.

Walking toward the stairs, I looked at my Duchess figurine, standing just where she was supposed to be, on the small table facing the doorway. On a wish and a prayer, I picked it up and looked through the little hole in the bottom – no rolled up note this time.

I stopped at the guest room, where Gregory's navy suit hung in the antique corner wardrobe, and his running shorts were folded neatly on the wicker chair. Even though the room was accessorized with Gregory's belongings, it felt empty, so I closed the door.

The ringing of the phone startled me so much I jumped, then stood still, as if mesmerized by its possibilities. Finally, I picked the phone up at the sixth ring.

"Meredith. It's Henry Jamison. We have some news."

My heart hammered in my chest as I sucked in a breath. Parker? Gregory?

"We're getting closer to linking Carlos to the illegal transportation of those cigars into the U.S."

I exhaled. "Oh, good."

"Before Parker, uh, disappeared in St. Thomas, he mentioned Telford's Pipe Shop in Cambridge," Jamison continued. "Said that's when he suspected the use of cigars in Carlos' drug trafficking. We're looking into it, but can you add anything to that?"

I thought back to Shannon handing me that chubby cigar at the subway station. "I know Parker was there. I think someone tipped him off about it, because we were having lunch, and then he got a phone call and flew off..."

Jamison chuckled. "His M.O., huh?"

"Yeah," I replied ruefully. "My friend Shannon was in Cambridge, and saw Parker arguing with the owner, Mr. Telford, but again Parker suddenly turned on his heels and left, so Shannon picked up one of the cigars and gave it to me later that night."

Jamison sounded excited. "Do you have it?"

"No, no. Carlos stole it from me." I heard a questioning pause on the other end of the line. "Long story."

"Well, this is good, Meredith. Confirms our theories. Seems that Gregory's the one who called Parker with the tip."

"Gregory?" My voice rose in shock. "I thought Parker didn't know that Gregory was working for the F.B.I."

"He didn't. Gregory did all this anonymously."

I made a sound between a grunt and a snort.

"Remember, Meredith, Parker resurfaced at your doorstep, and then everything happened too quickly. There was no time for Gregory to explain."

Explain what? I wanted to ask. That Gregory had pretended to be my boyfriend just to find Parker?

"So Parker rushed to Telford's," Jamison resumed, clueless about my discomfiture. "He got there in time to find boxes of the, as you call them, 'chubby cigars.' He figured out then what made them so chubby."

"Not tobacco, huh?" I asked.

"No, not inside the cigar. Crystal meth. Rolled in the tobacco leaves."

"God. How'd they get there?"

"That's where we're putting the puzzle together. Looks like they were made in Columbia, then boxed and shipped to the U.S...."

"Thanks to men like Roger Browning," I said, finishing off his thought.

"Yeah. Oh, and thought you'd like to know. If it wasn't for Gregory, Parker would never have been able to tip us off about those cigars."

"What do you mean?" I squeezed my fingers into the palm of my hand. I wasn't sure if I wanted to hear much more about secret agent Gregory.

"He's the one who warned Parker to leave the cigar shop - you know, when your friend saw him suddenly rush out? Gregory sent Parker a quick text, again anonymously, telling him to get the hell out of there. Carlos strolled in just a few minutes later. If Parker had lingered at Telford's just a little longer, Carlos would have had him. Single gunshot in the back room. No one would have ever found him."

I commented softly, "so Parker owes his life to Gregory."

"Well, I don't know if I'd put it that dramatically," Jamison replied. "Let's just say it was good teamwork."

"Teamwork?" I protested. But then I let it go. I was more anxious to see if Jamison had any news about either member of the 'team,' but he revealed nothing, and I hung up the phone as frustrated as when I had answered.

I began to roam again, from living room to kitchen, bathroom to guest room, and then to my favorite room in the house.

My bedroom looked serene and enticing, my fluffy white comforter inviting me to lie down on the bed and nap. But my nerves were jingling like a

Christmas tune, so instead I paced from the dresser to the window, back to the bed and to the dresser again. My string of pearls still lay where I had placed them last night. I picked them up and touched the smooth round gems, comforting me somehow. I slowly clasped them around my neck, as a talisman. I looked out at the beautiful Japanese maple tree that Parker had planted. The leaves were still green, but a touch of red here and there promised a vivid fall display.

Then my eyes traveled to a form standing below the tree. A male form, his face looking up toward my bedroom window. Our eyes met. Embarrassingly, I let out a squeal.

And then I ran to the front door and opened it wide.

~~~~~~~~~~~~~~~~~~~~~~~~~~~~

Parker was already standing at the threshold as my arms widened for an embrace. I didn't even wait for a "hello" or a "sorry, I couldn't call you and let you know I was okay because every single cell phone in the world was out of order." I didn't care. I was too happy to see the man standing in one piece with a loopy grin on his face. He took one step toward me, then stopped. "Are you sure?" he asked.

"More than anything else in my world," I answered.

Then he surrounded me in his embrace – warm, solid chest; strong arms; deep sigh. "I thought you'd never ask," he said as his hug tightened.

Then he pulled back and looked at me with an earnest expression. "First, I really need to apologize. I didn't know I was putting you in harm's way. We hadn't been a couple for half a year. I had no idea that Carlos was able to figure me out so well. That he knew how attached I still was to you."

I nodded. "And I to you. Parker, I'm sorry. I should never have kicked you out of my life like that. I should never..."

Parker put up his hand to stop me. "Yes, you should have. You were right."

I blinked. "I was right to break up with you?"

"No, you were right to be frustrated. I shouldn't have expected you to understand this job. I was away too often. And I could never talk about where I was and what I was doing. You were right. That was no way to deepen a relationship."

We stood and looked at each other. So where did that leave us?

"But it's better than no relationship at all," I finally whispered.

"We can do better than that, Merry." Parker drew me to him, his lips touching mine, lightly at first, then deeper. I sighed contentedly, and he stepped back. "TRMFY," he said, nodding his head.

Playfully, I poked him in the chest. "Okay, come on, what is TRMFY?"

Parker just looked away dreamily. Then his eyes snapped back toward me, a serious expression plastered on his face. "We got him."

"You got him?" I repeated.

"Gregory and I. We got him."

I winced at the sound of Gregory's name. Parker continued as if he hadn't seen my discomfort.

"We knew we had to find definitive proof of Carlos' activities. That had been my assignment before my cover was blown, and I had come so close." Parker put his thumb and index finger almost together. "Damn Carlos. He thought he had me. And then I disappeared. Well, Merry, I didn't know he would become as desperate as he did – looking for you to find me. I didn't know about Gregory's undercover work with Carlos, helping Carlos get to me through you. I could have killed Gregory when I found out. But, of course, that was his job. The F.B.I. is going to have to take responsibility for that. Wrong. Wrong."

Parker had become distraught in a matter of seconds.

"Parker?" I interrupted. "You're rambling. Get to the point. You know? 'You got him'? That point."

CHAPTER FIFTY-FOUR

First Parker insisted that we move inside. "The neighbors are starting to talk," he laughed. Then he wrapped me in his arms and kissed me long enough to let me know he couldn't care less what the neighbors thought.

I inched him away from the door and into the living room between kisses. "Okay, I'm dying to know. You got him. You mean Carlos?"

Parker's eyes lit as he sat down on the chair. "A joint F.B.I./D.E.A. raid at Telford's Pipe Shop this morning produced hundreds of boxes of tampered cigars, all filled with crystal meth. Not only that, computer records of Bob Telford, whose real name was

Hashim, traced money accounts from his shop to a Columbia bank statement under the name of B. Rodriquez, to a charity foundation called 'Children's Relief Fund for Afghanistan.' Floyd Denton says early reports indicate that the charity is a front for a terrorist organization."

"That's awful!" I exclaimed, causing Parker to look at me with alarm. "I mean, it's wonderful that you were right, and they got the evidence to convict Telford, and Carlos and his sister Bella. But God, to go to such lengths! And to spread these drugs all in the name of a charity that really funds terrorism." Inadvertently, tears sprung to my eyes. "What a waste."

Parker rose from his seat and sat next to me on the couch, picking up my hand and rubbing it with his fingers. "Yeah, you're right. It's awful." He paused and then added, "Sometimes I get so involved with the thrill of getting 'the bad guys,' that I lose sight of how vile this business is."

He looked at me intently for a long time, and finally, he said, "I've missed the hell out of you, Meredith Powers."

"I've missed you too," I responded, quietly.

"I'd like to try again. Make it as good as it was, only different."

I nodded.

We walked up the stairway, arm in arm, to my bedroom. Bright late September rays coated the room in gold. We didn't say a word as we slowly undressed, as if shedding everything that had gone on in the past. His blue polo shirt merged on the floor with my white lacy blouse; his blue jeans stacked on top of my khaki shorts. I faced him in my bra and panties. His hand reached out and gently touched the pearls around my neck. He grinned that wonderful dimply Parker grin, and then pulled his briefs off so quickly I was still holding my breath when he pulled me onto the bed.

We faced each other, nose to nose, knee to knee, both breathing heavily.

"Close your eyes," Parker whispered.

Following his command, my skin tightened into goose bumps as I felt his feathery kisses cover every inch of my body. He began on my toes, which curled in response to his soft breath. I never knew I had nerve endings on the heel of my foot. Up to the shins, the knees, and the thighs. By the time he was caressing my forehead with his tongue, my skin vibrated like notes on a scale.

Our lips connected, finally, and we kissed, and we kissed, and when we merged, I couldn't tell where Parker began, and where I ended.

ONE MONTH LATER

Life was back to normal. And everything was different.

Parker moved back in with me officially a week after we returned to Boston. He still had to travel a few days a week, but this time the trips took him to Washington, D.C., St. Thomas, and Miami to help with the prosecution of Carlos Medina and his associates, including Bella Rodriquez and her ex-husband.

Through plea bargaining and a damn good lawyer, Roger Browning would serve a five-year sentence and lose all of his investment holdings. Barbara Browning now needed Flack, Inc. more than ever, and the publication date of her occupational therapy book was moving faster than even I expected.

Arthur Flack gave me a big raise. I deserved it. He also added two more weeks vacation to my benefit package, which I demanded. Parker and I planned on a long vacation as soon as he figured out his career.

Shannon flew down to be with Dad every other weekend, and Dad flew up to be with her the weekends in between. I loved seeing them both so happy, but I admitted to Parker that now that the novelty had worn off, I felt a little strange about it. I mean, my dad and my best friend! Mom certainly hadn't gotten used to the relationship yet. She called me every day to give me reasons why it was a bad idea. I hadn't determined whether she meant for Shannon or Dad. Parker guessed Mom meant for herself.

And still, I had not solved the puzzle of TRMFY.

I woke up with the initials drawn on the bedroom mirror with toothpaste. After my morning shower, I'd look up to find TRMFY written on the steamed mirror. When I served one of Parker's favorite meals – roast beef with all the fixings – I'd find TRMFY etched into the mashed potatoes.

On a Sunday morning in late October, I looked out the bedroom window and saw red, orange and yellow leaves dancing dramatically in the fresh autumn air. Attached to some of those leaves were swirling pieces of paper that spelled TRMFY in large black letters.

"Parker!" I yelled. He ran up from the kitchen as if I just shouted "Fire!" But instead, I cried uncle.

"Enough. I just need to know. What does TRMFY stand for?"

Sending me one of his wicked Parker grins, he deflected my question by suggesting, "Let's go for a run at the Great Meadow." Without waiting for me to acquiesce, Parker put on his fleece and ran down the stairs. I grabbed my own jacket, and away we went.

As we drove to the wildlife preserve, I mused that I had been wrong about myself. I did like spur-of-the moment activities and a little adventure in my life. And I didn't need my man to be totally predictable all the time. Of course, I never had that anyway with Gregory, since he turned out to be even more of a mystery than Parker ever was.

Gregory's disappearance was the talk of the F.B.I. and the D.E.A., according to Floyd Denton. My guess was that Gregory was undercover again, but Parker and I never discussed it.

Thirty minutes into our drive, we parked in the empty lot, thankful that we had Great Meadow to ourselves. We began a slow trot on the trail that circled the large pool of water, covered with tall brown reeds, cat's tails, and grasses. The sounds were more subdued from the last time we ran here; the red-winged black birds had already flown south for the coming winter. Geese honked overhead, on their own instinctual path away from the impending cold.

I looked up as I heard another more mechanical honking sound approach us. A small, single engine airplane flew directly above, waving a long banner behind it that read: TRMFY.

I stood still, head raised, and watched the banner until it became a tiny dot in the sky.

Then Parker enfolded me in his arms, whispering, "See? I knew it all along. I'm **T**he **R**ight **M**an **F**or **Y**ou!"

ACKNOWLEDGMENTS

The Right Wrong Man began as a sentence and
10-minute writing exercise with my first California
writing group, which has been meeting on Thursdays
for over 20 years. Astrid, Claire, Janice, Joan, Sara –
thank you for being such incredible students and
teachers of writing.

Many chapters of this novel first came to light
with my New England writing group – Anna Marie,
Bonita, Jean, Katie, Mary, Ruth, Verna – the truth of
your writing always brings light to my life.

The Right Wrong Man has seen the light of
many, many drafts thanks to my hard-working, always-
encouraging, but always truthful Concord Critique

Group. Charity, Lee, Rhoda – *The Right Wrong Man* is right, because of you.

Pamela Wight is a successful author of romantic suspense. Her novel, *The Right Wrong Man*, received rave reviews for taking readers "on an exciting adventure with lots of intrigue, unexpected plot twists, and romance."

She earned her Master's in English from Drew University (Madison, NJ), continued with postgraduate work at UC Berkeley in publishing, and teaches creative writing classes in Boston and San Francisco.

She lives in the San Francisco Bay area with her "right man," and her sidekick, Henry, a 12-year-old soulful golden. Together, they hike the hills of Marin

County while concocting stories full of romance and suspense.

Many readers enjoy Wight's "weekly blog on daily living," *Roughwighting* (www.roughwighting.net.)

If you enjoyed *The Right Wrong Man*, you'll want to download her book TWIN DESIRES, available through Amazon and Barnes & Noble.

Twin Desires, a romantic suspense set in San Francisco and the quiet CA town of Stinson Beach, follows Sandra Eastman and the two men who almost destroy her world. Blake Sinclair, Sandra's boss and president of a prestigious investment firm, is successful and charismatic. But his twin brother, Alex, is his opposite - a twisted, tormented soul. Sandra becomes a pawn in a deadly game between these powerful opposing forces.

In this fast-paced thriller, Sandra is scooped up into a whirlwind of suspense from the mansions of the S.F. elite to a remote beach house 30 miles north. As each page turns, she becomes more entangled with the skeletons in the Sinclair closets while desperately confronting her own skeletons and discovering strength she never knew she possessed.